THE URBANA FREE LIBRARY

3 1230 00935 9866

S0-BYF-113

Praise for
Trouble in Rooster Paradise

The Urbana Free Library

To renew: call **217-367-4057**
or go to **urbanafreelibrary.org**
and select **My Account**

Finalist, "Best First P

"Emory's first novel vividly evokes the ambiance of classic American hard-boiled crime writing. [....] Emory, a Seattle native, captures the period setting well."
—*Publishers Weekly*

"Seattle-area writer T.W. Emory's debut, *Trouble in Rooster Paradise* is an affectionate nod to noir fiction and its tough guys and dolls. [....] Good, vivid stuff. And who can resist a book with a cover featuring a fedora-wearing private eye, a shapely dame … and the Smith Tower?"
—Adam Woog, The *Seattle Times*

"The story has numerous twists, the characters are interesting, and there's plenty of local history. I'd gladly read another book featuring Gunnar Nilson and his friend Walter."
—Jeff Powanda, in "Ten Seattle Novels," *Read+Write+Watch*

"Gunnar Nilson, Emory's clove-chewing gumshoe with an eye for the ladies is every cliché in the book when it comes to hard-boiled detective stories, but to great extent that's what makes this novel such a pleasure. [....] The characters in the 1950s sections (which make up the bulk of the book) are well-drawn, quirky, and a lot of fun to get to know. The setting—

Seattle in the 50s when it was a working-class backwater—is also evoked well…. Readers will want to follow this detective and his delightful supporting cast of friends."
—Meredith Frazier, *Reviewing the Evidence*

"Emory skillfully evokes this era of class distinctions and gender inequity. The murderer's motive is inspired by both of these inequalities. The tale is peppered with recognizable 1950s characters—the world-weary waitress, the damaged World War II veteran, the thwarted career woman [….] I was happy to be plunged into Nilson's tale in the 1950s."
—*Historical Novel Society*

"Seattle has changed a lot in 50 years, and of course in 1950 the second World War is only just over, so Gunnar is able to talk about how the war affected various people, and what life was like then. The novel is filled with interesting characters, particularly those who live in the boarding house where Gunnar resides."
—*Mysteries in Paradise*

"When perfume is the smell of death, a private eye needs to be careful around the ladies. That's a tall order for detective Gunnar Nilson in T.W. Emory's thrilling debut set in post-war Seattle. Nilson meets many a lovely beauty as he tries to find out how one of them ended up murdered with his business card in her pocket. He's a tough-minded, smart sleuth, unwinding a plot layered with deception and driven by sins going back decades. Call it Queen City noir; this is an enthralling look at Seattle when it was a working class town populated by tough guys and great smelling gals, many with black secrets."
—Rich Zahradnik, author of the Coleridge Taylor Mysteries

CRAZY RHYTHM

CRAZY RHYTHM

A Gunnar Nilson Mystery

—

T.W. Emory

cp
coffeetownpress
Seattle, WA

coffeetownpress

Coffeetown Press
PO Box 70515
Seattle, WA 98127

For more information go to: www.coffeetownpress.com
www.twemoryauthor.com

All rights reserved. No part of this book may be reproduced or transmitted in any form or by any means, electronic or mechanical, including photocopying, recording, or any information storage and retrieval system, without permission in writing from the publisher.

This is a work of fiction. Names, characters, places, brands, media, and incidents are either the product of the author's imagination or are used fictitiously.

Cover Illustrations by T.W. Emory
Cover design by Sabrina Sun

Crazy Rhythm
Copyright © 2018 by T.W. Emory

ISBN: 978-1-60381-752-3 (Trade Paper)
ISBN: 978-1-60381-759-2 (eBook)

Library of Congress Control Number: 2017952771

Printed in the United States of America

To my wife and sons for their ongoing support of my one-morning-a-week stints at the keyboard.

———

Once again, I wish to thank my publishers, Catherine and Jennifer, for their helpful input and kind assistance.

Also by the author

Trouble in Rooster Paradise

Chapter 1

—

An assisted living home in Everett, Washington
Sunday, July 6, 2003

S HE WAVED THE SMALL microphone in the air like it was
a conductor's baton and I was her orchestra as she asked,
"So, is this another *murder* case you're going to tell me about,
Gunnar?"

The pretty young woman who'd fired the question at me was
Kirsti Liddell. She was seated on a wooden bench facing me,
and at her request, I'd begun telling her about my private eye
days back in post-World War II Seattle.

"Well, as it happens, blue eyes, it turned out that way," I said
wistfully. "But like I've told you before, a lot of my work then
was fairly humdrum. Bumping into the occasional homicide
was just a slim piece of Gunnar Nilson's overall pie."

Her mic had stopped waving and she was mulling that over
as I went on, "I guess you could say that this particular incident
was an example of something simple and harmless on its face
that turned out to be thorny and ... well, *lethal.*"

"Huh ... okay."

Kirsti had parked my wheelchair and me in an outside courtyard of the care facility where I was staying till my broken leg mended. Since early the previous month, she'd been one of my caregivers. We'd become friends. I'd quickly pegged her as the idealistic dreamer type. For some reason, she wanted to record and transcribe anything I cared to tell her about my time as a private detective. I didn't pretend to be Dr. Johnson, but she saw herself as my James Boswell and was willing to devote some of her off hours to that role. Like I said, a dreamer type.

A cassette recorder sat on Kirsti's lap and she gripped the mic in her right hand. Two weeks before, on a Sunday and a Monday, I'd told her about the investigation into the murder of a sales girl with whom I'd been briefly acquainted. Since then I'd merely related a few brief stories when she'd come by my room. This was the second time we'd arranged to formally meet so she could record what I had to share.

"And so this case involved this Rune guy you started telling me about?" she asked.

"Uh-huh. Blanche DuBois may have depended on the kindness of strangers, but Rune Granholm was past-master at banking on the kindheartedness of suckers."

"So, you're saying he was a real user, huh? Is that it, Gunnar?"

"That he was. A user with a reckless and fertile imagination that might have been a real plus, if it wasn't for the faulty moral compass that went along with it."

"So, a real sleazeball."

"That'll work. Sure. But he had a certain charm about him and didn't lack for company. But it was a *raffish* charm. Rune's engaging manners and buoyant spirits were somewhere between those of a baby-kissing politician and a snake-oil salesman."

"Snake-oil salesman?"

"A guy who knowingly sells bogus goods."

"So, he was a con man," she said in her clear, pleasant voice.

"Almost. Except in Rune's case, it wasn't a profession. He was more of an earnest dabbler."

"Sure. Okay. I get that. So, let's hear about this murder and how it connects with your sleazy friend Rune."

"Well, first of all, blue eyes, Rune wasn't really what I'd call a *friend*. I want to be clear about that."

"Got it. Not a friend."

Kirsti was a petite girl with blonde hair worn in what used to be called a Prince Valiant haircut back in my day. All in all, a pretty young woman who definitely rated a double-take and a first-rate look-over. She was a twenty-year-old college student working at Finecare for the summer, who toyed with becoming a journalist, and figured she might parlay my memories into some sort of extra-credit paper when she returned to school. It was Sunday, and Kirsti's day off, so instead of scrubs, she wore a pink blouse and denim pants that she called hip-huggers. She smiled a crooked smile at me as she turned on the recorder.

AN OLD SUCRETS TIN I kept filled with cloves was perched on my right leg. I opened it, separated one clove from the others, and slipped it into my mouth, moving it to one side with my tongue as I said, "I'll definitely need to take periodic pee breaks."

"Sure thing."

"And, like the last time, I'll probably get talked out eventually, so this story might have to be told in two sittings."

"Got it."

"And keep in mind, blue eyes, I'll be harking back to a totally different era, so don't be surprised if you hear the glacier move."

She made a face at me.

"Okay," I went on, "but just remember, I'll be talking about a time when Google was the name of a comic-strip character, gay meant merry and light-hearted, and if you looked at television at all, you were sure to be watching Uncle Miltie."

"Uncle Miltie?"

"Skip it."

Kirsti's forehead was creased and her eyes had a glint in them as I began my story ....

Chapter 2

———

Seattle, Washington
Monday, July 10, 1950

ONCE UPON A TIME, Seattle's Fremont district was its own little city. But it wasn't the "center of the universe" that it's claimed to be today. And in my day, no one would ever have considered setting up a statue of Vladimir Lenin there. Not hardly. No, back in 1950 it was definitely in its pre-gentrified period.

The heart of Fremont was an aggregate of churches, stores, taverns, and fabrication shops surrounded by old houses and dilapidated tenements built back when it was annexed to Seattle about the time the nineteenth century was about to give up the ghost. Fremont was also where you could find one of the many watering holes of Rune Granholm.

I parked my '39 Chevy Coupe on a side street a few blocks north of the place. As I stepped out of my car, I glanced at my left wrist out of habit, forgetting I'd failed to put on my Longines after showering that morning. It didn't matter. I wasn't exactly meeting up with Mr. Punctuality.

I'd just finished a job for a middle-aged woman up in Everett who'd got my number from a friend I'd worked for once. My client had an heirloom stolen—an expensive necklace that had belonged to her grandmother. I got it back to her after a two-day search that led me to her shiftless nephew and a pawn shop he frequented over on Hewitt Avenue. So, money-wise, I was flush, but still feeling somewhat slimy from the experience, and all I really wanted at the moment was take a nice, long Epsom salts bath to relax my body with the radio playing Hawaiian tunes to soothe my spirit.

But instead I'd gone to Fremont.

The sign above the entrance to the Flying Clipper had a small anchor and frayed ship's rigging hanging from it. I went in through swinging doors with portholes for windows. Inside, the place was shaped like a rectangle with the short ends front and back. There was a bar on the right, and directly above it, suspended from piano wires, was a three-foot-long scale model of a clipper ship with yellowed, drooping sails.

Here and there, numb or getting-numbed customers sat in booths or at small tables. A jukebox played, and two couples were dancing. A man and a woman chewed face while propping each other up in their version of a slow dance, painlessly unaware that a livelier tune now filled the air.

At one end of the bar sat three local workers in a lively discussion that shifted from English to Swedish and back to English again.

Some trace the term "dumb Swede" to the struggle immigrants had learning English. Maybe. But I'm inclined to believe it was because Scandihoovians came from a forthright culture and tended to be just a bit too trusting.

As I approached the three Swedes, the guy nearest me challenged one of his pals in a strong Scandinavian accent, "*Ja*, was you there, Charlie?"

To which the third guy chimed in, "*Ja*, I *knew* Squeaky Anderson up in Alaska. He was a *real* guy!"

The Swedish began again in earnest as I passed by, making me think of the way my fellow boarder Sten regularly parodied the language.

"Hewta, hewta, hewta," I said under my breath.

I sat at the other end of the bar and nodded at a middle-aged barge worker two stools down on my right. He was glassy-eyed, looked to be long past settling his jitters, and didn't seem to notice me. Still, hope springs eternal, so I asked him, "Do you have the time?"

He pulled his lips back so that his teeth showed. It was probably the closest thing to a smile he had. His eyes showed a spark of amusement as he said, "No man has the time, young man, just the crude means of calculating it."

"It's five after six," said the bartender. He was burly and had a cauliflower ear. He looked at me expectantly with heavy-lidded eyes.

"Could you possibly be any more typecast?" I asked him.

"Huh?"

"Skip it. I'll have a beer. Pabst on tap if you have it."

"We got Rainier."

"Rainier it is."

Rune's idea of being on time was arriving within an hour of the time designated. So, I had no qualms about starting without him.

Fifteen minutes later I was studying the bottom of my empty glass when a customer whisked through the swinging doors.

It was Rune Granholm.

Rune moseyed over my way and planted himself on the empty barstool to my left. His face was sun-flushed, which made his dreamy brown eyes look dreamier than usual. He blew a plume of cigarette smoke past my left ear, and said, "And how's Gunnar?"

"Rune, why am I thinking it's a favor you want and not my pleasant company?" I asked dryly.

He gave me a lopsided grin. "Boy, you're not just a gumshoe.

You're a mind reader," he said, signaling the bartender to get us each a beer.

When our beers were brought, Rune ground out his cigarette in a blue-glass ashtray that sat on the bar and then drank a big gulp from his glass. I took a small sip from mine and watched him struggle to gather his thoughts.

I knew Rune far too well to be impartial about his physical appearance, but I suppose women would consider him reasonably attractive. He was twenty-six and was just beginning to show traces of every fast-lived minute of it. His sandy hair was combed straight back off his high forehead and pomaded to where you could almost see your reflection in the shine— that is, if you could take your eyes off his perpetual thin-lipped smirk. He wore a cream-colored linen sports jacket, with tan slacks, and a loud and busy open-neck Hawaiian shirt—all of which hung nicely on his lean frame and were all-of-a-piece with his brown and white shoes.

"I know what you're probably thinking. I'm not in a jam or anything," he said, giving me a sidelong glance. "Actually, it's about me collecting a fair-sized debt. So, it's a good thing. You follow?"

I didn't say a peep as I continued to study him.

I suppose some people found Rune charming. He was a two-fisted drinker, a partygoer, a gambler, and a self-styled ladies' man—the kind of guy my grandpa Sven disparagingly called a "good-timer." He apparently worked, but at what, and when, and where, were like the things that made up the nebula.

"I won three-hundred bucks at pool this past Saturday night," he announced smugly. "The guy I won it off of was a newcomer to the 211 Club, and he didn't have the cash on him to back his play. So, he staked his watch. He said if I won it, he'd buy it back from me in a few days when he got the dough. Since it was a fancy gold Cartier watch, I told him okeydokey."

I swallowed some beer and said, "I take it he lost the watch."

"You bet he did," said Rune cheerily.

He pulled a pack of Camels from an inside coat pocket, snagged and lit a cigarette, and took a draw on it.

"So, let me take a look at this gold Cartier watch," I said flatly.

Rune's startled face was luminous with meaning. "Oh, I don't have it on me," he said in a high, thin voice. "No. It's … it's over at my place. In my chest of drawers. I wanted to keep it safe."

"Uh-huh," I said in a casual tone. He was quick on his feet, I'd give him that. It was guys like Rune who eventually got me to believe that the human race was for me to learn from, when I wasn't bent over laughing at it.

"So, what do you need me for? Sounds like you've got everything pretty well covered," I said.

"Well, not exactly," he said, his voice sharpening. "I've set up a meeting later tonight to trade this guy his watch for my cash."

"Like I said, where do I fit in?"

"Well Gunnar, like I told you, this guy's practically a stranger to me. And he's pretty big. I mean Charles Atlas big, if you follow me. And you know how some guys will make a deal in a roomful of people but welsh on it in private. Do you follow?"

I told him I followed. Rune was pretty easy to follow, only I usually didn't enjoy the trip. I gave him a cool, level stare and asked, "What's the catch, Rune?"

"No catch. I swear it."

Rune's swearing to it was no confidence-builder. But instead of saying so, I said, "So, you want me to ride shotgun for you. You want me there for protection just in case this exchange goes sideways."

Rune blew a blimp-shaped column of smoke and fanned it away from me as he said, "That's about the size of it. So, what do you say? Will you do it, Gunnar?"

"Don't tell me you plan to meet this guy in some back alley?"

Rune faltered for only half a second. "No, no, not an alley. We're meeting later on tonight over at Green Lake. In a parking lot. Near the bathhouse."

Green Lake, a freshwater glacial lake surrounded by

residential neighborhoods, was a short drive from Rune's apartment in Wallingford. The lake drew people during the day, but a late-night meeting there would mean few people on hand.

"Rune, if you're nervous about this meeting, why didn't you set it up in a café or maybe a bowling alley? Some place with more people around?"

His face was blank for a moment as he dreamed up what to tell me next. "Yeah, maybe that would have been better. But I can't change it now. I … I don't have the guy's number. Besides, I don't want him to think I don't trust him."

"But you *don't* trust him."

"Yeah, yeah, I know … but I don't want *him* to know that," he said testily. "Come on, Gunnar, be a pal. Help me out here, will ya? The swap will probably take a minute, tops. All you have to do is be somewhere nearby to keep an eye on us. Just to be on the safe side. It'll be easy-breezy."

Safe side. Easy-breezy. I didn't think I could muster the stomach for such tomfoolery. Besides, Rune had a habit of leaving out disturbing facts and inconvenient details, so I was morally certain I wasn't getting the full story. Probably not even half the story. Such mischief had "walk away" written all over it.

So, why didn't I walk away?

If there were ever two brothers more unlike each other, it was Nils and Rune Granholm. Nils was one of the nicest guys I've ever known. The stark differences between the Granholm brothers made a solid case for genes over environment in the nature versus nurture argument.

Before the war, I lived in a fifth-floor studio apartment on Eighth Avenue, north of Seneca. Nils and Rune shared an apartment on the fourth floor. I got to know them, and I really liked Nils, and in the few months we were neighbors, Nils and I became pretty good friends. He and I ended up in different branches of the military and fought in different theaters during the war. Rune joined up a little too late to see combat around the time the news came that Nils had been killed in action.

If I felt even an ounce of obligation to help out this piece of work in a Hawaiian shirt, that ounce stemmed from my friendship with his older brother Nils.

I reached into my shirt pocket for a clove. As I slowly lifted it to my mouth, I said, "You say you set up this meeting last Saturday at the 211 Club. Why then so last minute about getting me involved?"

"I dunno … I guess I just started getting nervous about it this morning. So, what do ya say, Gunnar? Will you be a pal and do it?"

According to Rune, the guy was to meet him for his gold Cartier watch at 9:30 that night. I told him I'd be on his doorstep about nine o'clock. As my grandmother used to say: "The stupid one does what the crazy one says." It sounded less insulting in Swedish. I must have heard her say it a hundred times growing up. A hundred times more wouldn't have hurt.

BEFORE THE CRASH OF 1929, resulting in a slump, Wallingford had been touted as one of the finest residential sections of Seattle's newer neighborhoods. The area began to revive after World War II.

Apartment houses and businesses lined both sides of Wallingford's main commercial strip like Shawnees forming a gauntlet. All around and beyond this gauntlet were one-and-a-half-story bungalows with low-pitched gable roofs and two-story box houses tricked out with ornate windows. Both designs suited middle-class households, whose worldly display consisted of cars, kitchen appliances, lawn furniture on well-trimmed lawns, and porches where family members languished on rain-free summer evenings wearing polite, vacuous smiles as they read, listened to the radio, chitchatted, played Parcheesi, or just stared at the stratosphere and asked themselves every question but why.

Whether or not P.T. Barnum actually said it, the phrase "There's a sucker born every minute," was the motto Rune Granholm seemed to live by. It was how he'd probably wangled a small apartment with cheap rent above a bakery in Wallingford. The bakery was owned and operated by a friend's mother who I imagined had fallen for one of Rune's creative sob stories. But at the moment, I was in no position to fault her for being taken in by the man.

I parked my coupe on Forty-Fifth Street. It was still light out when I arrived. My Longines said 8:53 as I slammed my car door shut.

The bakery was a two-story brick building shaped like a rectangle. I walked around back to an outdoor stairway that led up to a small deck enclosed with a three-foot-high wood railing that served as Rune's front porch. The apartment had likely once been home to the bakery owners, but now it served as a caretaker's flat—though "caretaker" is not the word I'd have used to describe Rune. I'd have dropped the word "care" altogether.

I could see his door was wide open, so I went up the back stairs slowly, making thumping noises to let him know I was coming. You never know what a young single guy might be up to—especially a guy like Rune.

Next to the front door was an adjustable canvas-and-wood lawn chair. Alongside it on the deck near where Rune would plant his feet sat a ceramic ashtray overflowing with cigarette butts.

I rapped loudly on the door frame with my knuckles and called out, "Gunnar's here!"

No answer. I stepped inside. Immediately my feet decided to stay put.

Each wall had a window with gray pull-down shades, and someone with a severe case of agoraphobia had them all pulled down to keep out prying eyes. But Rune was anything but an agoraphobic.

Only one light was left on. It was coming from one of those hula girl motion lamps with a swivel setting so that the bare-breasted wahine actually gyrated in her grass skirt. She wasn't gyrating at the moment, however. It was as if she sensed there'd be no point.

The walls had the kind of smooth patina that comes from numerous tenants and many layers of paint. If you didn't count a tiny bathroom and a tinier clothes closet with their doors left wide open, the place was just one big room. There was a small kitchenette in one corner off to my right, marked off by a small half wall with a countertop. Diagonally across the room from that was a mirror-backed putaway Murphy bed. The intervening space had a tan carpet and furniture of so-so quality but not much of it. A mismatched armchair was parked next to a sofa upholstered with clashing jacquard fabric. A small end table with the hula girl lamp was near the chair. Next to the base of the lamp was a pricey Contax camera that Rune had more than likely borrowed. I knew that Rune owned a Colt .32 automatic with mother-of-pearl grips, but it was nowhere in sight, even though an open box of ammunition was sitting right next to the camera. Beside the sofa was a small chairside radio stuffed with magazines that spilled out of its built-in book rack.

Peeking just past the radio was a pair of brown-and-white shoes. They were still on the feet that wore them when I'd seen them earlier in the evening. My stomach got tight and I suddenly felt crawly all over. His feet didn't move, so mine finally did.

I circled around the sofa.

He was on his back.

His dreamy brown eyes stared off at nothing in particular. His hair was tousled and his lips were parted and fixed in a grin, as if he was about to ask an important question. His arms were at his sides, the left hand out a bit, the right hand partially pinned under him. He wasn't wearing his cream-colored sports jacket, and the red in his Hawaiian shirt was now a deeper hue around his chest.

He was as motionless as his hula girl lamp. I kneeled down and touched his neck anyway. He was still warm, but there was no thump, no pound, no throb. His swivel setting had definitely been switched off. *Aloha* Rune.

A couple of cigarettes had fallen to the floor from an open pack of Camels in his shirt pocket. Near his right leg lay his wallet, a couple of bills leaking out of it. I took out my handkerchief and used it as a makeshift glove to pick it up. A quick look inside showed just the two dollar bills, his social security card, driver's license, and a business card. I closed the wallet and put it back where I found it.

Whoever had removed his wallet hadn't bothered to toss the apartment. If Rune had something he wanted, he had either found it or needed to get out in a hurry.

I stood and looked from him to the tiny bathroom. There I found a toilet, a tub, a sink, and a young man's medicine cabinet with contents having far more to do with personal appearance than personal hygiene.

Next, I looked in the closet. Jackets, shirts, and trousers were draped on hangers suspended from a rod. Several pairs of shoes were on the floor, intermingled with dirty laundry. A few wood shelves had been built compactly into one corner. On these were socks, underwear, and T-shirts that had been thrown in willy-nilly.

There wasn't a chest of drawers in sight. So, no drawer for a gold Cartier watch to hide in. And so, no Cartier watch.

I reached for the right sleeve of the cream-colored jacket Rune had worn earlier. As I expected, a few inches inside the cuff and fastened with a safety pin was a tightly folded fifty-dollar bill. It was a peculiar custom of Rune's, what he called "the old back-up plan." I unclipped the fifty, tucked it inside my hat band, and put the safety pin back where I found it. Better that I got the money than a cop or stranger—or worse still, that it perish in some trash heap.

One of the closed shades looked a little crumpled at one end. I pulled it aside. The window it covered was unlocked and led to a fire escape.

I let the shade drop to where it was closed again and went over to the end table with the hula girl lamp and Contax camera. Using my handkerchief, I flipped the camera on its side. There was no film in it. I flipped it back.

There were probably plenty of people who had reason to hate Rune Granholm—who maybe even wanted to shoot him, if they had a mind to. But I didn't believe he'd been murdered over a gold Cartier watch.

I thought about getting out of there and making an anonymous phone call to the cops. But instead, I went over to the kitchenette where I'd seen a wall telephone. A little wooden shelf was attached to the wall next to the phone. On the shelf was a pencil and a notepad with a name written on its top page in Rune's scrawl: Richard Liles.

I reached for the phone and began dialing. When a gravelly male voice answered, I said, "I'm calling to report a murder."

I gave him the address and my name. After he told me not to handle anything and to stay put, I hung up.

My reason for sticking around wasn't for fear that a neighbor might witness my coming and going. And I certainly didn't stay because of Rune Granholm. I stuck around because Rune had been Nils Granholm's kid brother.

I waited for the cops outside on the small porch. I sat in Rune's adjustable canvas and wood lawn chair and munched on a couple of cloves.

Soon I heard the shrill yowl of a prowl-car siren.

Chapter 3

—

"Looks to me whoever plugged him was invited," said Detective Lyman Fitch. "The stiff ain't cold yet, so that seems to fit you sayin' you'd seen him a little more than two hours before you got here. If you're tellin' it to us straight, that is." He spoke in the self-assured voice of a man who never smokes, drinks, or gambles, and only occasionally dates loose women. However, Fitch *was* a smoker.

"Could be your arrival scared off the killer," he added. "The window leading to the fire escape ain't locked. That's probably how he made his getaway."

I'd concluded the same, but didn't say so. I'd done enough talking already to last me a week. Fitch had me tell my story three times. Trust me, three times isn't always a charm.

Detective Lyman Fitch was a stocky man in his mid-forties with sleepy brown eyes, a broad chin, and a folksy manner. He was wearing scuffed brown wingtip brogues, brown trousers, a dark-blue shirt with a reddish-brown tie, and a brown sports coat with shoulders you could do pull-ups on. His brown felt hat was pulled down to his earlobes.

We were standing inside Rune's apartment near the

kitchenette but within eyeshot of the body. The front door was still wide open, but it was now dark outside.

Two uniformed cops showed up first, soon followed by Fitch and his partner Alton Togstad. When the medical examiner arrived with a print and camera man, Togstad and the uniforms left to comb the area and question neighbors.

It wasn't lost on Fitch that I had a nodding acquaintance with the white-haired and paunchy medical examiner. A real image-maker. Gunnar the Coroner's Pal.

Squatting, Doc Pimm shifted his black bag on the floor and made a faint guttural sound as he maneuvered around the body. Looking over at us, he said breathlessly, "I'll know more when I get him on the table, but he looks to have been shot only once. Small caliber." He began fumbling in his bag for papers.

Fitch nodded at Doc Pimm and then turned back to me and said, "Since there was some money in his wallet, it don't look like no robbery to me. But since the dead guy's wallet was on the floor, it makes me think the killer mighta been lookin' for somethin'. He mighta found it, but maybe not. Who knows? So, I'm thinkin' it might be a good idea to post a patrolman on this place for a few days, just in case the killer sneaks on back here for another look-see."

I nodded and told him it was probably a good idea.

Fitch squinted at me and went on in his folksy way, "I gotta tell ya, this whole story of the dead guy wantin' you to tag along for when he sells a guy back his watch sounds like a lot of hooey to me. A lot of hooey."

"I agree. It was a load of crock. No argument from me," I said. "But like it or not, it's the story Rune told me. Don't you think that if I was making up the whole thing, I'd at least have tried to come up with a better story?"

He considered that for a moment. "You seem like a bright fella, so I'll give you that. *Maybe*. But if it's as you tell it, then why'd you even bother comin' over here to go along with him?

Make some sense of that for me if you can, 'cuz that don't make any sense to me at all. Not at all. No sir."

"Like I said, Rune was worried. That seemed genuine enough. He was nervous about something, and he really did seem to want my help. That much I believed. That much rang true to me. Can I help it I'm a curious guy? It's a burden, but there it is. Naturally, I got curious as to what kind of mess Rune had actually gotten himself into. So I came here to go with him and find out."

"Uh-huh," Fitch said, though his tone was puzzled and he had a doubtful look on his face. "So, do you think your friend was involved in somethin' shady, and that's what mighta got him killed? Is that what you think?"

I nodded. "That's my guess, sure. Rune was no paragon of virtue."

"Pair of what—"

Fitch was interrupted by the return of his partner, Alton Togstad, who announced tonelessly, "The neighbors had nothing helpful to tell me or the prowl-car boys."

Togstad was short, quiet, unblinking, and dressed in a battleship-gray suit and matching fedora. Under forty, I guessed, not over. He was a habitual gum-chewer who snapped his gum more often than he spoke—one of the open-mouthed kind who resemble a small cow chewing a very large cud.

He continued his report, "Nobody saw any visitors come or go from here. But that's no surprise, since the stairs leading up here face the side of the house next door. Plus, the fence and that row of tall poplars that line it give plenty of cover for both sight and sound."

"Uh-huh," Fitch said in a hollow tone.

Togstad's report finished, he stood there motionless. The only disturbance to his placid features came from his ongoing battle with his spearmint wad.

Fitch turned from his partner and shot me a sleepy-eyed glance but said nothing for a minute or two.

Nothing seemed to be the smart thing for me to say as well.

Finally, Togstad punctured the silence with a snap of his gum.

Fitch plucked a pack of cigarettes from his coat pocket, gave it a practiced flick until a couple inched out, and then pulled one free with his lips. As he lit up, he mumbled, "You bein' a keyhole peeper, I can't help but be thinkin' you're not tellin' us all you know. Was you followin' the dead guy for some reason? Was you *hired* to tail him? Is that it?"

"Uh-uh," I said, shaking my head. "Ask around. You'll find I've known Rune for years. Ask at the bar where we met earlier. The bartender will probably remember us having a drink together. It's as I told you, his hooey story and all."

Lit cigarette in hand, Fitch cocked his head back and chuckled. "Why, you coulda struck up a conversation with him in the bar as a cover. You seem the clever sort. Ain't that right, Togstad? Don't he seem the clever sort?"

Togstad merely nodded and kept chewing.

Fitch said, "Listen, Gunnar, me and Togstad know you private peepers have to protect your clients and all that. We get that. We really do. And we ain't necessarily interested in your client's business, unless of course it ties to this here murder somehow."

"I told you, I have no client. I'm between jobs," I said flatly.

Fitch waved that away along with the plume of smoke he'd just exhaled. "Sure, sure. So you say. So you *been* sayin'. But what *I'm* sayin' is you should level with us. Better now than later on. You gotta know that, right?"

Fitch didn't really expect me to reply to his folksy appeal. And I didn't disappoint him.

He went on, "I'm just givin' you a word to the wise, is all— like it was served up on one of those silver platters. It would be a real pity if we was to find out later on that you was holdin' out on us. Yes siree, a real pity. Ain't that right, Togstad?"

Togstad simply snapped his gum in a way that sounded like he heartily agreed. The talent of some people.

"Just so's you get that we're tryin' to be fair and all, do you know any cops who can vouch for you?" Fitch asked.

"Talk to Detective Sergeant Frank Milland about me. We're not exactly bosom buddies, but we're not enemies."

Fitch nodded, pointed me to the door, and said, "Come in and give us a signed statement in the morning. But think good and hard about what I said before you do."

As I was leaving the apartment, I saw that somebody had switched on the hula girl's swivel setting. She was gyrating up a storm.

It was nice to see someone feeling festive.

Chapter 4

—

I LIVED IN A residential area located in Ballard—once a city all its own until annexed to Seattle in the early 1900s. Some dubbed Ballard Seattle's Brooklyn. Others called it Little Scandinavia, Snoose Junction, or Halibut Alley. They all fit.

I boarded in a two-story house built during the Spanish-American War by a shingle-mill owner who favored gabled roofs and the box-style look. What set it apart was that years before I became a boarder, my landlady's husband Otto Berger had enclosed the huge front porch to turn it into a small parlor and then painted the entire house forest green. With the porch gone, the steps led straight to the front door. Another Swedish proverb my grandmother used to quote describes a tactless person as someone who has no porch for their house. That fit my widowed landlady to a T.

"HELLS BELLS AND WHISTLES, we've had another killing," Mrs. Berger said breathlessly, her face buried in the *Post-Intelligencer*. Mrs. Berger liked to keep close tabs on Seattle's crime waves.

We fed ourselves on the weekends, but Mrs. Berger dutifully

served us breakfast, lunch, and dinner on Monday through Friday, so all three of us boarders were on deck for a breakfast of pancakes, grapefruit, and coffee the Tuesday morning after Rune's murder.

Mrs. Berger went on, "Happened above a bakery over in Wallingford. Police don't have a suspect yet. There's no picture of him, but the young fellow killed was named Rune Granholm."

"That wouldn't happen to be the Rune you know, would it, Gunnar?" asked Walter Pangborn. "If memory serves, you've mentioned that name before."

Walter came from a wealthy family and had attended Princeton a while before going off to fight Huns in World War I as a private in a Pennsylvania company. He was badly burned while standing near a fuel wagon when it exploded. He could hide the gruesome red scars on his chest and right arm, but not those on his right ear and right side of his face and throat. My old partner Lou Boyd used to say that you don't really know what people look like till you get to know them. Those of us who knew Walter Pangborn forgot all about his disfigurement.

"It is, or it *was* the Rune I knew, all right. I heard all about it last night. Pass the grapefruit, would you, Walter?"

"Rune bought the farm, eh?" Sten Larson said emptily, a spoonful of grapefruit in one hand and a smoldering cigarette dangling between two fingers of the other.

Sten was Mrs. Berger's nephew, the only son of the late Otto Berger's sister, Lena. He was in his late twenties, and like me, a veteran of World War II, still trying to make sense of civilian life. Sten's approach to sense-making was multi-faceted. It included work, women, billiards, card playing, chain-smoking, and bimonthly attendance on Sundays at a Lutheran church over on Twentieth.

I sat directly across from Mrs. Berger, so all I could see was the top of her head and her hands holding the spread newspaper. Most of her fingertips were wrapped with frayed

Band-Aids to help prevent nail-biting—a futile plan, it turned out.

As she liked to repeatedly tell it, Mrs. Berger had once been an extremely gifted fan dancer, but marriage to her late husband Otto had taken her from the world of burlesque. Now about fifty, she was still a fine figure of a woman with a handsome, sharply defined face. She was generally good-natured, made liberal use of synthetic perfumes from the five-and-dime, and was often flirtatious.

"Any other details on the murder?" I asked her as I spooned out some pulp from my grapefruit.

"Lemme check," she said, the newspaper rustling as she hunted for the remainder of the article on another page. Her search over, she folded the paper to make it smaller and easier to wield. At last she told us, "It says, the police ruled out robbery and figure it was probably some sort of argument gone wrong."

"Gotta wonder what old Rune was up to so as to get himself offed," Sten said coolly, voicing what the others were probably thinking. The smoke from his cigarette was a thick cloud off to one side of him.

Mrs. Berger handed the paper to Sten and said in a sorrowful tone, "It's the family that suffers most. It's always the family."

Walter was about to agree with her when I cut in with, "Rune had no family. He had an older brother who was killed in the war."

"Well, still, *somebody'll* miss him," she said. "After all, he didn't live in a vacuum cleaner."

I could see Walter struggling with whether to amend her remark before he decided to give it up as a bad job. Prudence is the better part of pedantry.

I didn't say anything about those who might be grieving for Rune. Instead I asked Sten, "Were you at the 211 Club last Saturday night?"

He nodded.

"There long?"

"Long. Way too long. Twenty bucks too long."

"Was Rune there?"

"Nope. I haven't seen him there in weeks. Why?"

"Oh, just wondering what his haunts might have been the last few days of his life. It's nothing." Nothing but another one of Rune's lies.

Mrs. Berger got up to fetch another cup of coffee from the stove. When she returned to the table, she said, "What kind of person does such horrible things, anyway? *Murder*, I mean." She was looking at me for the answer.

I took a sip of coffee and looked down at my half-eaten pancakes. "Cops could be right about it being a dispute gone sideways," I said. "Rune ran with some pretty rough customers at times."

Sten rattled pages as he turned to the comics section and said, "Who knows? Maybe we've got a Jack the Ripper on our hands." He puffed on his cigarette and slowly blew a hazy plume of smoke. After watching it drift for a second, he added, "But this time, instead of foggy London, it's drizzly, foggy Seattle."

Mrs. Berger looked worried, her imagination taxiing down the runway Sten had put it on. With her fancy now in full flight, she asked, "You don't think it's some kind of Jack the Ripper killer, do you Gunnar?" She fanned Sten's smoke away from her face with her hand but kept her eyes on me.

"Better make sure all the windows are locked tonight, Aunt Nora," Sten said with a mischievous grin. "Some addle-headed fiend might come breaking in *and* ...." He made a ripping noise as he drew his index finger across his throat.

"That's *not* funny, Sten," said Mrs. Berger, screwing up her face and regarding him sourly. "It's not a damn bit funny. Besides, he was *shot*, not knifed."

"In all likelihood, Nora, it was simply a tragic case of a hothead acting without thinking," Walter said calmly, a reassuring smile on the undamaged side of his face.

Sten worked for a plastering and painting contractor named Sully, who picked him up for work each morning. We soon heard the sound of Sully's car horn. As Sten rose from the table to leave, I got up and walked him to the door.

"Do me a favor, Sten," I said under my breath. "Call around later and find out who of Rune's crowd owns a Contax camera that he might have borrowed."

Sten eyed me speculatively. "You think it has something to do with what got him killed?"

I shrugged. "Probably not, but I've got reasons for wanting to know."

Sten nodded and went off to join Sully.

Walter and I helped Mrs. Berger clear the table, and then Walter went upstairs to his room and I poured myself another cup of coffee. As my landlady began doing dishes, I sat back down at the table to think.

After leaving Rune's, I'd removed the fifty-dollar bill from my hatband. When I unfolded it, I discovered a claim check inside from Spud's Camera Shop near Market Street.

Curiosity got the better of any guilt I might have felt for withholding evidence. I wanted to know what Rune had been up to. If the pictures appeared directly tied to the Fitch and Togstad investigation, I'd come up with some way of turning them over without getting hit with an obstruction charge for my troubles. So, I headed over to Spud's to see what developed.

SPUD'S CAMERA SHOP WAS off of a part of Market Street that was only a few blocks south and then east of Mrs. Berger's. So, since the sun chose to show a little bit of its face and it was a nice mild morning, I walked the few blocks down and over.

As I neared my destination, a car horn tooted lamely in the distance like some parting shot signaling that the early morning comings and goings had begun to ease, and at ten minutes after nine I went into Spud's and strolled up to the counter.

Behind the counter was an appealing woman in her late twenties with dishwater-blonde hair, wide-set blue eyes, and pouty lips with just a whisper of magenta lipstick.

"Don't tell me *you're* Spud," I said good-naturedly.

"No. No I'm not," she said, her pouty lips curving into an uncertain smile. "Spud's across town on an errand."

I handed her Rune's claim check and said, "I'm picking this up for a friend."

She slowly looked from me to the slip of paper and back to me, and just as slowly she dropped her chin and raised it up to show me she understood. "I'll see if it's ready," she said in a subdued voice that a sleepy camper might use to tell a late-night story around a dying campfire.

Spud's employee was slim and willowy, but her main frame had enough curves to make it pleasant to watch her as she sauntered leisurely over to a section of shelves stuffed with small packages. Moving at a speed just above snail's pace, she compared the claim check with the items on the shelves until she finally found the match she was looking for.

By the time she got back with what I wanted, I felt like I needed another shave.

"So, you're a friend of Rune's," she said lazily as she handed me the package with his name written on it. It was more a question than a statement.

"Not really. I'm just here as a favor. You know Rune?" I asked.

Slowly but surely, she shook her head. "He just made an impression, is all. He came in here yesterday morning, and was fit to be tied when his pictures weren't ready. He was pretty rude to Spud."

"That would be Rune, all right."

"Uh-huh. He'd given his film to Spud last Friday or Saturday," she said lazily. "Seems Spud owed him somehow, and had promised to develop his pictures special so they'd be ready yesterday. But Spud had a big fight with his wife and didn't get to 'em as planned."

"So, what happened?"

"Oh, Spud calmed him down easy enough. Told him they'd be ready today. And there you have 'em. Besides, most guys can't stay mad at Spud for long. He's as big as a house." She said all this in a lackluster tone. She wasn't lackluster herself, but I imagined her actually producing tedium in all those with whom she spent much time.

However, in one matter she didn't dawdle. Not at all. When she dropped my change in my hand, three of her fingertips touched my open palm and were in no rush to move away. I looked up and saw her eyes going over me through those lowered fluttering lashes that mothers warn their sons about. I pocketed my change while her eyes and a sensual smile let me know right where I could find her.

I also knew right where I could leave her.

I touched the brim of my hat and did so.

All things considered, her feminine charms didn't seem worth the price of ending up in some yawning Black Hole of Tedium.

KIRSTI TURNED THE RECORDER off and said, "If I know my mom, when she hears that last part, it's sure to get a huge eyebrow raise out of her."

"Oh? How so?"

She appeared a little embarrassed and looked like she was working up the nerve to say something. "Well … I let my mom and dad listen to the tapes I made of you telling me about that case dealing with the fancy boutique with all those beautiful salesgirls."

"Uh-huh. And …?"

"Oh, they both really enjoyed your story and all that. My dad found it real interesting and entertaining. And of course, my mom loves a good mystery."

"But …?"

"Well, Mom thinks that all those women being attracted to

you is just you wanting to remember things that way. A *guy* thing. And she also kind of doubts that back in 1950, gorgeous women would have been used to … so *blatantly* sell products in a place of business."

"Well, as to your last thought," I said, smiling nicely, "it's a sales ploy as old as the hills. A case in point to tell your mom is that from just before the Second World War on up into the early fifties, there was a roadside diner and drive-in on the northern outskirts of downtown Seattle that intentionally employed attractive women to pull in male customers."

"Really?"

"Really. The eatery was called the Igloo—one of those oddball attention-getting buildings in the shape of two side-by-side igloos. The two guys that started the place scoured local office buildings and movie houses purposely hunting for pretty elevator operators and usherettes they could hire away as their carhops and waitresses."

"Really?"

"Uh-huh, really."

"I'll have to tell that to Mom."

"You do that. In addition to the eye candy, it was also a great place to get a double-malted and a cheeseburger."

Her eyes gleamed at me.

"Now don't tell your mom I said so, but with due respect to her, I think she's being more than a little naïve when it comes to what's gone on between the sexes in bygone days."

Kirsti nodded slowly and smiled. "I think my folks would like to meet you some time."

"I'm open. Now, as to women being attracted to me in my younger days, well, I guess you and Mom will just have to take my word for it that I did all right for myself."

I let that sink in a moment before I went on with my story.

I ASSUMED MRS. BERGER was shopping, because the first floor was quiet when I entered the kitchen side door. I went into the small hall that served as a pantry and reached for the telephone that sat on top of a lower cupboard.

I had a small office in Ballard over on Market Street a little west of Twentieth, that neighbored the larger office of my landlord, an attorney named Dag Erickson. The rent I paid Dag also bought me an additional phone line in Dag's office and his secretary's services as my message-taker. But Miss Cissy Paget's help with my filing and typing was a negotiable extra.

I dialed.

Cissy picked up after two rings.

"Hello, sweet knees," I said cheerily. "Do me a quick favor. I won't be in till this afternoon. If you happen to notice any hazy silhouettes passing by your door's frosted glass, go out and ask what they want, and then tell them I hope to be in later today."

"Okay, will do."

"Thanks. You're a doll."

"I feel more like a puppet."

I laughed, said goodbye, and dropped the phone in its cradle.

From the pantry, I entered the dining room on my way to the stairs. Try as I might, each time I went up or down that flight of steps I couldn't help but steal a glance at some framed photos and a wooden display case on the wall at the foot of the stairs. This was Mrs. Berger's monument to her life on stage. Behind the glass of the case was displayed her ostrich feather fans. Next to the case were three photos; each showing a different pose of a young and G-string-clad Mrs. Berger prancing across stage in high-heeled slippers, using her fans for cover. If Mrs. Berger noticed you noticing, she'd holler something about how she kept them mesmerized or she'd remark on what a grand and glorious time it had been.

Walter Pangborn's room was across from mine in the upstairs hall.

I knocked.

"Enter at your own risk," he said breezily.

I opened the door and stepped inside.

The smell of Walter's room was a pungent blend of paint, coffee grounds, tea leaves, pipe tobacco, and the grassy-sweetness of old books. At one end was a neatly made bed. One wall was taken up with a floor-to-ceiling bookcase. Against another was a bar-high wooden table, on a corner of which sat a hot plate, electric percolator, a can of Hills Brothers Coffee, and a bowl of Lipton Tea bags. In the center were paint pots and worn brushes clustered in jars. This table was Walter's ten-foot-wide workbench where he read, typed, and regularly painted toy soldiers for a soldier-making company back in Massachusetts. The proceeds supplemented a trust fund allowance that needed no supplementing.

"I thought it might be you, old socks," Walter said in his curious tone. "I have no coffee brewed, but like me you've probably had your fill for the day. And I'd offer you a shot of Black & White, but it's a bit early."

"Not necessary, Walter. I'm only here for a chat."

Walter had an open book in front of him on the table and was sitting on a stool, looking at me over his shoulder. I knew that he'd recently finished painting a set of toy soldiers from the Napoleonic era, so he was free to do some research. Walter indicated that I should sit in his channel-backed chair. I sat as he turned on his stool to face me more directly.

"From what little you said to Sten at breakfast, I gather that the murder of Rune Granholm has piqued your interest."

"Mrs. Pangborn raised a discerning child."

"Well, at least the governess she hired did," he said matter-of-factly.

Seeing only the undamaged left side of Walter Pangborn's face, you'd say he was youthful for a man in his early fifties. His brown hair was combed back and sprinkled throughout with wisps of gray. A paint-smudged white apron covered a tan shirt tucked into brown corduroy pants. He was lean and about an inch taller than my own six one. Despite the damage, one had to admire the dark brown eyes, set of perfect white teeth, and the one good ear that might have been sculpted by Michelangelo. He had a long narrow face with thin lips, and on its left side he usually wore an ironic grin. Walter's outstanding feature was his kind, steady gaze that inspired confidence, or at least made you believe panic was not necessary.

I got right to the point. No reason not to with Walter. I told him of my meeting with Rune at the Flying Clipper, the dubious favor he'd wanted me to do for him, and how I'd discovered him later on.

Walter grimaced, cradled his elbow with his left hand, and began kneading his chin with the fingers of his right hand as he looked up and off to one side.

"Sten's telling you at breakfast that Rune wasn't at the 211 Club last Saturday seems to confirm that his story was indeed invented," Walter said in his almost a musical voice.

"Not that I needed confirmation."

Walter nodded. "It does sound like the police might be on to something with their argument-gone-bad theory. To shoot someone at point blank, you'd either have to be good and angry with them, or leastwise, very, very thorough. But such thoroughness might suggest calculation, not spontaneity, don't you think?"

"Uh-huh."

"Still, you say there was money left in his wallet. That the bills were partway out does hint that the murderer made a quick search for something. Something *small*. And as you say, if he heard your noisy arrival, that's what cut short his search."

Walter's eyebrows rose when I told him about the claim check I'd found with the money pinned inside the sleeve of Rune's jacket. I handed him the package I'd picked up at the camera shop.

"Inside are the prints and the negatives for an entire roll of film," I said. "I leafed through them on my walk home. I can't see that there's anything special about them. Just a hodgepodge of unrelated pictures."

Walter turned on his stool to face the workbench again and laid out the prints. I got up and moved next to him so that we could study them together. Some of the pictures were scenic shots that looked to have been taken on a ferryboat ride in Puget Sound. A few shots were of some guys playing pool at the 211 Club. Rune was in two of the pictures. A couple of the shots looked to be of a newer model Ford. Several pictures appeared to have been taken in downtown Seattle, showing pedestrians on sidewalks with traffic in the background. Two pictures were of two couples seated at a table. One couple was drinking and laughing as the other smooched. Others could be seen seated behind them, but they clearly weren't the focus of the picture-taker. The final two shots were of the smoochers dancing while the other couple stayed seated in the background. All in all, nothing too out of the ordinary.

I told Walter about the empty Contax camera at Rune's place. "I'm sure he borrowed it. He was no photo buff, and I can't see him shelling out for that kind of camera just to take a few snapshots like these."

Walter kneaded his chin some more as he pondered my words. Then, reaching for his pipe, he began filling the bowl. "At first blush, Gunnar, I confess that it's difficult to deduce the nature of the jiggery-pokery your friend Rune might have been party to."

"I wouldn't call him a *friend*, Walter. Not as I like to define the term. Maybe this roll of film was taken so he could get used to the camera. But the girl at the camera shop says Rune was really upset because these pictures weren't ready for him yesterday morning. That got me wondering."

Walter acknowledged my point with a nod as he lit his pipe. "With that kind of camera, Rune wouldn't have needed flashbulbs," Walter said dryly. Taking a puff on his pipe, he added, "So, while the people in some of these snapshots may have known he was taking their picture, it's not necessarily so. Rune could have taken these pictures surreptitiously."

"That sounds like the scheming Rune I knew. But to what end, Walter? I'm seeing nothing unusual in any of these pictures. His pals shooting pool seem harmless enough. Even the shots of the couples laughing, smooching, and dancing seem fairly innocuous. The men look like typical working men. The women could be their girlfriends, or shop girls, or even a couple of tarts, given the way they're dressed and made up."

Walter agreed. "Yes, as you say, fairly ordinary pictures about commonplace happenings. But I gather you were supposing that maybe Rune had taken some photos that he planned to use in a blackmail scheme?"

I nodded. "Blackmail would be a new low even for Rune, but I wouldn't put it past him. When the girl at the camera shop told me Rune was upset at not getting these pictures yesterday morning, I got to thinking that maybe he'd planned to have them in his hands for later in the day when he met up with his blackmail victim. Which means he could only have described to them what the pictures he'd taken were all about. But with the pictures not ready to sell and deliver, I'm guessing he wanted me on hand as some kind of buffer while he bluffed his way to a postponement, with me being nearby but none the wiser. Granted, not a good plan or a smart one. But that was Rune for you."

Walter took another puff on his pipe and said, "Given how you characterize him, it has a certain logic to it."

I went on, "The cops will be sure to check Rune's phone calls. But if he *was* putting the bite on someone, he'd at least have been smart enough to use a payphone. But none of these pictures seem to show anything that would worry anyone. So, a blackmail angle seems to be a dead end."

Walter nodded and shrugged. "However, the fact that Rune was so upset that these pictures weren't ready yesterday morning does seem to argue that one or more of these shots was significant to him *and* to someone else."

I kept quiet and watched Walter's mind work. Finally he smiled and added, "And, if as you suggest, Rune took these pictures to practice with the camera, isn't it possible that it's the pictures at the end of the roll that the other practice shots were leading up to?"

I studied the sequence indicated by the negatives. "The last pictures taken were these four," I said, pointing to the two pictures of two men and two women sitting at a table drinking and laughing or smooching, and the two others of one of these couples slow-dancing while the other couple remained seated in the background.

Walter removed his pipe from his mouth and shook his head. His smile disappeared as his lips straightened into a thin line. "Unless we're missing something, a blackmail scheme based on these pictures is a bit thin for a hypothesis. I could be mistaken, but I'd wager that the men in these shots with the women couldn't care less who knows *what* they do in their off-hours or with *whom*. And that likely goes for the women as well."

I glanced at the four pictures again. Both women had shoulder-length hair. One was a peroxide blonde, the other had dark hair. While in each picture their facial features were crinkled by laughter, or smooching in the case of one, both women appeared pretty, though I'd say the dark-haired one— the smoocher and dancer—was the more striking. "And so, whether shop girls or tarts, where's the leverage on *them*?" I said woodenly.

We continued to study the prints for a while.

"Maybe there's some significance as to *where* one or more of these four pictures were taken," I said absently. "Though, if that's the case, it's lost on me." The twinge of guilt I'd felt for withholding evidence suddenly vanished. In other words, I wasn't feeling too rushed to get these pictures to Detectives Fitch and Togstad.

Walter agreed and relit his pipe. After a moment of silence, he said, "You didn't tell me what was on that business card in Rune's wallet, or what was written on that notepad."

"Probably neither of them mean anything, since they weren't taken by the killer," I said grimly.

Walter raised his good eyebrow and said, "Still, old thing, since they apparently weren't what the murderer was looking for, in his haste he might have ignored them and whatever their incriminating import might be."

I considered that a moment and said, "The business card belonged to Rune's mechanic. It was well worn and sweat-stained, so it had probably been in his wallet for quite some time."

"And the notepad?"

"It had the name Richard Liles scrawled on it. No address. No telephone number. Just the name."

"Ah … have you checked for this fellow in the directory?" Walter asked.

"Not yet," I said evenly. "The claim check for these pictures got me distracted."

Walter smiled.

"I guess I'd hoped I'd been dealt a pat hand," I said.

That made him laugh. It was a laugh that came from deep down in his belly. "I didn't think you trusted pat hands, old top."

"Normally I don't. I just don't see Rune getting himself killed over some lame argument. He was a lover, not a fighter. I've seen him either back down from or talk himself out of more than one dicey situation. Despite the story he spun for me, he was hedging his bets. For whatever reason, he wanted me on hand in case something went south. That much seems certain. By now the cops have been tracing the movements of Rune's friends and contacts and are checking on their alibis. I'd be smart to let it drop and leave the cops to dope it all out."

"But you won't."

"Oh? And why are you so cocksure about it, Mr. Pangborn?"

"Because, old top, you *want* to dope it out. My guess is, you *need* to dope it out. You said as much when you took note of that business card and the name written on the notepad. Not to mention your interest in these pictures taken by Rune."

I didn't say anything. No point. Why butt my head against sound logic? Instead I popped a clove in my mouth and began massaging it with my tongue. I pocketed one of the pictures of Rune and asked Walter if he'd hang on to the rest for me.

"It's probably a fool's errand, but I should at least try and earn that fifty bucks I took from Rune's sleeve. Besides, I don't have a client right now, so I'll nose into it until one comes knocking." I spoke casually. Probably too casually.

With a knowing grin, Walter said slowly and distinctly, "I'm sure I don't need to mention that in addition to your innate inquisitiveness, your very high regard for Rune's brother Nils also incentivizes you in this matter."

"And yet, you *do* mention it," I intoned sarcastically.

"Couldn't resist, old socks. I just couldn't resist."

Chapter 5

A<small>FTER</small> I <small>LEFT</small> W<small>ALTER</small>, I went and gave my statement to the cops. Detectives Fitch and Togstad were nowhere to be seen. They were probably off checking on the whereabouts of Rune's friends and acquaintances at the time of his murder. I also phoned Doc Pimm and learned that Rune had been shot with a .32. So, since the cops hadn't found Rune's gun in his apartment, I figured the killer probably used it and took it with him, which seemed to suggest his killing was a spur-of-the-moment thing.

At the Seattle Public Library, I found three Liles in the city directory for 1950—but only one Richard Liles. It listed his occupation as "Security," whatever that meant.

According to the directory, Richard Liles lived over on Capitol Hill. For all I knew, the Richard Liles I was actually looking for didn't even live in Seattle. But I had to start somewhere, so I wrote down the address and phone number and left. If later I needed to consult other directories at the telephone office, I'd cross that bridge then.

Seattle started off as a logging town, and lumber was squarely behind its first real economic boom. Thanks to regrowth, the city and the surrounding areas still have plenty of evergreen trees to help mask suburban sprawl, but it's also got its fair share of deciduous trees. A practical lot, the early pioneers chose to replant their clear-cut neighborhoods with fruit and nut trees. Capitol Hill settlers were more well-heeled, so early residents could afford to be impractical. That's why the streets there tend to be lined with a variety of ornamental trees. The tree of choice growing in rows along Richard Liles' street were cone-shaped Hornbeams, with their dense branches and dark-green leaves.

I arrived around 12:45. It was still mild out, and the sun was managing to show its smiling face despite a few sneaky clouds trying to move in and mask it. I found a shady spot on the street for my coupe just in case the sun was able to fend off the clouds.

I hadn't called ahead, so there was no telling whether Liles would be at home. I figured I'd stop back if I missed him. Besides, sometimes you can tell a lot about a guy simply from his chosen surroundings.

It was one of those chronically quiet neighborhoods probably inhabited by the likes of keeps-to-herself Gladys, minds-his-own-business Axel, and never-says-two-words Bob. Just the kind of locale that could easily harbor a homicidal maniac—if your imagination nudges you in that direction.

Richard Liles didn't live in one of the mansions on the four- or five-block stretch of Fourteenth Avenue called "Millionaire's Row." His house was several blocks west of there and a little north of East Aloha Street. But judging by the kind of mansion-wannabe he did live in, I'd say Dickie boy wasn't suffering. Whatever "Security" entailed, it seemed to be paying him well.

Richard's house was a "Seattle box"—a regional design about as common to Seattle as hops are to a brewery, and built in that period before the War to End All Wars and right on into the Big War that followed. Variation to these "boxes" was achieved by builders splicing facets of other styles onto them.

I'd say Victorian elements had been generously grafted onto Richard Liles' house.

His two-and-one-half-story box was mustard yellow and perched above the block a bit. Brick steps led up to more brick steps that led up to a wide front porch made of even more bricks. Much of this porch was swallowed up by ferny leaves of several goatsbeard plants thriving in shade provided by the sloping hipped roof. A narrow driveway led back to an average-sized carriage house turned into a small garage. Sitting in front of that was a newer model red Oldsmobile with a wax job you could use for a mirror if you were in desperate need.

I slipped a clove in my mouth and rapped on the front door. It opened immediately. A man stepped out and quickly shut the door behind him, which told me I wasn't going to be invited in for a glass of cold lemonade.

Richard Liles' self-satisfied face looked familiar. Or maybe he just had one of those familiar-looking self-satisfied faces. Underneath dark bushy eyebrows were heavy-lidded blue eyes that possessed a subtle menace—steely eyes that probably wouldn't blink if they witnessed a criminal being hanged and then drawn and quartered. The manly but manicured fingers of his right hand fondled his flinty jaw, while those of his left hand held a brown fedora, permitting me to see his head of wavy brown hair. He wore a dark-brown business suit, a white shirt and display handkerchief, and a ruby-red necktie.

Richard Liles gave me a once-over as he would a car he had no intention of buying or a boat he wished he'd never bought. He was thirty-five or maybe forty years old. A little shorter than six feet, he stood as stiff and upright as a soldier on parade. He was short-legged and long-waisted, with shoulders trying to burst the seams of his coat. Something bulged on his left side. It was an ominous bulge and it wasn't glandular—the kind of bulge a small cannon might make. I could've been mistaken, but Richard struck me as dangerous.

"Liles? Richard Liles?" I asked.

He gave me a smile of polite contempt and said in the smooth, sure voice of an undertaker during a cholera outbreak, "Everything about you says cop or gumshoe. Since the cops already came by to see me at my office this morning, I'm thinking gumshoe."

I'd been high-hatted plenty of times by people with much higher hats than his. I said in an airy manner, "I hear gumshoes are some of the finest people one could ever hope to meet in life."

His lips formed a slight smirk that quickly became a small sneer.

I reached for my wallet and showed him my Photostat license. He gave it a cursory glance.

As I put my wallet away, I said, "Your line is 'Security'—or so the directory says."

"Uh-huh, but you're not here to hire my services, are you now, partner? Nor could you likely afford them," he added in a cold and condescending tone. "So, what *are* you here for?"

"Since you've talked to the cops, you probably know about the guy murdered over in Wallingford last night, and that your name was written on a notepad next to the telephone in the dead guy's apartment."

A General Electric light bulb went on in his head. "Ah, yes ... the cops said the dead guy was found by a gumshoe. You must be him."

"I am."

"Well, as I told the cops, I didn't know the dead guy. And to my knowledge, I've never met this ... *what* was his name again?"

"*Rune* ... Rune Granholm."

"Fine ... okay. I've never met him."

I slipped my hand in my coat pocket for one of the pictures of Rune I'd brought with me. I let him take a look at it. "Maybe you haven't met him, but did you ever happen to *see* him?"

He studied the picture a moment and quickly shook his head as he handed it back to me.

"I can assure you that I have never met or seen this man—this … Rune Granholm." He spoke in a voice that was clipped and precise. Then he added, "Surely the cops have this case well-covered, partner. So, what's *your* interest in it?"

"The interest of a family friend."

I watched him rattle that around in his brain much longer than he wanted to before I asked, "Do you have any idea why Rune jotted your name down on a notepad?"

He gave me an icy look. "That's *assuming* that I'm the Richard Liles the note refers to."

"Uh-huh. But since we're in Seattle, and you're the only Richard Liles in the city directory, the odds and Occam's razor make it a fair bet that Rune meant you."

That got his dark bushy eyebrows to rise. "An *urbane* gumshoe, no less."

"It's been a struggle, but I've managed to read a book or two along the way."

He ignored my flip remark as if he were a past master at ignoring flip remarks.

"Well, as I said, I've already had my chat with the cops. And even though I'm under no obligation to answer *your* questions, I'm happy to tell you exactly what I told them." He paused for effect. "I haven't the slightest idea why your friend Rune wrote down my name."

"No possible connection to your line of work?"

"None that I can see, partner, unless your friend was thinking about coming to me for a job. But it's news to me if he was. And I highly doubt he was interested in hiring me, as my clientele tends to be big earners and the affluent. I gather this Rune was neither."

"What exactly is your line?"

"I provide personal security."

"So, bodyguards and doorknob rattlers."

"Sure … if you prefer those terms." He clearly didn't.

"Planting bugs and running tails—that sort of thing as well?"

He gave a slow nod. "It can be. But once again, *your* terms, not mine. I prefer to call it 'surveillance.' We act strictly within the law in whatever we do, and we only do what a given situation warrants." His tone was curt. "As I'm sure you realize, the well-to-do face difficulties at times that are peculiar to their station in life."

"So, you protect big earners from enemies they've made and you shield the affluent from friends they don't want. Is that about the size of it?"

"An oversimplification, to be sure, but something along those lines, yes," he said coolly.

Richard Liles put on his hat. That light bulb in his head must have gotten a little bit brighter, because for some reason he'd decided to change his tack with me. "Why don't you give me a couple of your business cards," he said in a smooth, almost honeyed tone.

He was holding out an open palm. I looked at his hand and then back at him for an explanation. "In case I learn something that might interest you," he said. "Also, a gumshoe who's managed to read a book or two along the way could be of use to a company like mine."

I shook my head. "I've paid my fair share of dues working for a large company. Trust me, I do best when I work solo."

"That may be," he said unctuously, "and I'm sure you drive a brisk trade as a private eye. But you never know what kind of change you might want to make, and *why*. For one thing, I guarantee you'd make a lot more money than you do now."

I dug into my wallet for a couple of my cards, but as I handed them over, I said, "For when you might learn something."

He took out his wallet and opened it to tuck my cards away. As he did so, he pulled out one of his own and handed it to me, his smile tight-lipped.

I slipped his card into my shirt pocket, where it joined my stash of cloves. That way, the next time I looked at it, it would have that earthy, spicy, and sweet smell.

Liles went on, "But just to repeat, partner, I never met your friend. And as I told the cops, my secretary couldn't find any record of his having phoned or visited my office."

We exchanged stares for a moment.

"Well, like you said, maybe Rune was simply toying with becoming one of your *bodyguards*." I emphasized the last word, knowing he didn't like it.

"Perhaps so," he said smugly. "Your guess is as good as mine, partner. Now, if you'll excuse me, I just stopped by home on my way to meet someone, so I really need to be moving along." His tone was firm and final.

We shook hands. But I don't think it was because Richard Liles wished to be particularly cordial. I think he wanted me to experience his manly, bone-crushing handshake.

He went down and over to his shiny Oldsmobile, and I went down and out to the street to my not-so-shiny Chevy Coupe, bending and flexing my sore right hand as I went.

At least the sun was still out.

If Richard Liles had lied about not having known or even seen Rune, he was awfully good at lying. And it was also possible that his initial menacing demeanor might simply have been his normal way of dealing with uninvited door-knockers. And maybe, just maybe, his taking on the ingratiating manner of a snake oil salesman toward the end of our talk had revealed the *real* Richard Liles. But not likely. In Dick's line, his stock-in-trade would include lies and intimidation. So, something during our conversation had triggered his sudden change.

Chapter 6

—

B Y THE TIME I moseyed into a café over in Wallingford, the lunch rush had died down to where it was buried and gone, and empty tables were for the taking. I spied a small one that suited me near the big front window.

A waitress with lank ash-blonde hair came over to me with clean utensils, a water glass, an empty ashtray, and a fixed smile that was no longer believable. A light-blue dress clung to her gangly figure like a draped dishtowel that harmonized with her sagging nylons. Still, she was nice-looking, and I could imagine how such a job could drag you down. I hoped the rest of her life somehow compensated for what she put up with here.

"Whattaya havin', hon?" she said in an impassive tone, as she swiped the full ketchup bottle from a nearby vacant table and traded it for my almost-empty one.

I asked for a pastrami sandwich and a cup of coffee. When she brought my order, I pointed to the shop diagonally across the street and said, "I see the bakery is still closed since that murder."

"Uh-huh," she said flatly. "Cops told her she can reopen, but

Mrs. Brooks don't want to for now. I ain't heard why. Maybe Clara figures it's too soon or just too creepy."

It was no shock that Rune was still managing to get others to reap what he'd sown. It's a talent some have, dead or alive.

The sandwich was better than okay and the coffee wasn't half bad. After I paid and tipped the waitress, I slipped over to the pay booth and checked the phone book for the name Brooks, of which Seattle had plenty, though only one Clara Brooks. Her address was just a few blocks over and down on Burke Avenue.

I DROVE PAST MRS. Brooks' house, made a U-turn at the end of her block, and parked kitty-corner across the street. Sitting behind the wheel, I looked over at a moss-green two-story box house built from Douglas fir around the same time another Douglas was wowing silent film-goers with his swashbuckling antics. I got out and strolled over.

Clara Brooks' front yard was a good four or five feet above sidewalk level and kept from landsliding onto it by a cement retaining wall topped with bricks. The wall had a slight slant to it from years of ground shift. I mounted the concrete steps that cut through this wall and spiraled up to the right to reach a walkway shaded by a large but lonely-looking elm tree. More steps led to a wide front porch with a potted scrawny palm placed on each side at the top.

I popped a fresh clove in my mouth and rang the bell. A half minute later, unhurried steps came clomping, and the door swung open. Clara was nearer to fifty than forty-five. Someone forgot to tell her that the Axis powers had been defeated, because her graying hair was swept up and out of the way in the unrelenting utilitarian braids worn by women factory workers during the war effort. All she lacked was Rosie the Riveter's bandana. She was on the tall side of short and wore a yellow house dress that would have been flattering on a less stocky body. Her face was pale and fleshy. She had a small but bulbous nose, and round eyes that looked a bit too shrewd to go with the angelic smile with which she greeted me.

"Mrs. Brooks? Mrs. Clara Brooks who owns the bakery?" I asked, tipping my hat.

"Well, you can't be another policeman; otherwise you'd know the answer to that question already," she said in a deep, gravelly voice, her smile still intact. "So, who might you be, young fella?"

"My name's Gunnar Nilson," I said. "I knew Rune Granholm."

She raised her thick, full brows and tightened her lips. "Another Scandihoovian, huh? A *close* friend of Rune's, were you?" She spoke in a frank manner that encouraged me to return the favor.

"We were only so-so friends," I said, waggling my flattened right hand in the air. "The Granholm I was close friends with was Rune's older brother Nils."

"Uh-huh," she said, her smile returning. "So, o'course I'm guessin' that Rune was one of them by-products they talk about."

I didn't say a peep. I just smiled.

"So, what brings you to my door, young fella?"

I reached for my wallet and opened it to show my Photostat license for the second time in one day.

She studied it a few seconds before making friendly eye contact again to say, "So, you're a private eye, then. Are you like the detectives in them pulp magazines?"

"Not nearly as colorful, I'm afraid. Not most days, leastwise."

She laughed abruptly, and her eyes squinted and the flesh around them crinkled. "So, you don't always riddle the crook with bullet holes," she went on, "or get to kiss the pretty girl afterwards. Is that it?"

"You've sized things up nicely."

"So, how'd you come to be a shamus?"

I shrugged. "You know how it is. You reach a point where you start asking yourself, 'What am I going to do with my life?'

Before you know it, you're doing something, yet you never really got around to answering that question."

She gave another abrupt laugh. "So, you're helpin' out the police then, I take it."

"Not officially," I said, shaking my head. "I was the one who found Rune dead in his apartment. I'm just looking into what happened all on my lonesome and on my own time."

She liked that. "On account of Nils, but not on account of Rune," she said quietly, a perceptive look in her eyes.

I shrugged.

"I think I understand, young fella. Believe me, I truly do," she said thoughtfully. "I'm keepin' the bakery closed a while out of respect for my late husband's notions of what he called 'propriety.' If not for that, I'd be up to my elbows in flour right now. You can bet it. But Charles started the bakery, and he had very strong feelin's about what he called propriety and decorum. And o'course I still have very strong feelin's about Charles. He was a man of rock-solid pure morals but with an illogical mind. But that was part of his charm and why I loved him." She sighed before adding, "So, o'course I told my daughter and son-in-law that we're all takin' a few days off on account of Charles."

Leaving the front door wide open, she stepped out on the porch and pointed off to her right at two metal motel chairs placed across from a glider with a threadbare hassock in front of it.

"Take a chair, young fella. No reason I can't talk to you a few minutes, particularly if you have no objections to how we talk about the dead."

I told her I had no objections whatsoever.

She liked that, and I was beginning to like her.

Mrs. Brooks lowered herself onto one end of the glider and put her feet up on the hassock with the smooth and seamless ease of a one-time gymnast. For a woman her age and size, she was definitely limber. Her white leather oxfords were the kind worn by nurses and meant for comfort and not fashion. But she wasn't wearing socks.

The chairs were spring form, so it took me a moment to get my bearings as I pitched and bounced into the one directly across from Mrs. Brooks.

Next to her end of the glider was a small metal table that held an empty glass, a full ashtray, a book of matches, and an open pack of Lucky Strikes.

"I understand that your son and Rune were friends."

"If *friendship* is what you want to call it," she said carelessly as she reached for the cigarettes. "My Stanley turned out all right in the main, but he's inherited the soft heart and the questionable sense of his father. And he's just a little too quick to call someone a friend. O'course I could tell when I first laid eyes on that Rune he was a freeloading scalawag and a four-flushing son of a gun. Seen his type many, many times. I worked in the circus as a young gal before Charles took me away from the life. Part of a trapeze act. Travelin' about, I seen plenty of no-goods, let me tell you. But sad to say, Stan's gullible streak made for a real blind spot when it came to Rune's glib tongue and tales of woe."

"It's what keeps guys like Rune in business, and what makes the world go 'round."

She nodded, and for just a split-second her smile turned rueful. She put a Lucky Strike in her mouth and offered me the pack. I told her no thanks.

"So, I'm guessing it was your son who persuaded you to rent the apartment to Rune."

"You're a good guesser," she said as she lit her cigarette and then pitched the match in the ashtray. "For darn cheap too. Too darn cheap." After inhaling and exhaling a lungful of smoke, she added, "O'course, just like I figured, and true to form for a freeloader, that young ne'er-do-well got behind in his rent after the very first month."

She was clearly on a roll, so I let her keep rolling.

"Why, only a day or two before he got hisself killed, I told Rune that if he didn't pay what he owed me, I'd have him evicted," she said dryly. She gave me a conspiratorial wink and added, "It seemed like a good time to lay down the law, what with Stan away this summer workin' on a fishin' boat belongin' to an old friend of mine, so's he'd be none the wiser. You understand."

I told her I knew all about none the wiser. "How'd Rune react to your eviction threat?"

"Oh, Mr. Smooth-talker tells me how very soon he'll be payin' me in full, and then some," she said, as she blew smoke in the air. "He goes on and on about his ship comin' in real, real soon. The kind of claptrap typical of a sponger dodge."

"You didn't believe him."

She waved smoke away with her plump hand. "O'course I believed he had somethin' in the works he hoped would pay off for *him*. What I didn't believe was that I'd be gettin' my rent money anytime soon because of it."

"Did Rune tell you what he meant by his ship coming in?"

"Nuh-uh. All he would tell me was to be patient, and he'd have my money quicker than a New York wink. So, on account of my Stanley, I decided to give Rune one last chance." She added grimly, "But o'course he goes and gets hisself killed. Talk about throwin' good money after bad, I tell ya."

"Cops think the killer heard me coming up the back steps and left down the fire escape."

"That's what they told me, too. My Charles had that fire escape special built. Seemed needless at the time, it bein' only a two-story buildin'. But Charles was thoughtful that way. A truly honorable man. That he was. A big part of his charm and why I loved him."

I noticed the uneven wear on the heels of her oxfords as Mrs. Brooks put her thick right ankle over her thick left one and sat silent for a moment, gazing down at the street behind me. A shroud of smoke hovered above her head. She shifted her eyes and stared at me coolly, as if studying every little hair and miniscule pore on my face. Finally she asked, "Do you think Rune's ship comin' in had somethin' to do with him bein' murdered?"

"I don't know, but I wouldn't be at all surprised."

"That makes two of us," she said softly, as she ground out her cigarette stub in the ashtray.

We were both quiet. A blue Plymouth Sedan went slowly by on Burke Avenue, its motor making a sputtering noise. I couldn't make him out from the porch, but the driver seemed to be looking for an address. I turned back to Mrs. Brooks as she lit another Lucky Strike.

I said, "Know anything about a Contax camera that I found in Rune's place?"

She nodded and took a drag on her cigarette. "It's one of my son's." Her angelic smile returned. "Photography's been a hobby of my Stanley since he was in high school."

"When did Rune borrow it?"

Her bushy brows went up and down a few times as she thought about it. "Maybe a month ago or so, now. But no more than that. It was just before my boy left. I was with both of 'em in the kitchen here when he asked Stan could he use it. Why? Is it important?"

"Could be," I said with a shrug. "Did Rune tell Stan *why* he wanted to borrow it?"

She puffed quietly on her cigarette and considered that. As she dropped ash into the ashtray, she shook her head. "Nuh-uh. Not really. O'course I'm sure you know what an 'Unsteady Eddie' Rune could be, all the time goin' from job to job, not stayin' put. That kinda thing. He worked for a paintin' outfit for a month or two, when outta the blue he asks to borrow Stan's camera. Suddenly it's no more paintin' for Rune and he's braggin' in that highfalutin way of his about makin' some money takin' pictures of people. You know the kind of folks what take your picture on the street or at some tourist spot or some such, and then try and sell it to you as a sort of keepsake. O'course I just seen the whole thing as another one of Rune's four-flush boasts."

"That's probably a safe bet," I said in a tone that was a wee bit too even.

Mrs. Brooks regarded me curiously. "Say, are you maybe thinkin' that this harebrained scheme of his is some kind of clue to his bein' killed?"

"Don't know. I play plenty of hunches in my line of work. I find it pays to look under rocks that others ignore."

Her angelic smile broadened into a beatific one.

"Do you know if Rune was regularly seeing someone?" I asked.

"A steady girl, you mean?"

I nodded.

"I doubt it. His kind play the field and break hearts and have a special way of spreadin' ill will like most people spread butter."

It was hard to disagree with her, so I didn't. Still, I figured I'd quiz Sten about a possible girlfriend later. We talked for a few more minutes and then I thanked her for her time and gave her one of my cards.

As I got up to leave, Mrs. Brooks asked, "I don't suppose the police found anythin' that resembles my rent money?"

"They didn't tell me if they did. Sorry."

She was a likeable old gal and I really was sorry Rune had stiffed her. But I wasn't about to tell her about the fifty-dollar bill I'd found pinned inside the cuff of Rune's jacket. Word of that getting back to Detectives Fitch and Togstad would only make them wonder what else I might've glommed onto.

Gunnar the Oh-So-Cautious.

Partway to my coupe, I looked back at her. A hazy column of smoke wafted from the ashtray. Her feet were still resting on the hassock and her hands were now clasped over her bosom. Her head was tilted back and I think I heard faint snoring.

I hopped in my car and nosed down Burke to circle the block. Just before turning right, I peered in my rearview mirror and saw the driver of that blue Plymouth Sedan a few car lengths behind me. He was still going slow and still appeared to be hunting for a particular house. So, just in case I was wrong, I sped up and circled a few more blocks until I was satisfied I wasn't being followed.

Gunnar the Little-Bit-Edgy.

I mulled things over as I moved through traffic on my way to Ballard.

My chat with Clara Brooks got me rethinking what might have happened to Rune and why. He was plainly up to something that he expected would pay off in a big way; instead it got him killed. But my photo-blackmail theory now looked like a dead end. He'd probably promised to sell one or more of the pictures he'd taken on the day they weren't ready for him, which was why he blew up at Spud at the camera shop. There seemed to be nothing more to it than that.

So, the question still remained: what had the old four-flusher been up to?

I pondered that question a time or two the rest of the day, which I spent in my office reading mail and newspapers from the previous two days, waiting for clients who never showed.

Chapter 7

——

LATER THAT SAME DAY, while eating dinner at Mrs. Berger's, I asked Sten Larson if Rune had a steady girlfriend.

Sten shook his head. "I didn't see Rune all the time, but when I did and a girl was with him, it was always somebody new. You know Rune … he was strictly a new-flavor-of-the-week kind of guy."

What was it Clara Brooks had said about Rune? He spread ill will like most people spread butter.

After swallowing a mouthful of food, Sten added, "Gunnar, after work today I made some calls and asked around as to who mighta loaned Rune that camera. But I got nothin."

"Thanks, Sten. I appreciate it," I said. "As it turns out, the son of Rune's landlady loaned it to him."

"Why'd he want it in the first place if he weren't really a photo nut?" asked Mrs. Berger.

"His landlady told me Rune planned to take candid pictures of people with the idea of selling them to those he could get interested. One of his many money-making schemes."

"The air-castle talk of a dreamer, if you ask me," said Mrs.

Berger. "A pipe dream if I ever heard one. And believe me, I've heard my share."

Walter, Sten, my landlady, and I were sitting at the kitchen table eating boiled potatoes, steamed carrots, and a small roast. The reliably slow kitty-cat wall clock read 5:10.

"Why, a body might say I was led into an airy-fairy world of dreamers and their chatter one summer during my flapper days," Mrs. Berger announced crisply.

"And what was it that happened to you that particular summer, Nora?" asked Walter, genuinely interested in the details of our landlady's life. He sat directly across from her.

"Any of you ever hear of a magician called Flanders the Fantastic?" she asked.

None of us had.

Mrs. Berger looked a bit disappointed with us. She told us that one Malcolm Flanders was a magician on the Pantages Theatre Circuit back in the 1920s.

Mrs. Berger went on, "I suppose it was a bit of luck for me that the girl who was Flanders' regular assistant broke a leg while out on a tear one night, so's he needed a stand-in for her, and pronto. A fellow I knew who knew Flanders, recommended me to him."

"*You* were a magician's assistant, Aunt Nora?" asked Sten, waiting to put a forkful of meat in his mouth.

She nodded vigorously.

"Well how come this is the first I'm hearin' about it?" Sten added.

"It's never come up before, is how come. Besides, it was only for three months," said Mrs. Berger in a brittle voice. "After a crash course in my stage duties, I joined Flanders the Fantastic on the Pantages Circuit."

"Did you like that particular end of show business?" I asked.

Mrs. Berger scrunched up her face. "Not nearly as much as my later burlesque work. But I'll admit it had its moments. That Flanders … he tied me up, squeezed me into boxes, stuck swords in me, sawed me in half, and did a helluva lot more to boot. But quite a bit of the time, when he was doin' his solo magic tricks, he just had me prancing around him on stage in a flimsy silk outfit so's to distract the audience."

"Ah … classic *misdirection*," Walter intoned knowingly.

"No, Walter. I always did exactly what I was told to do … *on stage*, that is."

Walter attempted to clarify but was cut off by Mrs. Berger, "Of course, womanizer that he was, that Flanders wanted me to do *everything* his other girl had done for him—if you catch my drift." She surveyed us with an up-from-under look.

We all caught her drift to the point where we stopped eating and stared at her expectantly.

"But I told Flanders nothing doing. And that, as they say, was the end of that."

"Good for you, Nora. That's the girl. You stood on your principles," said Walter confidently.

"It had nothing to do with school masters or standing on them, or standing on anything else, Walter. It had everything to do with me choosing not to *lay* down."

"You mean *lie* down, Nora," said Walter the Ever-Helpful.

"No, I definitely mean *lay*. Trust me, Walter, there was no question in my mind that Malcom Flanders wanted me *laying* down."

Walter wisely gave up his grammar lesson as a bad job, and instead said, "So, you refused to submit because you had scruples."

"I refused to submit because Flanders was a homely son of a seacook whose mere touch gave me the dry gripes. Thankfully he wore gloves during his act. So, believe you me, I told him to keep his pudgy clammy hands to himself during our off-hours or he'd be out an assistant faster than he could say hocus-pocus."

Walter, Sten, and I reached an unspoken agreement not to

ask any more questions on this particular subject, and for a few minutes we ate our meal without further conversation.

Finally, between bites, I asked Mrs. Berger, "So, you say you were led into a world of dreamers and their talk that summer you were on the Pantages Circuit. How so?"

"Because up till then I'd never in my life met such a pack of people always talking about coming up with bigger and better acts, so as to become big and famous somebodies, so as to make more and more money, is *how so*."

On that note Mrs. Berger got up to get us coffee and our dessert of apple pie she'd bought at a bakery—her own baking being pretty much limited to failed cookie experiments.

Mrs. Berger ate only a couple of bites of her pie before putting her fork down and dabbing her lips with a napkin. She sipped some coffee and put a Chesterfield in her ivory holder. When she lit up, she looked at me and said, "About your friend, Rune—"

"He wasn't really my friend."

"Well, whoever's friend he was, Gunnar, I'll bet Walter's dollars to Sten's doughnuts that it was some pie-in-the-sky scheme that got him killed."

KIRSTI'S MIC CLICKED OFF suddenly and she said, "The way you talk about your landlady …. I mean, she sounds nice enough, and all … but a bit of a whack-job. Am I getting her right?"

"Mrs. Berger *was* a bit unconventional, I'll grant you that. A little eccentric even. Or maybe just plain old *quaint*."

"I guess," Kirsti said, screwing up her face in thought. She shifted the cassette recorder on her lap as she crossed her denim-clad legs. Her raised sandaled foot began to bob up and down.

"Well, part of what made Mrs. Berger what she was were the phrases she'd blurt out. They were usually colorful, if not downright politically incorrect by today's standards. Out of the blue she'd say things like, 'When I was young, everyone had to work … even the cat.' Or, 'Times was so tough, we'd be happy to work for a cheap pair of shoes.' Walter and Sten and I could usually dope out her meaning … at least we could if provided with sufficient context."

Kirsti smiled and nodded. "You'd said that Mrs. Berger believed in chewing her food a lot, right?"

"Uh-huh. She was a fanatical believer in Fletcherism. And, thanks to Walter, around the time I'm telling you about, oil-pulling had become her latest craze."

"Oil-pulling? Never heard of it. What is it?"

"It's a folk remedy that apparently traces back thousands of years."

"How'd your friend Walter learn about it?"

"Well, owing to his disfigurement, Walter usually ventured out only at night. He had his usual haunts where he could visit with people who knew him well. At one of his nightspots, he met a fellow who was visiting from India. They got to talking about oil-pulling. According to this guy, you're supposed to swish a tablespoon of either sesame, coconut, or olive oil around in your mouth for ten or fifteen minutes every day, and then spit it in the trash afterwards."

"What good does that do?"

I shrugged and chuckled a bit before saying, "It's a kind of oral hygiene that supposedly cures migraines, diabetes, asthma, and acne, while also whitening your teeth."

Kirsti regarded me skeptically. "Sounds a bit farfetched."

"Well, think what you will. But Mrs. Berger swore that oil-pulling ended her migraines. And I have to say that the coffee stains on her teeth did disappear."

Kirsti smiled and said in a thin, playful voice, "In your story about the boutique, you hinted that your friend Walter and your landlady had kinda started having a thing."

"Uh-huh … their relationship had definitely developed a new wrinkle. But around Sten and me they tended to act like everything was as it had always been. We played along and didn't pry. Of course, the two of them had the whole house to themselves for much of the day, so I can only guess what went on then."

Kirsti clicked on the mic.

Chapter 8

—

THE WEDNESDAY AFTER RUNE'S murder, my nosing around into his affairs was abruptly put on the back burner by a paying client.

My office in Ballard was on the second floor of the two-story Hanstad Building on Market Street. Dag Erickson, a local attorney, owned the building and worked out of the large office that neighbored my small one.

During the war, landlord Dag had his suite enlarged, which transformed the one I ended up renting into two adjoining walk-in closets entered by the outer door and divided by an inner door. Clients who weren't claustrophobic waited in the outer cubbyhole. At least Dag had left me a window in the inner one.

Around 9:30 that morning I was nearing my outer door and reaching into my pocket for the key when I heard a woman's voice call my name. Miss Cissy Paget stuck her pretty head out of Dag's office, where she presided as secretary. I turned to see her holding up a slip of paper, which she waved at me.

"A message for you, tough guy," Cissy said as she started to walk toward me, though *glide* was a better word. She had the natural stride and carriage of one of those finishing school students made to walk with a book on her head. Cissy's supple body swayed and quivered alluringly from heels to hindquarters. A whiff of sandalwood wafted under my nose as she reached me.

"Thanks, sweet knees," I said, taking the paper from her.

"Your wish is my ... *and all that*," Cissy said saucily. She could be cheeky, brash, and fun-loving, and her ready smile was often conspiratorial.

"You'll see that I wrote it all down for you," she said crisply. "An attorney named Ethan Calmer phoned. If possible, he wants you to come see him early this afternoon, or I suppose whenever you can work it into your extremely busy schedule."

I smiled. "I'll see what I can arrange."

Cissy Paget was a slender but shapely brown-haired girl with thin lips and sparkly eyes the color of chestnuts. She had narrow hips and medium-sized breasts that jiggled subtly when she swung those hips. And despite her businesslike attire—a skirt suit and round-lensed reading glasses similar to Mahatma Gandhi's—she was very pretty in a no-nonsense way.

"I don't suppose lawyer Calmer gave you a hint as to what this is about?"

Cissy shook her lovely head. "Only that he wants to hire you." As she turned to leave, she added, "You're to call his secretary for an appointment. There. I've told you everything. Now all you need to do is dial the number."

Cissy was easy to be chummy with, and I did my level best to view her as a pal. But when it comes to nice-looking gals, it's nearly impossible for the average guy to avoid carnal theorizing. I was not impervious to her physical appeal, and we both knew it. I ogled her as she glided back to Dag's office, which is what she expected me to do. Such was the nature of our symbiotic relationship. Or so I liked to think.

ETHAN CALMER'S SECRETARY ASKED me to come to their

offices on the eighth floor of the Ponn Building, a steel-framed skyscraper on Second Avenue near Cherry Street. When she asked if 1:30 would work for me, I told her it would be just ducky.

So, around 1:23, I passed through a small arcade with the requisite drugstore, lunch counter, and shoeshine stand to reach a lobby of gold-and-cream-colored columns and bronze friezes of ferns and sunflowers. I was feeling about as idyllic and pastoral as ornamental ferns and sunflowers can make you feel when I reached the bank of elevators to make my ascension.

I took a right when I stepped from the elevator and found the Mumford and Calmer shingle hanging two doors down and across the corridor. The door let me into a fair-sized room with several chairs facing a table with old magazines in a messy pile. This waiting area was separated from the entrance to the offices within by a rectangular desk large enough to hold all the dishes of a potluck supper at a family reunion, including the desserts.

At the desk was a strawberry blonde in her early twenties whose rectangular-shaped nameplate said Lillian Voorhees. There was nothing average about her. Soft curls that barely touched her shoulders adorned a beautiful face with a pale, fine-pored complexion. Bright-red lipstick caused lips that were pursed for effect to be moist and glistening. She wore a short-sleeved nutmeg-brown blouse that looked to be made of chiffon. On her right wrist was a shiny gold bracelet, but she glanced at the watch on the other wrist after we made eye contact.

I tried not to wince when a blast of perfume exploded in my nostrils as I sidled up to her desk. A lot of jasmine had died to create the quantities of toilet water she'd splashed on after lunch.

Lillian Voorhees fluttered her thick lashes at me as she unpursed her lips and asked, "Mr. Gunnar Nilson?"

"That would be me."

She showed me at least six of her thirty-two teeth and said in a sweet, melodic voice, "We talked on the phone earlier. Please, have a seat. Mr. Calmer will see you shortly."

There was a *Look* magazine from earlier in the year on top of the stack on the waiting area table. On the cover Bob Hope stood next to a gorgeous brunette. In the upper right-hand corner, I read, "How F.D.R. Planned to Use the A-Bomb." I thought about checking into F.D.R.'s plan, but instead I snagged a copy of the *Saturday Evening Post* and sat in the chair nearest Miss Voorhees.

I studied a picture of Anne Baxter in a Chesterfield ad. Holding up a cigarette, she smiled and told me that she preferred Chesterfield because it was milder. But before I could leaf through the magazine, I learned that Miss Voorhees' "shortly" was indeed *shortly.* I heard her say, "Mr. Nilson, you may go in now."

As I walked toward her desk, she pointed over her left shoulder at an archway and added, "The door to your right. It's open, and Mr. Calmer is expecting you."

Like me, Ethan Calmer was in his early thirties, and when I finally saw him stand up, I made him to be about my height— six one. But for now, he sat in a high leather chair behind a huge desk made from some sort of dark wood that was doubtless imported at great cost. He had wavy brown hair and eyes that were light blue and sparkly. Broad-shouldered and just a tad on the pudgy side, he had small ears, a broad pug nose, full lips, and far more teeth than anyone would ever want or need. By no means good-looking, but not exactly homely. An in-betweener. He wore a nicely pressed dark-brown suit, and a diamond pin pierced a necktie cinched tight around a short and thick wrestler's neck.

There were three other chairs in the room for clients. I sat in the chair directly in front of his desk and started fishing a clove out of my front shirt pocket.

His office telephone rang. He said he was sorry and answered it, listening quietly while I popped a clove in my mouth and bit down.

Calmer told the party on the line that he'd call back later. Then he hung up and said he was sorry again.

I told him no problem and gave him an expectant gaze.

His fast speech and sudden movements told me he had a quick mind, and his hail fellow well met demeanor that he liked to get along with people—or at least give them the impression that he did.

Giving me a level look, he said, "Dag Erickson recommends you highly."

"Are you a friend of Dag's?"

"No. We're merely professional acquaintances, and I know him by reputation. Our paths have crossed enough times over the past few years to where I've come to respect his opinion." This was said matter-of-factly, as if he'd told me it was rainy or sunny outside and that I'd be very happy to know it.

"You've discussed some details with Dag, then? Details as to why you wanted to see me?"

"No. No, I haven't. I merely told him I needed help with a very delicate situation. I knew he used a private investigator from time to time. He recommended you."

I wondered why Calmer wasn't talking to the one or more investigators that his firm probably used, but since I needed the work, I decided not to mention it. Instead, I nodded and let his words bounce around the room awhile before he spoke again.

"You'll want a retainer, of course."

"If I agree to do what you want done, Mr. Calmer," I said. "I charge thirty dollars a day plus expenses. In your case, a hundred-dollar retainer should do it."

"Fine, fine," he said, and stared at me thoughtfully for a long moment. "I'm acting for my fiancée in this matter. She was against the idea at first, but she's authorized me to speak with you and possibly hire you."

"After you've sized me up?"

He shot me a shrewd glance and nodded. "She'll also want to meet with you, of course. But I'll get to that in a few minutes."

Calmer opened one of his deep desk drawers and came out with a bottle of Paul Jones Whiskey and two shot glasses. Maybe he really liked that brand. Or maybe it was just an office bottle, and he saved the kind he really liked for special occasions. One never knows. He filled the glasses and put the bottle away.

I reached for the glass he'd slid over to me and took a sip. He downed his in one practiced swallow.

"Here's the situation, Mr. Nilson," he said as he pushed his glass to one side. "I recently became engaged to a wonderful girl. Miss Mercedes Atwood. Perhaps you've heard of her father, Chester Atwood?"

I told him I'd heard of him. Chester Atwood, the well-known scion and heir of a fortune-maker from Seattle's early boom years, Tobias Atwood.

His lips formed a big smile. "Then as you may know, Chester is somewhat of a local legend. His inheritance permitted him to become a world traveler and collector," he said proudly. "Miss Atwood, my fiancée, maintains a display room in her home of some of the souvenirs and artifacts that her father collected during his many adventurous years. It's her own private monument to him, you understand."

I smiled my understanding as I thought of Mrs. Berger's bump and grind shrine. Everybody's got a story to tell, and their own way of telling it.

Calmer added in an awestruck tone, "Of course, the majority of the really valuable pieces of Chester's collection have been loaned to museums by Miss Atwood."

"Of course," I said, just to say it.

He went on awhile about various pieces housed in museums, and about something in particular that was supposedly worth a small fortune. The man practically drooled as he spoke of it.

"When Chester Atwood was in Shanghai in the mid-thirties, he purchased a set of porcelain incense burners from a collector who was liquidating his assets. This fellow was a British expatriate who saw the writing on the wall when it came to Japanese imperialism, and he was doing what he had to do to get out in front of it, if you understand me."

I told him I understood him. I understood him in spades.

"Anyway, as this fellow was hurriedly taking his leave of Shanghai, Chester Atwood was able to acquire this very rare Dehua porcelain set for a song. A truly amazing stroke of luck for him."

It was plain that Ethan Calmer took great pride in this aspect of his fiancée's life.

"But please forgive the digression," he said. "To get to the point: Miss Atwood and I announced our engagement less than a week ago. Late afternoon yesterday, my fiancée received an anonymous telephone call. And she received another one just like it very early this morning. The calls are menacing." He looked like he wanted me to ask him a question.

"*Menacing* how?" I asked, taking another sip of my whiskey.

"Mercedes—my fiancée—says that it's a raspy gruff sort of voice that does the talking. But she doesn't recognize it. So, unless he's a total stranger, he's likely disguising it. Both calls were not long. But the message of both was the same."

"Which is …?"

"Each time the raspy voice said, 'If I can't have you, no one else will. Break off the engagement before the end of this month, or else.' And then he hung up."

"Did he say what he meant by 'or else'?"

"No, he did not. Just 'or else.'"

"And you say he's called two times?"

"Yes."

"At different times?"

"Yes. Late afternoon yesterday and early this morning. Mercedes dismissed the first call as a mean prank. But the second call really shook her up. She masks it well, but she's both frightened and angry."

I nodded my head slightly.

"She told me about the first call immediately, of course. And at first I, too, thought it was just a cruel joke. But not anymore. Not after the second one."

Two calls still seemed a nasty prank in my book, but Calmer seemed genuinely concerned. Being a lawyer, maybe he had good reason to be. So, I said, "Have you talked to the cops?"

"No, Mr. Nilson. Mercedes asked me not to."

"Look, Mr. Calmer, this caller gives you till the end of the month, whatever he means by that. Police manpower and resources could make far better time than one man in locating this guy, if that's what you're going to ask of me."

"I understand that, of course. But as I said, Mercedes didn't even want me to talk with *you*. She's a very private person. She's also concerned for me. She says she doesn't want my firm dragged into anything that might tarnish its reputation— though I don't really think this would." Calmer shrugged his broad shoulders. "For that matter, I told her that I was certain my firm could easily weather something like this, and if anything, should it become known, it would more likely garner public sympathy than scorn. But she's insistent on the point. She can be like that. And again, she's a very private person. A lovely girl with a resolute spirit," he added almost dreamily.

I kept quiet to let his dreamy remark dissipate.

He went on, "I don't believe this is a prank. It can't be a coincidence that these calls began not long after we announced our engagement. And I imagine that whoever is making them is most certainly unstable. Deranged. I suspect he's someone with a grievance against me, and that by frightening Mercedes with his threats, he's actually targeting me. I've concluded that he's either a disgruntled former client or someone who lost a case to us. In my practice, I've learned it doesn't take much to send some people over the edge."

I finished my drink but kept the glass in my hand. I said evenly, "Have you considered that this menacing caller might possibly be a former suitor of Miss Atwood's?"

He took a deep breath and let it out slowly before answering. "Yes, we discussed that very thing. But from how Mercedes tells it, most of her prior beaus are now married, and she ended things on amicable terms with one and all. Besides, Mercedes has actually been out of circulation for quite a while. She was somewhat reclusive that first year or two after her father died. She took his death pretty hard, you see. During that time, she didn't socialize much, and she dated no one. I happened to meet her through mutual friends at one of the rare dinner parties she attended. You might say I swept her off her feet and got her to rejoin the world. We've been going together for almost six months now."

I put my empty glass on his desk and sat back a bit as I planted an ankle on my knee.

"How can I help you, Mr. Calmer?"

"As you surmised, I want you to try and find out the identity of this anonymous caller and stop him from tormenting Mercedes. Do you think you can do that?"

"It's possible," I said coolly, "as in *anything is.*"

"Good. You'll at least try, then. That's all I can ask. I'm chiefly concerned with Miss Atwood's safety, of course. I'm having the alarm system in her home revamped. The caller stipulates she has till the end of the month to break off our engagement, but we're possibly dealing with a lunatic here, and we can't be certain what he might do, or when."

"Uh-huh," I said dryly. One of my grandmother's sayings came to mind: "Fools and stubborn people make wealthy lawyers." But I didn't say this. Instead, I added, "You've likely got a fair idea of past clients or legal adversaries who might be nursing a grudge against you. I'll need a list of any you think may be addle-brained enough to make this sort of phone call."

He nodded. "I've already come up with names. But it's a short list, I'm afraid." He pulled an envelope out from under his desk blotter and slid it across the desk to me.

I put the envelope in my coat pocket and said, "A list of the names and addresses of Miss Atwood's former boyfriends would be good to have as well."

"Do you really think that's necessary, Mr. Nilson? As I told you, she insists she's on good terms with all of them."

"Listen Mr. Calmer, if I'm to do this job right, it makes sense for me to give a hard look at the men in Miss Atwood's past. She may be right about her old beaus, but experience has taught me that people aren't always the best judge of character when it comes to their romances. After all, your caller makes *romantic* claims on your fiancée. Ex-suitors go to the front of the line, the way I see it. It would be foolish to ignore them."

"I suppose you're right," he said bleakly. He curled his lip a little and fumbled with the knot of his necktie. "Miss Atwood will provide names and addresses for you, of course. You can get the list when you see her. She'd like you to call and arrange a time to meet—sometime this afternoon, if possible. As you leave, just ask Miss Voorhees, my secretary, to give you Miss Atwood's address and telephone number."

I said I'd do just that.

"From what Mercedes has told me, a couple of her former suitors now live in other parts of the country, so it's hard for me to believe one of them would be the guilty party. So, if I might suggest, perhaps you could primarily concentrate on those living in the state of Washington."

"I can do that. But Mr. Calmer, I'm sure you realize that my job demands that I look under rocks. And there's no telling where I'll eventually find those rocks."

"I fully understand, Mr. Nilson. But please check into those on my list first. If that should disclose this phone menace, then

Miss Atwood's former suitors can be left out of this entirely."

"I can do that."

"Fine. Now, should you have to look into Miss Atwood's suitors, treat it as the delicate matter that it is. Neither one of us wishes to offend anyone unduly. So I ask that you be *extremely* discreet."

As we stood up to shake hands, I told him I was the soul of discretion.

I went back to the reception area to where Miss Voorhees still manned her post. Being a glutton for punishment, I lingered right next to her chair, where her perfume caused my eyes to water. I said, "Boss man says you'll provide me with the address and phone number of Miss Mercedes Atwood."

Her eyebrows rose ever so slightly and her lips momentarily formed a lowercase "o," prior to her reaching for a pad and pencil on her desk and opening the drawer in front of her. Next, she did some quick rummaging in the drawer, studied what she found, and began writing on the pad. Finally, she tore the top page free and handed it to me.

She'd clearly been a keen student of the Palmer Method, because her penmanship was a work of art. I looked at the address and then back to the girl before saying, "Broadmoor, huh?"

Miss Voorhees unpursed her lips and smiled a modest, eight-toothed smile.

I made to leave, but continued to watch Calmer's secretary as I added, "I was once hired by a lady living in Broadmoor. All she wanted was for me to fire her houseboy."

That won me a high-pitched titter and a glimpse at two more teeth.

I FOUND A PAYPHONE down in the arcade near the lunch counter. I put in a nickel and dialed the number Miss Voorhees had given me.

A commanding but toneless voice on the other end

answered. The voice wasn't Miss Mercedes Atwood's, but I was pretty sure it was a female with a Scandinavian accent. I was going to make a quip but figured it wouldn't get me anywhere. My guess was the voice was unsmiling and liked it that way. Instead, I said, "My name is Gunnar Nilson. Miss Atwood is expecting a call from me."

The voice told me to wait.

After about two minutes, the voice returned and said, "Miss Atwood wishes you to be here at four thirty, sharp."

My Longines said 2:15. I told the voice that I could fit that into my busy schedule.

"Do you have the address?"

I told the voice I did.

The voice said, "Good," and hung up.

Next I called Sam Kelly, a reporter at the *Seattle Times*. When we'd finishing swapping barbed witticisms, Sam agreed to check out what their morgue had on the Atwoods for me and call me back on the payphone number.

That gave me time to slip over to the lunch counter for a late lunch. I had a tasty turkey sandwich and a cup of bitter coffee. The payphone rang as I was paying my bill.

Sam told me a few things I knew and several I didn't about Miss Atwood and her father. "The old man was quite the world traveler—his home in Seattle was where he occasionally hung his fez and pith helmet. By many he's considered a local legend. But if you ask me, Gunnar, from how I read it, he seemed a bit buggy. Maybe not bughouse buggy, but oddball buggy. You know what I mean?"

I told him I understood oddball buggy.

"Anyway, some of what Chester Atwood collected over the years might make for passable window dressing—if you like that kind of stuff, which I don't—but there are a few really rare and extremely valuable pieces the daughter has loaned out to museums. In particular there's this pair of ceramic incense burners made in China during one of those dynasties that sounds like a musical note when you say it."

"Old, huh?"

"Yeah. They're supposedly made from some special kind of porcelain. The covers of these burners are shaped like grotesque-looking lions called Foo Dogs."

"Imperial guardian lions."

"Ah, so you've heard of them. It figures. Anyway, supposedly this pair of Foo Dogs is Pricey with a capital 'P,' and the Atwood dame loans them out to be seen only once in a blue moon. Mainly they're kept in some bank vault gathering dust."

This had to be the special set Chester Atwood bought in Shanghai, which Calmer had raved about. I thanked Sam and hung up.

I passed through the small arcade and out.

Chapter 9

——

Located on the east side of Capitol Hill and bordered on the west by the Arboretum, Broadmoor was a logging site for many years before finally ending up as an affluent community with its own golf course. The original idea of making Broadmoor a kind of country club within Seattle was derailed by the Depression, so it wasn't until after World War II that the neighborhood started coming into its own as an enclosed haven for the upper crust. While Broadmoor's birth and development isn't exactly a "rags to riches" story, it comes pretty close to being a "logs to luxury" one.

I got over to Broadmoor around 4:20. I drove past what looked to be a green '47 Dodge Sedan parked kitty-corner across the street from the entrance. The lean, hatchet-faced driver had his window rolled down and looked a lot like a plainclothes cop on a stakeout. Though it wasn't any of my concern, of course, I made a note of the numbers on the license plate.

If you live in Broadmoor, you don't hire a crass and shabby private detective; you engage a polite and tidy confidential inquirer. And you prefer to do your engaging by proxy.

And you don't go to him. That just isn't done.

He comes to you, and he enters a neighborhood as far removed from that of the hoi polloi mainstream as a three-tier wedding cake is from a lumber-camp flapjack.

I nosed my coupe into a sweeping oblong section of Miss Atwood's long driveway, parking behind a blue Cadillac Sedan that looked like it had just been delivered yesterday. In front of it was a newer model red Buick that was probably acceptable for driving to market. Off to one side, looking as lonely and as out of place as a brewmaster at a temperance meeting, was a weather-beaten Dodge Coupe that had come off the assembly line during Franklin Roosevelt's first term. The Dodge probably belonged to one of the help.

The main building on the Atwood property was a three-story brick and columned Colonial that made most homes in Ballard look like low-rent summer cabins. I stared up at a series of little balconies and huge windows as a cool breeze jostled me out of the beginning of a daydream. I followed the flagstones to the front door.

The bell was answered by a bony middle-aged woman in a plain housedress the color of an old ashen mare. She had wide-set probing eyes underneath thin arched brows, an ordinary face, and graying hair parted in the middle and hanging in straight strands that almost touched her shoulders. She eyed me suspiciously, looking me up and down as if studying a bad cut of meat.

I tipped my hat as she asked me what I wanted. It was the same Scandinavian accent and commanding voice from the phone call earlier. I'd assumed it was the only voice she had. But I was wrong about that.

I told her I was Gunnar Nilson and gave her one of my cards.

That made a small difference. She actually smiled and said in an almost pleasant tone, "Please, come in."

I removed my hat and did so.

The huge vestibule had a high, coffered ceiling that could

make you feel insignificant if you stood there too long and thought about it more than you should.

She said, "Please follow me."

She led me through an oak-paneled reception room past a broad, sweeping staircase with a banister that looked like it might be fun to slide down. We ignored the closed door leading to what I assumed was a drawing room and went down a hallway that led us to a pair of doors that opened into a living room that didn't look like it was meant to be lived in. She pointed to one of four Chinese wing chairs with coral-pink upholstery that surrounded a large glass and dark-wood coffee table in the center of the room. A plain white envelope sat squarely on top of it.

As she turned to leave, she said, "Please, have a seat."

I hugged my hat to my lap and planted myself in a chair that faced the doors we'd come through.

Before she left me, my escort added over her shoulder, "Miss Atwood will be with you soon." The doors quietly closed behind her.

I picked up the plain white envelope from off the coffee table, saw that it was sealed, and put it back as I'd found it.

It was a warm, dry, stuffy room with the odors of the priceless, the remarkable, and the old. It felt like a museum. An easy room to feel uneasy in.

One large wall had several paintings hanging on it, only one of which seemed familiar. The remaining walls had objects suspended from them or were lined with large cases, towering shelves, and pedestals loaded with sculptures, bric-a-brac, and travel mementos that looked like they'd come from South America, Africa, Europe, and the most baffling parts of the Orient. It was a great room to be in if you went in for Traditional Mausoleum.

A collection of headdresses and spears got me out of my chair. As I went over for a closer look, I started to reach for my stash of cloves in my front shirt pocket.

I hadn't heard the doors open, but behind me a woman said in a quiet but firm tone, "I'd prefer you didn't smoke in here, Mr. Nilson. We try to keep this showroom unspoiled."

I turned around and said, "I don't smoke. I was reaching for one of these." I waved a clove that was clamped between my thumb and index finger. "I suck on cloves. It's an old home remedy for toothache."

"And you're suffering from toothache?"

"Not at the moment, no."

She looked mystified but the moment faded so quickly, I wasn't sure what I'd seen.

Miss Mercedes Atwood had an oval face that was lovely in a proper, solemn kind of way. Like her tone, she had the authoritative air of someone used to getting her own way. She was probably twenty-six years old—give or take. She neither smiled nor frowned.

"You must be Miss Atwood," I said cheerily.

She nodded brusquely. Her raven-colored hair was glossy, parted in the middle, and swept up in a kind of regal updo with soft waves, supple rolls, and precise curls.

My old partner Lou Boyd, from back in my Bristol Agency days before the war, would have said Miss Atwood had a come-hither figure trying but failing to hide itself in don't-touch-me clothes. She wore a navy-blue sheath frock with gold buttons along the left side from underarm to mid-thigh that for all its simplicity drew the right sort of attention to her shapely figure and her midsized but well-formed bust. She had pallid skin like an elegant but fragile China teacup. Not too much makeup but not too little, either. Her crisp, small but sensual lips were as red as newly plucked cherries and as lustrous as rubies. She had a cute little snub nose and dark and lazy brown eyes with lashes that might almost provide cover from the sun's glare. Her looks would have been striking if it wasn't for her looks.

Miss Atwood gestured for me to sit. I chose a wing chair across the coffee table from where she sat. She carefully crossed her legs, thought better of it, and just as carefully uncrossed them. They were a nice pair of careful legs in sheer stockings that made them look naked. Her painted toenails were showcased by peep-toe pumps. It was as if she was trying *not* to look alluring, but only succeeding in a half-baked fashion.

As I slipped the clove in my mouth, I recklessly planted my right ankle over my left knee.

"I've never met a private detective before, Mr. Nilson. To hire, I mean. I've always imagined it to be a rather tawdry and distasteful line of work."

"It has its tawdry and distasteful moments, Miss Atwood."

That seemed to sail right over her head, but I was left to wonder because we were interrupted. The doors swung open and my escort from earlier came in with a tray and a thin smile. She placed the tray on the coffee table next to the white envelope. It held a teapot, two cups and saucers, two spoons, a cream dispenser, and what appeared to be a little bowl of sugar.

"Thank you, Nadia. That will be all," Miss Atwood said softly. Nadia vanished, taking her thin smile with her.

"I hope you like Oolong, Mr. Nilson. It's the tea I prefer."

I told her Oolong was just fine as I helped myself.

"Mr. Calmer tells me that a fellow attorney highly recommends you. After his conversation with you earlier, he immediately telephoned and told me that he'd hired you."

"Uh-huh," I said, as I poured cream in my cup of tea.

"As Mr. Calmer surely told you, I agreed to use your services against my better judgment," she said gravely, taking a little sip from her cup.

"If 'better judgment' always won out, Miss Atwood, I wouldn't be in business."

"No, I suppose not," she said a bit frostily, and then studied me a moment. Her naturally arched eyebrows gave her an indefinable imperiousness. "If you don't mind, Mr. Nilson, tell me something of yourself."

"All right," I said, tasting my Oolong as I weighed what to

say. "But be forewarned, Miss Atwood, if I wrote down my life's story, it wouldn't make for good reading." I considered how my old partner Lou Boyd used to get a read on people by saying something shocking. I toyed with Lou's tactic as I began, "I was raised by my grandparents in a little whistle-stop upstate called Conway. My grandfather ran the local feed store. After high school and a series of odd jobs, I ended up working for a big detective agency in Seattle. The war interrupted that. Following my discharge, I attended college for a year on the G.I. Bill—just enough to learn that Proust is pronounced *proost* and not *prowst*. After that I decided to go it alone as a detective. I'm thirty-three years old. I'm single, mainly because I see no point in buying a coffee percolator when I can easily get coffee for free."

She sucked in a harsh breath. "You confuse wit with being boorish and offensive," she said, her voice well-bred yet drenched in vinegar.

"I guess that all depends on what it was *you* thought I meant by *coffee*, Miss Atwood."

That nearly got her to smile, but not quite. She apparently only gave those out on real special occasions. Still, it suggested she had a pulse and a sliver of personality.

After a respectable pause, she asked a bit icily, "Do you know anything about *me*, Mr. Nilson?"

"Your family is old money by Seattle standards. You were raised by a widowed father who inherited his wealth from your grandfather Tobias, who started off logging, worked as a carpenter, then as a shopkeeper, till finally he made a bundle in land investments. This allowed your father Chester to become a world traveler and a collector." I gestured to the exhibits in the room. "Some of the things your father collected are rare and quite valuable and have been loaned out to museums. Your father died four years ago, leaving you everything. You're not married but you soon will be, to Ethan Calmer."

"I'm rather impressed, Mr. Nilson," she said in her stiff, unruffled way.

It was nothing that couldn't be gleaned from the morgue file of the *Seattle Times* with a little help from Sam Kelly, but I let her be impressed. She seemed to like it that way.

My reference to her father's collecting jaunts got her talking about him. "My father was a local celebrity of sorts," she said evenly. "Travel was his chief passion." She spoke with no emotion. In fact, during this conversation, if a muscle in her face moved even a tiny bit, you'd need time lapse photography to prove it by me.

"So, I suppose you've been all over the world."

"Oh, my father never took me with him," she said flatly.

"Never?"

"No. Not once."

I decided to pour myself another cup of tea.

Miss Atwood's eyes got distant as she quietly said, "From what I've been told, before I was born my mother would accompany my father on some of his trips. But that ended when I came along. She died when I was two, so she's nothing but a faint memory to me now."

Miss Atwood paused for a long moment, so it seemed like a good time to sip tea. She was in her own little world, so much so, that if I was a smoker, I could have lit a cigarette just then and I don't think she'd have noticed or objected.

"No," she said finally, "I remained at home during Father's many absences."

"You mean you didn't even go with him once you got into your teens?"

She looked at me now. "Oh, no. Father believed that I should remain at home during my formative years."

And your father should have remained at home with you, I thought but didn't say. I actually began to feel a little bit sorry for this poor little rich girl, but my pity had barely started to take shape when she obliterated it by continuing on like an automaton, "Next to travel, my father was devoted to his collecting." She pointed to a few of the displays. "And while much of what he brought home is interesting but not exceptional, still, as you remarked, some of the items my father collected are extraordinary and even precious."

"Like those priceless porcelain incense burners he bought in Shanghai? The ones shaped like Foo Dogs?"

"So, you've heard of them."

"Mr. Calmer went on about them with some enthusiasm."

My mention of the love of her life barely evoked a nod. "Yes, Mr. Calmer is very proud of my father's rare acquisitions. The porcelain set you mention has particularly captured his fancy." There was no modulation in her voice, whether talking of her father or her fiancé.

Miss Atwood abruptly stopped talking, as if she suddenly remembered with a start that we were meeting for a purpose other than idle chatter.

We gave each other level stares. Hers was quite a poker-face. She had probably learned not to show feelings from the time she was in rompers. My expression was just mildly expectant.

Miss Atwood reminded me of a grim-faced Swedish accordion player I'd known as a kid. He ran the gamut of emotions from A to almost B, which meant you might get a handshake from him at Christmas and New Year's. But never expect a smile or anything even resembling a hug. Not unless something stronger than clam nectar was being served—then watch out.

"Mr. Calmer said that he told you all about the anonymous telephone calls I've received." She relayed this information as if she were an elevator operator on sale day at the Bon Marché, rattling off floor-by-floor patter.

I nodded. "Can you think of anyone in your circle of friends who might do such a thing?"

"I fail to see how a *friend* would behave in such an appalling manner," she said stormily—at least it was stormy for her.

"Uh-huh. I meant *friend* in the sense of acquaintance or associate." I added gently, "But Miss Atwood, hard experience has taught me that sometimes even those close to us may not always be what they seem to be."

She almost looked offended. As offended as she could look, anyway. And pale as she was, she seemed to get even paler. All the same, I could tell she was considering my remark.

"Perhaps so, Mr. Nilson," she said after a moment, her cool stare restored. "Perhaps so. But it's very difficult for me to think ill of any of my friends—and my old beaus in particular." This flat voice of hers was starting to grow on me like a bad case of athlete's foot. "None of my relationships ended sourly. They simply ended. We all moved on."

"I see," I said.

She lifted her already arched left eyebrow. "You see *what*?"

"I only meant I understand, Miss Atwood."

Her eyebrow returned to its usual position.

"I'm more than willing to believe it's probably true that you ended all your relationships on friendly terms. But, as I told Mr. Calmer, to do my job right, I still need the names and addresses of your former suitors. I have to be thorough. And your mystery caller does sound *romantically* fixated on you."

"So it would seem," she said, slowly nodding. "What then can be done, Mr. Nilson? Surely you've dealt with this kind of thing before."

"Not exactly this, but similar things, sure," I said. "It's why I asked about the people in your life. That has to be the starting point. Given what the caller says, the motive seems connected to an obsession with you. But that might just be a ruse. Calmer could be right. Maybe someone is trying to hurt *him* through you."

She didn't say anything. She just stared at me. She looked puzzled. Puzzled for her, that is.

Believing that I'd made my point sufficiently, I put my empty tea cup down and asked, "Who all do you employ here?"

She stiffened visibly and I thought she was going to spill her Oolong. "*Excuse* me?" Her arched eyebrows collided as her eyes narrowed. "What are you insinuating, Mr. Nilson?"

"I'm not. Given the situation, it's just a good idea to check into *anyone* with whom you have close contact on a regular basis."

"I'll have you know that my help is like family to me, and I do not at all appreciate the direction you're taking with your line of questions." She sounded out of breath.

"I don't either, Miss Atwood. But it's my job to ask what I'm asking. At the very least, it may be that one of your employees has seen or heard something that could be of help to me."

As she took this in, her nostrils flared a tiny bit. She stared at me a long moment and didn't seem to enjoy the view, but I could tell I'd won her over to the idea when her nostrils finally relaxed.

I said nothing as I reached for another clove. I popped it in my mouth as Miss Atwood again placed one knee carefully above the other. With one thigh resting over the other and her hem slightly hoisted, both knees showed to advantage. I furtively inspected the impressive contours of her raised leg until she started fidgeting her foot so that her peep-toe pump began to dangle. If the rest of her wasn't so controlled and impassive, I'd have found this alluring in an off-key way. For the first time, I imagined that I saw actual evidence of an underlying emotion. I was even starting to pick up on what Ethan Calmer might see in her, when she noticed me noticing her dangling foot and promptly uncrossed her legs and delicately cleared her throat.

After a very proper "ahem," Miss Atwood said in concessionary tone, "You'll want the names of all whom I employ."

I nodded.

She thought about it a good long minute before replying. "Nadia Forsgren. She's the woman who showed you in and brought us our tea. And Isabella Oscarson. She's the cook. She also helps Nadia with the housekeeping. They both live here with me."

"How long have they worked for you?"

"Since I was too young to remember. They've lived with us for years. They were with us when we used to live on First Hill. As I said, I was only two when my mother died, and Nadia and Isabella practically raised me. They took care of me when father was away on his trips. I trust them *implicitly*," she added firmly.

I scratched my chin and asked, "Any other employees?"

"No. I let the driver go after father died. I do all my own driving. And the gardener comes only once a week. He's in business for himself, and so strictly speaking he's not an employee. But I've used his services for years, and I've never had any problem with him or any of his helpers."

"I'll still need the particulars on him."

She gave me an abrupt nod.

"Other than the gardener and his helpers, has anyone else done work on your house in the last month or two?"

She thought for a moment then shook her head. "The house was painted inside and out well over a year ago. And then six or seven months ago, I believe it was, we had a plumbing problem that resulted in plaster repairs and the re-painting of two walls. But that's it."

We talked a little bit more. She told me that against her better judgment—and thanks to Ethan Calmer—she'd already typed up a list of the names and addresses of her former suitors. She reached down and picked up the plain white envelope from the coffee table and held it out to me. I took it and stuffed it in my inside coat pocket.

She talked some more about the amicable relationships she'd had with all her former suitors. To hear her tell it, her romantic breakups were as smooth and uneventful as turning the page of a calendar. And I was willing to believe that might indeed be the case for someone as staid as she was.

After Miss Atwood finished her second cup of tea, she stood up and told me, "As I said, Nadia and Isabella live here with me. I'll take you to both of them. But first, we'll go and get the particulars for my gardener. His name is Toshio Ito. Not counting his internment during the war, Toshi has worked for us steadily since I was a little girl. He's a decent man who has suffered enough unkindness from our race. So, please treat him respectfully. His address and telephone number are upstairs where I do my billing. Follow me, please."

She led me out of the living room back the way I'd come with Nadia. We climbed the staircase to the next floor, where we went down a long, quiet hallway with a blood-red runner slinking down its center. This floor was less formal and cheerier, but that didn't mean it was informal and cheery. It wasn't.

Miss Atwood was a no-nonsense and brisk walker, so while I took much longer strides than she did, she had no problem keeping well ahead of me. This gave me another opportunity to gain sympathetic insight into what Ethan Calmer surely found appealing about her.

My eyes were riveted on Miss Atwood as she moved swiftly down the hallway. War production and textile conservation had hiked up hemlines during the war. So, while they'd now dropped to around the knee again, they weren't so low that I couldn't see her shapely calves tighten as she careened along to a quick but respectable drumbeat all her own, gently teeter-tottering her hips to where her sheath frock defined each mesmerizing swing and sway, causing her very proper fundament to gently waggle up and down like the wings of one of those signaling biplanes back in World War I. But Miss Atwood definitely struck me as a girl who didn't intentionally send out signals.

We entered a dark-paneled study with a window looking out at her well-kept flower gardens below. There was a heavy dark desk in the room and two chairs to match. Near the desk, a hooded typewriter was perched on its own little stand with locking casters.

A notepad and pencil sat on the desk blotter. Miss Atwood picked these up and then opened the desk drawer and found what looked to be an invoice. After jotting something down on her pad, she tore off the top page, poked it at me, and said, "My gardener's telephone number and home address."

I took it.

"Unless you have any further questions for me, Mr. Nilson, please feel free to talk with Nadia and Isabella for as long as you feel it necessary. Isabella knows nothing of what's been happening. While Nadia knows no details, she does sense that something's amiss, and she perceives it's why you've come."

That helped explain why Nadia's commanding voice had become almost pleasant when I'd told her who I was and gave her one of my cards.

Miss Atwood went on, "Still, I suppose you'll need to acquaint both of them with at least the bare minimum of what's been happening before you can effectively question them."

I nodded.

"Please be as prudent as possible, won't you?"

"Prudence is my middle name," I said airily.

The humor was lost on her.

Miss Mercedes Atwood was physically attractive. No question about it. But she sort of reminded me of the girl I'd met in Spud's Camera Shop. Though instead of lethargy, I decided Miss Atwood sucked the life out of every room she entered. But apparently Ethan Calmer believed she was well worth whatever tradeoff he was willing to make for her. To each his own, and variety is the spice of life, and all that. Or to quote George S. Kaufman: "One man's Mede is another man's Persian."

Once again I appreciatively studied Miss Atwood's derrière as she led me on another engaging trek to the kitchen where we found both Nadia and Isabella. Miss Atwood told them to fully cooperate with me and that I had a few questions to ask them. She then told me to please show myself out when I was finished, and scurried off in her very proper manner.

My brief explanation of why I'd been hired was met with a perplexed look from Isabella and a stern-faced grimace from Nadia. Both agreed to let me interview them separately in the dining room off the kitchen, where we sat at the corner of a long table—me at the head, and each woman, in turn, to my left.

Isabella Oscarson was a much older, plumper, white-haired version of that famous watercolor painting *Scandinavian Peasant Woman in an Interior*, replete with dark skirt, orange and brown vest, and starched white bonnet. Isabella's white apron and blouse were food-stained, and it was probably rare when they weren't.

While clearly devoted to Mercedes Atwood, Isabella was basically a nice but simple soul and not much help at all, since she approached both life's joys and duties like an unquestioning worker bee. I seriously doubted she'd spent any of her spare time gathering raw material for original thought, let alone rubbing thoughts together to come up with conclusions. H.G. Wells wrote that throughout time people have commonly been illiterate and incurious. Isabella was definitely the latter, and she was probably pretty much the former, if not bothering to read puts you on par with those who can't—to paraphrase a line from Mark Twain. Extracting answers from Isabella was about as problematic as getting out of quicksand. However, I did eat a fresh-baked biscuit she offered me, and I can attest that her baking skills were masterful.

Nadia Forsgren I've already described. She too was clearly devoted to Miss Atwood—fiercely loyal, even. Though she had more going for her wit-wise than Isabella, and she readily answered my questions, I didn't learn much that might help with solving the mystery of the menacing caller.

However, at one point Nadia did speak of their house as

having had some "unhappy times." When I pressed her for details, she flushed and clammed up, behaving as if she'd begun telling tales out of school—which was doubtless the case.

So, after we talked about a few useless incidentals, I decided to take a different tack.

"Miss Atwood told me she never went along with her father on any of his trips abroad. Sounds like she didn't see him for months at a time."

Nadia's eyes darted to the swinging doors leading into the kitchen and Isabella. You could practically cut with a knife her discomfort at my question.

She looked back at me and said, "She came to understand … *in time*." That was all she'd say, but I sensed she could say plenty if she felt free to.

I wanted to say plenty more, but I held my tongue. What I wanted to say was that Chester Atwood sounded like a colossal piece of work.

As I thanked them, I gave them each one of my cards, asking that they please call me if they thought of anything that might help, or if they noticed anything suspicious in the days ahead.

I figured I'd phone Toshio Ito the gardener a little later on and determine from that call whether a personal visit would be necessary. I said goodbye to the ladies and told them I'd see myself out.

I LEFT THE KITCHEN with hat in hand, questions about Mercedes Atwood bouncing around inside my head. She was a looker. No doubt about it. But she was such a prim, straight-laced nice-nelly that it neutralized the overall effect. A genuine iceberg if I ever met one. I had a hard time seeing how a normal warm-blooded guy would become fixated on her romantically. But then again, maybe her mystery caller wasn't normal.

I went down the long hallway past the pair of living room doors and the drawing room. But before I could go through the oak-paneled reception area that led to the huge vestibule, I heard a hushed voice behind me say, "Psst."

I turned around and saw that the drawing-room door was slightly ajar. Protruding from the darkness beyond was the back of a hand with its fist clenched and its index finger sticking straight up and then closing on the fist—a gesture the hand performed repeatedly, beckoning me to come closer.

It was a female hand. A female voice said in a sultry tone, "Come over and talk to me, won't you, handsome?"

The voice and hand had the words "Turn around and walk away," written all over them. So of course, I heeded the voice and moseyed right up to the beckoning hand—close enough so that it grabbed my wrist and pulled at me. I didn't struggle, so the hand easily yanked me into the drawing room. I heard the door shut behind me and the lock click. Inside was as dark as one of the coal mines over in Black Diamond.

The hand let go of my wrist and a lamp was switched on that provided the dimmest of dim lights. I stared down at a shadowy female form with hazy but alluring curves that gradually became more distinct as she slowly worked the dimmer switch to give us more light. She reeked of the cheap perfume my landlady favored. If the girl standing in front of me hadn't looked so very, very different from Mercedes Atwood, I'd say she looked an awful lot like her. A dead ringer, in fact.

Instead of a navy-blue sheath frock, she wore a flimsy red dress—an off-the-rack type that a shop girl might wear if she wanted to pass for a streetwalker at a costume party. It looked to be made out of crepe and clung to her curves like the intestine casing of a frankfurter. And thanks to one of those bullet bras with pointy cups, her midsized breasts protruded like a couple of elliptic paraboloids. She'd swapped her sheer stockings for gray nylons and had traded her peep-toe pumps for a pair of black T-straps. But clothes weren't the only difference. Gone too, was the imperious air.

Letting the lamp alone, she moved directly in front of me,

her warm hands enclosing mine. She stared up into my startled eyes with her lovely mascara-encircled brown ones. Her updo of earlier was now a little undone so that dark curls hung down on the sides of her head in reckless strands, and as lovely as her face was, it wasn't the face your mother wanted to meet. Not hardly. She wore a lot of makeup but most of it where it counted. Her cheeks were artificially rosy and her bright-red lipstick formed an unnatural crimson heart-shape when her lips were in repose, which wasn't often because she'd somehow learned to give glamour-magazine smiles.

She'd also learned how to kiss.

Suddenly she let go of my hands, reached around my neck, and tugged till our faces nearly collided. I dropped my hat on the floor and automatically took her in my arms as she planted her mouth firmly on mine and held it there.

I let her.

But only for about thirty seconds.

Okay, maybe forty-five.

Halfway into this ferocious kiss, I tasted gin. It was then that I also heard faint mood music coming from a phonograph somewhere in the room.

I couldn't believe the transformation. Mercedes Atwood had struck me as a no-lips-have-ever-touched-mine kind of girl, but now she was the gal who clearly knows her way around all the local necking spots.

She unclamped her lips from mine, disengaged her right hand and lowered her heels to the floor again, the better to see me. With her free hand, she gently tapped the tip of my nose with a finger and said in a throaty purr, "Yeah ... you want me. I can tell."

She looked down and started to take a step back so I let her go. She raised her eyes slowly and gave me one of the most mischievous looks I'd seen that week. A soft, lazy smirk crept across her face.

I found myself grinning, but rather than experiencing the

pride of male conquest, I felt like a bewildered bull that's just shuffled into a slaughterhouse.

My chat with Nadia and Isabella had given Mercedes ample time to change outfits, paint her face, and hide in here to waylay me when I showed myself out. But I was having a deuce of a time figuring out why.

She pointed at the sofa, cooing softly, "This is a sofa bed, handsome. Help me unfold it, and we'll see about putting it to good use."

It's not that I wasn't tempted.

I was.

No question about it.

But I tried to stick to a hard and fast rule not to chase after married women, clients, or bughouse escapees—and especially the latter. And what was happening seemed more than a bit buggy. I wanted no part of it. Well, no part of *most* of it anyway.

Mercedes Atwood started to undo the sofa bed and noticed I wasn't helping. Her eyes looked puzzled and then shrewd. She shot me what was meant to be a reassuring look through fluttering thick eyelashes.

"Don't worry, handsome. Those two old ladies won't hear a peep. These rooms are soundproof. Trust me. I should know."

"That's not it," I muttered lamely.

She was puzzled again and then shrewd once more. "Oh, I get it," she said with a tight, nasty little laugh that reached right down and vibrated my toes. "You're the kind of guy who needs to have a drink first. Not a problem, dreamboat. We've got fixin's right here. I'll make us each a highball."

Her eyes sparkled and her well-formed chassis did a titillating cha-cha as she sashayed over to a miniature bar.

Drawing rooms were typically where guests could be entertained, but what she was offering was far from typical.

While Mercedes Atwood—or whoever had taken over her body, for clearly she was possessed—was at the bar making a dull jangle sound, tinkling ice, and clinking glasses, I managed to pull my eyes away from her to scan the room, which was like no drawing room I'd ever been in.

It lacked the feminine touch and a few other touches besides, and for an upper-crust drawing room it was oddly furnished. First off, it was cell-like, as there were no windows. The entire room was wainscoted with vertical tongue-and-groove panels of knotty pine—the kind of knots that you can see faces or objects in, if you have the time and are in need of amusement. All the upper walls and the ceiling were painted a calming light green. I noticed what looked to be a closet door, and there was also an open door leading to a small bathroom. In one corner was a radio-phonograph console, and in another, a river-rock fireplace. The andirons were shaped like owls with glass eyes that probably glowed when a fire crackled. A huge Persian rug depicting an exotic-looking harem scene covered most of the dark hardwood floor. The rug was itself partly obscured by two Mohair chairs and the aforesaid matching sofa bed, which was flanked by two small end tables, each supporting its own slag glass lamp. One of these lamps gave us our light. Then there was the miniature bar. Above it was a print of Edvard Munch's painting, *The Scream*. An inside joke? Maybe.

But all these were mere side details, because the transformed Mercedes Atwood was the magnet that really drew my eyes. Her back was to me as she mixed our drinks and hummed. Her well-rounded fundament no longer seemed so proper, and I suspected that those sleek legs weren't quite as careful as I'd originally assumed.

"There," she said. "Drinks are ready."

She turned around and gave me a teasing smile that offered the unspoken invitation wanton women have been tendering for centuries. "I'm going to step into the john a moment, handsome. So, why don't you make yourself at home, sip your drink, and get in the mood?" Her dulcet tone caused my spine to tingle and my whole frame to quiver. "And when I return, we'll get to work on this sofa."

Her face actually glowed. Her lower lip curled, and she tossed her head provocatively as she slunk sexily into the bathroom and shut and locked the door.

Her bothering to lock the door under these circumstances made no sense to me at all. But then, none of it did. More to the point, what had Gunnar Nilson gotten himself into?

I could hear Mercedes humming on the other side of the door. I decided I could have none of this—whatever *this* was. I also knew that if I kept standing there, it would be nearly impossible for me to leave. And if I didn't leave, I'd hate myself in the morning. Well, maybe not *hate*—but I'd be really disgusted with myself. Okay … fairly disappointed.

So, while Miss Mercedes Atwood hummed away in the bathroom, I picked up my hat from the floor, hopped out of the drawing room, skipped through the oak-paneled reception room, and jumped from the vestibule. Then I shot out the front door.

Once safely at the wheel of my coupe, I wiped the lipstick off my face with my handkerchief and turned the motor over. I didn't even bother to let it idle.

I rocketed out of the driveway.

But I didn't rocket out of Broadmoor so fast that I failed to spot the green Dodge Sedan I'd seen when I arrived. Instead of making a right on East Madison, I hung a left.

That green Dodge Sedan was still across the street, but parked in a new location so that I couldn't see the driver clearly this time. But as I cruised on by, I noted that the license plate numbers were the same.

He might have been a cop. But I didn't think so. Instead, I decided one of Broadmoor's Brahmans had hired some extra security for the day. Was it to keep people out, or to keep some of them in? That was the question.

OFF WENT THE RECORDER. Kirsti immediately wanted to know what I'd concluded about Miss Femme Fatale of 1950.

"I'll be getting to those details in good time," I said. "I'm not going to rush through this. You'll just have to let me tell it in my own way, blue eyes."

She scowled at me but agreed to wait.

We decided to take a short break to eat some of her mom's homemade lasagna that Kirsti had tucked in her tote bag. Since she'd also brought along a thermos of coffee and another of lemonade, we decided to stay in the outer courtyard to eat. Having seen plenty of the cafeteria dining hall, we were both glad to avoid it—she for her employee reasons, me for my inmate ones. Still, Kirsti made a quick trip to microwave the lasagna.

"Lasagna's good," I said, after swallowing my third mouthful. "Be sure and tell your mom for me."

Kirsti nodded absently. Her mind was clearly elsewhere as she picked at her food. Her next words told me she was still back in Broadmoor at the Atwood residence—specifically in the drawing room.

"Of course, my mom's gonna think you've exaggerated about Mercedes Atwood hitting on you like she did," she said in an impish voice. "I'm just saying."

I merely smiled and took a sip of coffee.

My coupe was getting parched, so I got some gas at a filling station down near the ferry dock in the Madison Park neighborhood. The short ferry run to Kirkland was to finally halt by the end of the following month, thanks to several years of competition with the Lake Washington floating bridge.

I wasn't really thirsty, but I thought a beer was in order, so I stopped in at the nearby Red Onion Tavern.

For the time being, I decided to carry on with my mission for Ethan Calmer as if my escapade with his fiancée hadn't occurred. But only for the time being. The beer was helping gear my mind for a chat with Toshio Ito, Miss Atwood's Japanese gardener.

My fellow boarder, Sten Larson, harbored animosity toward the Japanese—but I figure he'd come by his feelings rightly enough. The Japs had killed many of his buddies and made him bleed as he'd bled them in turn. My own position toward the Japanese wasn't so cut-and-dried.

Don't get me wrong. Pearl Harbor broiled me as much as the next guy, but my personal and more direct war had been with the Krauts, not the Japs. And even though the Japanese had killed some of my friends—Nils Granholm among them—my feelings were a little thornier than Sten's. Probably because three Japanese families had farmed rented land in the rural community where I was raised by my grandparents. Also, I went to school with three Japanese kids, and was good friends with one of them, who we all called Munch because his given name was too hard to pronounce. When those three Japanese families were interned during the war, I learned that local farmers bought their stuff for a dollar at auction and kept it for them for when they later returned.

So again, my feelings about the Japanese were a little more nuanced than Sten's.

I emptied my glass and edged over to the payphone. Since it was only a little after six, I was hoping Toshio Ito would be home for the day.

I lucked out. He was home. I introduced myself.

He'd probably been raised in the U.S., because his English was better than Mrs. Berger's.

"Ah yes, Mr. Nilson. Miss Atwood just now called me and said you would be speaking to me soon," he said in a controlled, crisp voice.

"Just *now*, you say?" That surprised me.

"Yes. That is correct."

I couldn't help wondering if she'd bothered wriggling out of her bullet bra to slip back into her self-adjusting Maidenform before making the call.

Toshio Ito caught the surprise in my tone. "Is there something wrong, Mr. Nilson?"

"No, Mr. Ito. Nothing's wrong. Miss Atwood probably mentioned I'd have a few questions for you."

"Yes. That is correct."

From what Mercedes Atwood had told me of her history with the man, I placed Toshio Ito at around fifty years old. We talked for maybe ten minutes. I learned that the only helpers he ever used were his two sons and a daughter—and only when their schooling or other work allowed. He struck me as forthcoming, and not the sort who'd menace one of his customers—not that he was ever seriously on my suspect list. What I really wanted to know is if he'd seen or heard anything suspicious in recent weeks while working at Miss Atwood's. He said he hadn't.

Mercedes Atwood told me she'd had some work done inside her house six or seven months previously. But in case Toshio Ito remembered differently, I didn't want to put him in a position where he might be forced to contradict his customer. So I simply said, "Miss Atwood told me that she had some plumbing, plastering, and painting done a while back. Do you happen to recall that, and particularly *when* it was that the work took place?"

"Yes, I remember. It had to have been no more than a month ago."

"You sound pretty certain as to the time, Mr. Ito."

"Yes, I am very certain. My younger son was working with me then, and it was his birthday. The plumbing and plastering must have been completed by then because that day a painter came outside and overheard my son and me talking about it being his birthday. He wished my son a happy birthday and asked if there would be cake served later. We all laughed. So yes, I am certain of the time, Mr. Nilson."

Days run into weeks and into months so fast, they become blurred. So, Mr. Ito's recollection of when the work was done versus what Miss Atwood recalled was probably inconsequential as far as her version was concerned. Still, my money was on him.

I asked, "Do you happen to remember the name of the painting company this guy worked for?"

"I do not recall, Mr. Nilson. I am sorry."

I told him no worries and thanked him for his time. After I hung up the phone, I headed for home. Since I'd missed dinner, I raided the refrigerator for a quick snack, and then knocked on Walter Pangborn's door.

Chapter 10

———

"IT WAS THE GOOFIEST thing, Walter," I said, after I'd described my encounter with Mercedes Atwood.

"Curious word, 'goofy,' " Walter began in a learned tone. "The root of 'goofy' and its noun 'goof,' meaning 'silly or stupid person,' is from the now extinct English word 'goff' which meant 'fool' back in the late 1500s, and which appears to be closely related to the French 'goffe,' the Spanish 'gofo,' and the Italian 'goffo.' All in all, a rather good example of Grimm's Law, you understand—"

"Walter—"

"Sorry, old socks."

"So, what do you think I should do now, Walter? Return Ethan Calmer's check, or go on with what he wants me to do, acting as if nothing happened?"

We were each nursing a shot of Black & White. I'd quickly told Walter about my visit to Broadmoor, including Miss Mercedes Atwood's first and second acts.

"If I were you, I'd do the latter, old top," he said calmly. "I'd go on with the job as if nothing happened."

"You would? Why?"

"Because, under the circumstances, it seems the logical thing to do."

"I don't follow you," I said, "but I'll admit, I'm still probably not thinking all that clearly about this whole thing," I took a sip of Scotch. "So please, lay it out for me, oh wise one."

"Well, let's consider all the possibilities we can reasonably come up with," he began in an even, clinical tone. "It's possible that Miss Atwood finds you irresistible, and simply must have you. Had you considered that?"

"I think we can scratch that one, Walter."

Walter chuckled. "I had to at least mention it, Gunnar. In the interest of being thorough, don't you know."

I said nothing.

He went on, "It's possible that Miss Atwood was merely pulling your leg, and it was all an outrageous act, a performance meant to test you for some peculiar reason of her own devising. The unconventional conduct born of too much leisure time, and all that. If so, perhaps by fleeing the scene as you did, you passed Miss Atwood's test. Who knows? In any event, whatever her reason, I doubt this is something she'd wish to air to her fiancé. So, if you don't say anything about it to Mr. Calmer, likely she won't either."

I just looked at him and frowned.

"Admittedly, the theory that her behavior is merely an act and a peculiar test *is* a bit thin, old top. But it is a possibility, nonetheless."

"A pretty remote one by my way of thinking. What else can you come up with?"

"Hmm … well, it is possible that Miss Atwood is hypersexual. In other words, she may have frequent or unexpectedly enhanced sexual urges, an inordinate and intense interest in sex and in having sex."

"You're saying she might be a nympho?"

"Nymphomania *is* the better known and more common term for it, yes. All the same, what it refers to is a woman affected by abnormal and uncontrollable sexual desires. And if that is indeed the case, then Miss Atwood may be keeping this libidinous facet of her life hidden from Mr. Calmer—difficult as that might be for her to do. If so, then again, she's not at all likely to talk to him about what went on with you today."

I gave what he said some thought. "If Mercedes Atwood *is* a nympho, then it could have a direct connection to the menacing phone calls she's received, don't you think? It may also be why she didn't want Calmer to call the cops, and why she was at first reluctant to involve me. She's walking a pretty narrow tightrope she doesn't want jostled."

Walter nodded and took a sip of his drink. "Perhaps her attempt to seduce you was meant to embroil you in her dark secret—make it *your* secret as well. What better way to keep close tabs on you? Control you? And, if she is indeed hypersexual, it's very possible that a man from her past with whom she has had a casual tryst has become obsessed with her. That would explain the telephone calls so soon after her engagement. As I see it, all the more reason for you to proceed with your investigation as if nothing happened between you and Miss Atwood. As you say, you need report only to Mr. Calmer. After all, it was *he* who hired you."

I weighed his words, then said finally, "I've got another possibility for you, Walter."

"What's that, old thing?"

"Mercedes Atwood may simply be bughouse crazy."

He merely gave me his broken smile.

"So, you think I shouldn't tell Calmer that his girlfriend's a vamp and possibly a nympho, is that it?"

"Yes. Mum's the word. For now, anyway. Though eventually you may have to inform him, depending on what you uncover. I know it's not the first time you've had to be the bearer of disturbing tidings to a client. But, there's also the possibility that it might not fall within your purview, since the menacing calls may be solely connected to Mr. Calmer himself somehow.

Besides, without incontrovertible proof, you'd likely find it almost impossible to convince Mr. Calmer that his sweetheart is a seductress, let alone a nymphomaniac—so nothing good would be gained by it, especially for you. And that would also be true if she was simply playacting today or is indeed a mental case."

"You're probably right, Walter."

"I feel certain that I am. If I might quote Voltaire, 'It is difficult to free fools from the chains they revere.' I'd say Mr. Calmer reveres the chains he wears because of Miss Atwood."

I grunted.

We sat in silence for almost a minute. Finally I said, "As of now Walter, I've got a gut feeling those menacing calls *are* connected to Miss Atwood's dark secret. I don't like it, but there it is."

"You could be right, old socks. I'll be curious to see how it all plays out."

"You and me both, my friend. You and me both."

Chapter 11

———

MERCEDES ATWOOD'S BEHAVIOR GOT me really curious about what I might learn from her old flames, but since I'd promised Ethan Calmer I'd tackle his list first, that's what I did. I was a bit surprised that he'd provided me with only five names of unhappy clients and legal adversaries he considered more than a little shaky. I guess my opinion of lawyers made me think Calmer would have accumulated far more disgruntled and unstable enemies than that. Maybe he had, and he chose to grade his enemies on a fairly generous curve.

It took me the next two days to eliminate all five of them. During this time, according to Calmer, Mercedes Atwood had received two more menacing phone calls.

The first person on Calmer's list had died. The second one was dying in Providence Hospital and was in no condition to make any phone calls. The third was taking a liquor cure in a private sanatorium. Another had moved to Hong Kong. The last one I found living in Everett. He was shacked up with a rough-looking woman living in an apartment above a dingy storefront on Hewitt Avenue, where the two of them cheerfully made bad pottery together. He didn't even have a telephone. He was as mad as Alice's Hatter but as harmless as the Dormouse. As I was leaving Wonderland, his lady love gave me a mindless grin wider than the Cheshire Cat's but lacking incisors.

When I got back from Everett, it was 2:30 in the afternoon on Friday. I was strolling to my office when Cissy Paget stepped into the hall and handed me a note with a message from Calmer. He wanted me to call and arrange to come see him and report my progress.

"How would you say he sounded on the phone, sweet knees?"

Cissy thought for a moment. "Definitely anxious. Maybe even a bit harried."

"Stressed and annoyed, then."

She nodded. "Something you did to make him unhappy, tough guy?"

"It's not that. What I'm looking into for him is obviously taking its toll, is all."

I thanked Cissy and went into my office. I called and talked with Calmer's receptionist, the lovely Lillian Voorhees, and arranged to meet her boss at his office within the hour.

THOUGH NOW FULLY OCCUPIED with the Calmer-Atwood job, I hadn't entirely forgotten about Rune's murder investigation. Curious about how the cops were doing on it, I called and asked for Detective Fitch or Togstad.

I waited on the line for a couple minutes before I finally heard, "Detective Fitch speakin'."

"This is Gunnar Nilson. Just wondering if you've got any news to share on the Rune Granholm killing."

"Sure, sure … since there's really nothin' to share," Fitch said, chuckling. "And since your so-so pal Milland says you're almost a stand-up guy, I'm more than happy to share it."

"Decent of you."

"Uh-huh. We hunted down as many of Granholm's friends we could and checked on how they was spendin' their time when he was killed. I swear, the guy had more ex-girlfriends than Carter has Little Liver Pills," he said in his folksy manner. "If any of 'em knows anything worth sayin', they ain't sayin' it. And nobody seems too broken up about Granholm's passin', that's for damn sure."

"Rune had that effect on people."

"Uh-huh. A nice bunch of pals if you ask me, if 'pals' is what you call 'em. It's lookin' more an' more like Granholm finally wore out his last welcome with the wrong kind of pal. How 'bout you? You been nosin' around? Got anything helpful to give us?"

"Only to agree that Rune seems to have finally pushed his luck a bit too far."

"Uh-huh. So, nothin'. You got nothin'?"

"I got nothin'."

"Togstad said Granholm's funeral service was short an' poorly attended, an' that *you* wasn't there right along with several others."

"As I told you, we weren't close." I'd actually forgotten all about his funeral.

"Uh-huh."

Fitch said he had to go, so we ended our phone chat.

MY LONGINES SAID IT was 3:40 as I entered the law offices of Mumford and Calmer. The waiting area was empty and someone had transformed the pile of magazines on the waiting table into a neat, orderly stack.

Lillian Voorhees was dutifully at her station behind her big desk doing some typing. Her Remington ceased its clickety-clack-clacking when she saw me out of the corner of her eye.

This time she wore a plain-cut white blouse that still managed to prove she had curves. As she looked directly at me, I pointed my right index finger at my chin and asked, "Miss me?"

That got me a fourteen-tooth smile. It was progress. You try and make it when, where, and how you can.

"You already know the way, Mr. Nilson. Go right in. You're

expected." She spoke in a cheerful and lilting voice I hadn't heard the last time we'd met. Money and social standing aside, I found myself wondering why Calmers hadn't romanced the frisky Miss Voorhees instead of pursuing a girl whose personality appeared to blow hot and cold—particularly if all he experienced was the cold.

Lillian was still taking baths in jasmine toilet water, for as I passed the girl, my nose recoiled in protest.

The door to Ethan Calmer's office was wide open just like the last time, and just as before, he was planted in his high leather chair behind his huge desk, with another chair cozied up alongside it. In that chair sat the regal-looking Miss Mercedes Atwood.

My jaw almost hit my shoes when I saw her. I tried not to goggle. Miss Atwood merely looked at me and then through me with a vague expression, like she was making plans to trim her fingernails or perhaps shave her armpits later in the day. She had no more concern for me than she would a chewing-tobacco salesman, and probably far less than that.

I shut the door and stayed standing by it as they both stood up.

I closed my mouth and nodded at Calmer, whose lower half was hidden by the desk. He wore a Sulka tie with circles and dots and his broad shoulders were packed inside a dark-brown suit coat with pinstripes that helped make him look a little less pudgy. His lips parted to show me what Colgate toothpaste had done for him. "Thank you for coming, Mr. Nilson," he said in his rapid-fire way of speaking.

Miss Atwood gave me a crisp nod as if she was trying to recollect who I might possibly be.

I took her in at full length with a quick up-and-down once-over. She wore a dark-green pencil skirt topped by a peplum jacket, and beneath the jacket a lime-colored blouse, open at the neck to show off a pearl necklace. Her legs were in light tan stockings that ended in high-heel pumps the same color as her outfit. Her raven-colored hair was once again in a stately updo that was partly covered by a green toque hat. Her smart handbag and gloves were parked on Calmer's desk blotter.

They both resumed their seats and I sat in the chair in front of Calmer's desk that was directly in line with Miss Atwood. Her back was ramrod straight, her hands clasped on her lap, and her very proper fundament poised on the edge of her chair.

Calmer had steepled his fingers and was studying his fingernails as if inspecting a botched manicure. Miss Atwood was looking at Calmer. I was mainly watching her.

As Calmer cleared his throat authoritatively, his fiancée unclasped her hands and decided to slowly and deliberately place one leg atop the other. She must have felt my eyes, because hers narrowed and moved from Calmer to me. What she saw apparently caused her to lower her raised leg. The iceberg girl I'd first met had definitely returned with a vengeance, careful legs and all.

Walter was right. She hadn't and probably wouldn't tell Calmer about how she'd behaved with me in her drawing room. She had to be an actress, and a damn good one at that. She didn't seem the least bit self-conscious around me or show the slightest sign of embarrassment or discomfort.

Gunnar the Boggled.

Whatever Mercedes Atwood was—actress, seductress, nympho, parolee from a nut house, or all of the above—she didn't let on in the least. You'd think nothing more than a polite conversation had taken place between the two of us when we'd met the other day.

Calmer had been speaking, and though I'd missed his opening preamble, I caught his drift well enough when I finally tuned in:

"… so Mr. Nilson, we'd first like you to update us on what you've learned thus far from your investigation into those people I named for you."

Before doing so, I told them of my brief telephone conversation with Miss Atwood's gardener, Toshio Ito.

"I hope you took care not to accuse Toshi of anything," Miss Atwood piped up. "I don't want him thinking we suspect him of any part in this unpleasantness."

"I made no accusations, nor did I see the need to tell him about the calls you're getting."

That made Calmer smile and nod, and I think it mollified Miss Atwood. But with her, who could tell?

After that and in fairly quick order, I told them in detail what I'd discovered about the five people on his list.

"Damn," said Calmer, "I'd seriously hoped one of them would be our man."

"It's headway, Mr. Calmer. I'm eliminating likely suspects."

"Yes, of course," he agreed ruefully, looking at Miss Atwood. "Naturally, we've been hoping to resolve this matter as quickly as possible."

"I understand. But this sort of thing takes dogged legwork and a fair amount of time," I said matter-of-factly. "As you know, I'm a one-man plodder, and believe me, it wouldn't hurt my feelings if you'd like to engage one of the large agencies that can put several operatives on this before the day is done. Or, as I suggested at our first meeting, you can still get the police involved and draw on their resources and manpower." I'd added the last part out of sheer cussedness, just to see if I could rattle Miss Atwood's cage.

I wasn't too disappointed, though I got more of a quiet jingle than anything like a rattle.

She showed her disapproval of my suggestion by tightening her lips and shaking her head slowly. She then parted and moistened her lips with her tongue and swallowed before looking over at Calmer to say in her usual even, unemotional voice, "No police, Ethan. We agreed. And the fewer involved, the better. Let's allow Mr. Nilson to proceed with what he's doing."

"Of course, my dove," Calmer said in a tender and reassuring coo, as if I wasn't even in the room. He then turned to me. "This has been very unsettling for us both. I'm sure you understand."

I said I understood. I looked at Miss Atwood and said, "I assume your mystery caller still calls."

She nodded.

"Has he changed his message in any way?"

She slowly laced her fingers once again. "No. It remains unchanged," she said in a neutral tone.

I confess, having encountered her singing siren side, this rather stoical Mercedes was now much harder to take with a straight face. But, I fought back the grin that was struggling to surface.

Next we discussed my investigation into Miss Atwood's old flames. Both of them renewed their concerns about the necessity for such a move.

"I can't begin to conceive how you plan to find out about these fellows without causing them unnecessary offence," Calmer said in an anxious tone.

I didn't say anything at first, mainly because at the moment I didn't have anything like a real plan of action other than to take the direct approach. For the next few minutes I practically had to win both of them over again to the idea of questioning her former suitors. What tipped the scales was when I told them I'd have to quit if I couldn't do the job right.

"Just be discreet, Mr. Nilson. *Very* discreet," Calmer said with the uneasiness of a man who sees lawsuits everywhere he turns.

An unblinking Miss Atwood woodenly nodded her concurrence.

I couldn't help it. I smiled. Neither one of them seemed to notice or care.

Calmer went on, "These men are respected and influential. None will take kindly to unfounded aspersions. I can't emphasize this enough."

I stopped smiling and assured them I'd cast no unfounded aspersions.

Chapter 12

—

B~Y~ 5:20 I ~WAS~ back at my office desk looking over a used copy of the Western novel *Shane*, which I'd bought recently at Shorey's Bookstore downtown. It had come out the year before and I'd been meaning to read it ever since Sten Larson had recommended it to me. My copy still had its brown jacket, which showed just a bit of wear around the edges. Only Shane's head appeared on the cover, but even that showed him to be everything a smartly dressed gunfighter should be, and that he knew it. He was wearing a brown cowboy hat with its brim covering part of his eyebrows. The brown bandana around his neck looked like it was tied a little too snug for my taste. His rugged unsmiling face was drawn and solemn, and he had piercing eyes that had seen more than their share of rowdy ranch hands, tinhorn gamblers, flirtatious bargirls, and pointless violence. I found myself relating to Shane.

I toyed with starting the book, but instead decided I'd better do something about Miss Atwood's list of former beaus.

Apparently, the lovely but poker-faced Mercedes Atwood had attracted her fair share of suitors, because after she'd eliminated those now happily married or currently living out of state, her list of old flames was pared down to four. She'd put them in alphabetical order with their pertinent particulars placed in parentheses. Cynical me would also have liked the names of those who were happily married, but the list I had was a start.

The name at the top was George Aldrich, a bank manager who lived in an apartment downtown. I dialed his number. The phone rang three times before the line finally opened.

"Hello."

"Mr. George Aldrich?"

"Speaking."

I told him who I was and who I represented.

"Oh yes, Ethan Calmer told me to expect your call, though he was a little vague as to why. What's on your mind, Mr. Nilson?" He had a friendly voice.

"Mr. Aldrich, I'd like to meet with you some time tomorrow. I know it'll be Saturday, but I'm happy to meet you at your convenience. It concerns Mr. Calmer's fiancée, Miss Mercedes Atwood, and involves a delicate situation she finds herself in. I don't want to make this overly mysterious, but it's a private matter that I can better explain face to face."

"Hmm. I suppose I understand."

His tone told me otherwise, so I added, "For now I can tell you that I'm simply trying to gather background information from those who have been Miss Atwood's close friends."

"Ah, you're fact-finding. Hmm, I see. Well you've got me curious, I can tell you that," he said airily. "Mercedes and I went out for a while, if that's what you mean by close friends."

"Sure. That kind of thing. Like I said, I can better explain when we meet. I won't take much of your time. How's tomorrow work for you?"

"Hmm. Tomorrow's not good. Not good at all. As it happens, I'm leaving town tonight and won't be back till Monday. Perhaps we could set something up for the beginning of next week." He spoke a bit absently, as if his mind had drifted elsewhere. "In the meantime, do you care if I make a suggestion?"

"I'm all ears."

"Well, before you go any further, if you're wanting to talk to people who know Mercedes Atwood fairly well, you should really talk to Douglas Eagleson."

It wasn't a name on my list. "What's his relationship with Miss Atwood?"

"He's an old school chum of mine. He went out with Mercedes before I did, and he's known her for a number of years. Doug lives in Tacoma. He's a single man like me, but he's far more the socialite than I cared to be, if you understand me."

I told him I understood.

"I daresay Doug probably knows more about Mercedes than I ever will. So, he's likely the very one to provide you with the information you might need, whatever that might be. Or, I'm sure Doug will at least help steer you down the right path."

Aldrich gave me Douglas Eagleson's name and phone number. Since this Eagleson had been a suitor, was still single, and hadn't moved out of state, I wondered why Miss Atwood hadn't put his name on her list. I suddenly had a strong desire to talk to the man.

Aldrich and I arranged to meet up Tuesday of the following week. Before hanging up, he thought to say, "I'll tell you what I'll do. I'll phone ahead and tell Doug who you are and to expect your call. Give me your number and I'll call you right back."

I did as asked and dropped the phone in its cradle.

I had just finished the first page of *Shane* when the phone rang.

It was George Aldrich. He told me that if I could make it down there tomorrow about 7:30 in the evening, Doug Eagleson would be more than happy to talk with me.

Chapter 13

—

I SLEPT IN LATE Saturday morning. Since on the weekends we boarders were on our own when it came to breakfast, I wasn't surprised to find Sten alone at the kitchen table clutching and chomping into a five-inch stack of bread, lettuce, and cold cuts that completely covered the lower half of his face. When he came up for air to chew, morsels rained down on the newspaper laid out flat on the table in front of him.

I was inspired to construct my own, smaller version of his sandwich after pouring myself a cup of coffee. As Sten finished sections of the *Post Intelligencer*, he scooted them over to me so I could browse as I breakfasted.

After breakfast, I went into the pantry and telephoned Cissy Paget.

She picked up after two rings.

"Feel like an early movie and a late lunch, sweet knees?"

"Whatever happened to an *early* dinner and a *late* movie?"

"Can't. I have to drive to Tacoma this evening."

"Early movie it is."

I was interested in seeing a Randolph Scott Western at the Orpheum, but Cissy wanted to see a comedy about a talking mule named Francis at the Egyptian. So, the Egyptian it was.

After the movie, we found a nearby eatery to our liking. Cissy had a turkey sandwich, but since I'd had a sandwich for breakfast, I ordered a bowl of clam chowder.

Cissy talked awhile about what she did and didn't like about the movie. Mostly she liked it.

"But that's enough about an imaginary mule," she said finally. "What's taking you to Tacoma later on, tough guy?"

"Oh, just some nosing around I'm doing for a client."

"That Calmer fellow?"

"Uh-huh. Nothing I can talk about now, but I'll be happy to tell you all about it eventually, if you type up my final report."

"Think so, huh?" she said coolly, her eyes crinkling at the corners.

I asked, "You ever know someone with a secret life?"

"A hypocrite?"

"Well, yes ... but that's not exactly what I'm aiming at."

She looked thoughtful. "If you mean a person who acts one way with some people and another way with others, I'd say that describes most people to some extent, wouldn't you?"

"Sure ... but no, not that either. I guess I'm not sure what I mean to say. Just forget it."

She considered me a moment and then said, "If this has something to do with that final report you mentioned, I might just be willing to type it up for you."

I winked at her.

I finished my third cup of coffee, paid our bill, and we left.

MY LONGINES SAID 6:05 as I drove away from Seattle, headed south on Highway 99. I passed through long stretches of woodland and rural areas dotted with mostly small frame houses built on chicken farms or stump ranches that specialized in berries, vegetables, contented cows, and here and there a grumpy-looking one. Just outside of Des Moines, halfway to Tacoma, I grabbed a bite at an inn. I wolfed down their chicken dinner, and to keep it company, drank two cups of what they served for coffee. Then I continued on my merry way.

At 7:18 I was in the Point Defiance Park District, one of Tacoma's poshest residential neighborhoods. By 7:32 I was wending my way down a very long and winding driveway looking out at Commencement Bay. By 7:34 my Chevy Coupe was parked next to a newer model Cadillac Coupe de Ville with a dark-blue body and a light-blue hardtop, and fitting in like a well-worn dime alongside a spanking new dollar.

Douglas Eagleson lived in a Tudor-style brick mansion that was not quite as big as the Globe Theatre, but just might accommodate Shakespeare's players and the fashionable part of his motley audience. It had fewer bricks than the Great Wall of China, but probably had more beams than a three-masted tall ship. By Tacoma standards, it was downright regal.

I was shown into the house by a skeletal little man almost through middle-age and who appeared to be wondering what was taking him so long. He had an oblong head with cold, sunken eyes and the severest case of widow's peak I'd ever encountered. He looked as good-humored as a man with sunken eyes and a widow's peak can look.

I followed him as he turned left and went down a short corridor and through two glass-paneled doors already opened to the outside. We ambled along a cobbled walkway beneath a long trellis ruthlessly shrouded with unruly grapevines. Beyond this was a large, awning-covered patio. Still farther was an adjoining terraced walkway that cut across a well-trimmed lawn and led about thirty yards down to a gazebo overlooking the water.

A man and a woman sat in the gazebo, casually ignoring their rarefied view of the bay. As we neared, they stood up in an unhurried manner and came out of the gazebo to meet us. Both were smoking cigarettes, and each held a near-empty tumbler. The girl appeared to be in her early twenties.

Douglas Eagleson was maybe twenty-nine or thirty years

old. He reminded me of one of those bon vivants you see in Hollywood screwball comedies. He was a tall, slim man in a suit of white linen that played up his suntanned skin. His sandy-colored hair was slicked straight back. He had a pencil mustache under a thin pointy nose that went with a skinny neck sporting a scarlet cravat.

Describing Eagleson's companion as an extremely decorative woman who blended well with the décor would be a gross understatement. She was a statuesque lovely in a strapless, curve-hugging silk dress. Her cinnamon-colored tresses looked unnaturally curly and reached just past her bare clavicles. Her face had an off-color, sensuous allure. All she lacked to be overtly sluttish was excessive rouge and tawdry clothes.

"Mr. *Nilson*," announced my skeletal escort.

Mr. Eagleson smiled broadly. He flicked his cigarette out on the lawn, shook my hand, and said, "What are you drinking, Mr. Nilson?"

Wanting to be helpful, I said, "Scotch. Neat."

Eagleson looked at the skeletal man and said, "Be so kind as to fetch a drink for Mr. Nilson, Lloyd. And bring me another highball while you're at it."

Lloyd quietly left us and Eagleson said, "This is Miss … Miss …. "

"Dahl," she said with the languid ease of a girl accustomed to meeting strange men in unfamiliar places for well-known reasons. "*Penny* Dahl."

"Why yes. Yes, of course. Miss *Dahl*. Miss *Penny* Dahl," Eagleson said blithely. "Would you mind giving Mr. Nilson and me some time to ourselves, my dear? We shan't be too long, I promise. It's business. You understand. I'm sure you can find your way back inside the house. Just ask Lloyd to make you another drink and then have him show you to the parlor, where you'll find plenty of picture magazines. Or feel free to look at television, if you'd rather. Lloyd will direct you to a console with a combination television, radio, and phonograph."

Miss Dahl nodded. Her smile was nearly as heartfelt as her reason for being there. Eagleson and I appreciatively pondered her shimmying curves as she sauntered back to the house the same way I'd come.

"Shall we talk in the gazebo?" Eagleson said finally. He moved as quickly as an athlete and had a graceful bounce to his step as though he'd been rigged with shock-absorbers. "The bay provides such a calming setting, whatever the occasion," he added over his shoulder.

We went inside the gazebo and sat across from one another in reclining chairs, each with its own built-in ashtray. He lit up a Chesterfield, so I reached for a clove. I'd started to massage it with my tongue and waited for him to speak as the smell of his cigarette drifted over to me.

His smirk might have meant most anything as he said, "You don't look at all like I thought, Mr. Nilson. I suppose I expected a frumpy little man in desperate need of a shave and wearing a small battered derby."

"I left the derby at home today."

His smirk became a grin that said he liked that. He studied me awhile, then said, "George Aldrich explained that you've been hired to assist Mercedes Atwood. I understand it involves a *delicate situation*—a genuine euphemism if ever I heard one." He shot me a conspiratorial glance.

Douglas Eagleson wasn't on the list I'd been given, and he didn't strike me as the kind of guy I needed to walk on eggs around. So, I decided to level with him straightaway. I told him about the menacing phone calls and my reason for coming. I even let him read the names on the list Miss Atwood had given me.

When I finished, and he'd given the list a quick peek, he once again wore the broad smile he'd had when I first arrived.

"Anonymous phone calls. Bizarre claims. Vague threats. It

all sounds rather cloak and daggerish," he said lightheartedly.

"Uh-huh."

"I know all the fellows on that list Mercedes gave to you. I know them all very well. Very well indeed. Every one of them is a solid citizen of the first chop. All have flat sides, to be sure, but each one is a squared-away individual, in the main. I can't imagine any of them pulling such a stunt, unless it was done entirely in jest." His expression turned grim. "And this doesn't sound at all like a jest."

I agreed it was no jest.

"So, in my opinion, Mr. Nilson, your visits to the men on that list will be a waste of your time. And that insightful opinion is probably all the help I can offer you … leastwise when it comes to Mercedes' old beaus." His brown eyes had a gleam in them and were steadily and calmly probing my face.

"You have something helpful to say about Miss Atwood herself, then," I said, since he seemed like he wanted me to say it.

He puffed quietly on his Chesterfield and studied me some more. "You say Ethan Calmer hired you, but knowing her hands-on nature, I have to imagine you've actually met Mercedes in person. Am I correct?"

I nodded. "I talked with her at her home. And then again in Calmer's office yesterday."

We remained quiet as the skeletal Lloyd arrived with our drinks. After he left, Eagleson asked, "And both times you met with Mercedes, what did you think of her, Mr. Nilson? What's your detective's impression of her?"

He'd turned my interview into his interview, but it was okay by me. I liked the direction he was taking. I also sensed nothing was to be gained by being cagey on this one, so I said, "A lovely looking woman, but I don't think I've ever met one more deadpan."

He chuckled. As he ground out his stub in the ashtray built into the arm of his chair, he said sardonically, "Merely *deadpan,*

Mr. Nilson? Come, come. How about an out-and-out zombie of the first chop? Brief as your meetings might have been, doesn't 'zombie' do Mercedes better justice than deadpan?"

I grinned and took a sip of my drink. I was starting to like Eagleson a little. But only a little.

"Your grin says it all," he said brightly. "But, I'm afraid, Mr. Nilson, you've only met Dr. Jekyll. I'm two or three years older than Mercedes, but I recall first meeting her when I was in grade school. Our families ran in some of the same social circles, you understand. I'm confident that none who've simply *met* Mercedes in her normal routines and haunts have met her as Mr. Hyde. And when it comes to those of us on her social level who've gotten to know her, I daresay that none of us has met Mr. Hyde either, though I'd venture to guess that a rare few have caught a fleeting glimpse of *him*—you'll please excuse the pronoun. But I seriously doubt that Ethan Calmer knows that a Mr. Hyde even exists. I suspect it's only convenient strangers lower down on the social strata who are treated to that side of Miss Mercedes Atwood."

This Douglas Eagleson was a perceptive bird, and I didn't want to let on that I knew exactly what he was talking about, so I tried to keep a blank expression on my face. Taking another sip of my drink, I asked, "Mr. *Hyde*?"

"Oh, just my picturesque way of referring to Mercedes' alter ego. Her *second* side. A side that is far, far different than the one most people are treated to—particularly those who know her well."

"You're saying that *you* caught a glimpse of this alter ego?"

"Yes, but only once. Entirely by happenstance. And it was the sort of glimpse where one could later find oneself doubting whether it was real."

"Care to elaborate, Mr. Eagleson?"

"Certainly. But only because it's entirely possible that what I'm about to tell you may help you in your search for this lunatic caller. Believe me, I've never told this to anyone. I have facets to my own life I wish to keep private. I respect the same in others, and especially those I count as friends."

A code-of-conduct fellow. So, while I sensed in him the earmarks of a man who loved talking about people more than things, and things far more than ideas, still, I believed he was being truthful about having kept secret what he was about to tell me.

"And Mr. Nilson, I must insist that you agree not to tell Ethan Calmer what I'm about to share with you. He appears to love and adore Mercedes for the zombie that she is. Why, exactly, I don't pretend to know. Nor do I care. But as far as I'm concerned, some sleeping dogs are best left to lie undisturbed. That goes for zombies and their alter egos, too. Do you understand me?"

I finished my drink and said I understood him, but I made no specific promises. I asked, "Has Miss Atwood always been so impassive?"

"As in wooden, robotic, unemotional?" he asked and then nodded. "Yes, as long as I've known her." He gave me a level look. "I'm no psychoanalyst, but I've often wondered if her mother's death and her father's absences might have done something to her emotionally. Some sort of deep-seated harm, I mean. As you probably know, Mercedes was raised by her father— or more particularly, by those two old girls who work for her. Chester Atwood never remarried. Aside from the matronly hired help, there was no actual mother figure in Mercedes' life. Not really. And her father was a veritable phantom. Chester the World Traveler left Mercedes months at a time to go off on his exotic jaunts. However, I assume he must have more than made up for it on his returns, because Mercedes was undeniably devoted to the man. At least it seemed so from the way she spoke of him. And with Mercedes, you pretty much have to go by *what* she says, not *how* she says it."

It was clear Eagleson knew Miss Iceberg well.

He lit a fresh Chesterfield and took a puff. He blew a column of smoke toward the bay that a slight breeze caught and blew back toward his house. Taking another sip of his highball, he continued, "I was a bit sweet on Mercedes when I was in my late teens. I mean, as looks go, she's a knockout, as you know. But try as I might, I could never get past her stoicism—her lack of emotions. Her relentless zombiism. It took away from her feminine charms. Neutralized them. My brief pursuit of her was quite some time ago. I imagine that's why she didn't bother putting me on that list she gave you."

I shrugged.

I was enjoying this. As conversations go, this one called for buttered popcorn. But lacking that, I reached for a fresh clove.

"Owing to mutual friends, our paths crisscrossed many times over the earlier years, but we haven't really been what you'd call 'chummy.' We pretty much lost touch after Chester's death, and then I heard that Mercedes had become rather withdrawn. *Physically* isolated, anyway. It's not like she was ever really around much in spirit, you must realize."

"The zombie."

"Precisely. So, imagine how stunned I was to hear that Ethan Calmer was going out with her. Oh well, one man's meat, and all that."

"Uh-huh. You mentioned you got a peek at her alter ego."

"Yes," he said softly. He ground out his half-finished cigarette and grasped his high-ball glass with both hands. He sipped a bit from his drink as if tasting it for the very first time and checking to see if he liked it.

"Three or four years ago, a friend and I were driving back from a party in Everett when he suggested a nightcap. It was after midnight, but my friend said he knew a roadhouse over in Georgetown where we could snag a quick drink before our trip home. Mind you, it's not like we hadn't had enough to drink already, but off we went."

Eagleson suddenly decided he liked his drink after all and took two big swallows.

He laughed absently. "It was a shabby, rough-and-ready sort of roadhouse. A dive really. It was frequented by a tough-looking crowd of local workmen and the kind of women who like whatever money local workmen care to spend on them. But everyone there was quite tolerant of a couple of young swells like us, so we didn't feel unwelcome, and the liquor was decent enough."

Eagleson finished his drink and put his empty glass on the floor next to his chair. He chuckled wryly at his recollection and said, "As we were leaving, we walked by two men and two women at a table. One of the women was Mercedes Atwood, but at the same time *not* Mercedes Atwood."

"What do you mean?"

"This woman was dressed and made up as a tart. Like in that song 'Crazy Rhythm,' about the highbrow having no brow after meeting up with the lowbrow. Well, the highbrow Mercedes I saw that night clearly had no brow whatsoever, so to speak. She not only looked like a tart, she was laughing and carrying on as one. Rather loud and rather vulgar. You understand?"

"Loud and vulgar."

"Precisely. You can imagine what I thought. I stopped abruptly, looked right at her, and said, 'Hello, Mercedes.'"

He paused, so I asked, "What happened?"

"Why, she looked me in the eyes as if she didn't know me. She even had the cheek to tell me I had her confused with someone else. The burly fellow sitting next to her growled and made as if to get up, so I quickly apologized for my mistake and left."

"Did your friend recognize her too?"

"He didn't know Mercedes, Mr. Nilson. And when he asked me what the little ruckus was about, I simply told her I'd mistaken one tart for another. But I *wasn't* mistaken. That tart *was indeed* Mercedes Atwood. Reflecting on it the following day, I was forced to conclude that Mercedes sometimes leads a second life, slumming it, and wishes to keep that her own little secret."

I sat there wondering, looking at Eagleson as I did. He stayed quiet. There was a kind of thick, palpable tension in the air, the kind between spooners in the moonlight or two old friends fishing, when one party knows the other party's unspoken thoughts.

Finally I said, "So, you're thinking that this loon who keeps phoning Miss Atwood is an unsavory fellow from her second, *seedier* life—an unhinged pal she's picked up somewhere along the way. Maybe one whose personal brand of nuttiness has led him to stake a serious claim on her?"

Eagleson nodded briskly. "Social diseases aren't always contracted by the body, Mr. Nilson," he said sourly.

I figured he oughta know.

Chapter 14

—

IT WAS POURING DOWN rain when I reached the outskirts of Seattle later that same Saturday night. It finally stopped when I made it to Mrs. Berger's.

The kitty-cat wall clock in my landlady's kitchen read 11:05 as I came through the side door. Since the clock tended to run slow, it was probably more like 11:15.

On the table was Mrs. Berger's latest cookie experiment on a plate under a sheet of wax paper. I lifted the sheet and stared at the twisted, half-baked blobs of dough. What was it she'd called them earlier? Bohemian Teacakes? I grabbed one for the road and then tiptoed through the pantry past Mrs. Berger's bedroom off the dining room. She suffered from insomnia, and only somebody with a persistent death wish would wake her once she got to sleep. Her door was slightly ajar and I was pleased to hear light snoring. Always a good sign.

Bits and pieces of my conversation with Douglas Eagleson were still whirling around in my head, so that I almost went upstairs without taking my customary glance at the three framed photos of a nearly naked Mrs. Berger from her bump and grind days. *Almost.*

Owing to his marred appearance, Walter didn't go out much during the day, but he usually visited his haunts at night dressed in a dark-brown slouch hat and overcoat, with the coat collar flipped up and his hat worn in such a way as to help hide the right side of his face. His getup made him look like a cross between the Shadow and the Phantom of the Opera. As I reached the second floor, I was glad to see light peeking out from under his door.

I rapped lightly. Walter, Sten, and I were extremely vigilant when it came to the slumber of our resident insomniac.

"Enter," he said, his voice sufficiently muffled by the door.

I opened the door and stepped in.

Walter was sitting in front of his workbench reading a book but turned on his stool to face me as I entered. The left side of his mouth lifted in a grin. "Ah, Gunnar, will you have a spot of Black & White? You look as though you could use it."

"Make it two spots and I'll think you're on to something."

He noticed the half-eaten cookie in my left hand and said, "I see you've tried Nora's latest … *treat*." Reaching down alongside his stool, he picked up the waste can and swung it up to me with a knowing nod of his head. "Care to make a deposit?"

I dropped the remainder of the cookie in the waste can and heard it land with a dull thud. Mrs. Berger was a topnotch cook, but her baking skills desperately needed honing. Still, sampling her cookie experiments was a kind of daring duty that we boarders regularly and bravely shouldered.

I plopped in Walter's channel-back chair as he stood up to pour us each a Scotch. After he'd handed me my shot glass, he pulled his stool a little closer to my chair and sat so as to face me.

We both took a sip of whiskey. "What are you reading?" I asked, indicating the book he had quit.

"It's one of a few books I've recently borrowed from Dieter Feinberg."

Dieter Feinberg was a learned friend of Walter's—a fellow-frequenter of one of his nocturnal social haunts. As I recall, Dieter was a retired professor who had taught at some Midwest university but moved to Washington to be closer to his brother after his wife had died. According to Walter, Dieter's personal library was enviable.

"And what do these books of Dieter's deal with?"

"Psychiatry, psychology, and some of the twists and turns of human thinking and behavior. I've lately become curious about a few things, is all."

"*Light* reading then."

"Precisely, old thing," he said airily. "So, do you care to share how things are going with your ongoing saga? Any hurdles overcome? Any breakthroughs made?"

"That's just what I came to talk to you about, Walter."

Taking a big sip of my Scotch, I told him of the meeting I'd had the day before with Ethan Calmer and his pokerfaced lady love, and what the three of us had discussed.

Walter lifted his good eyebrow. "Ah ... so. Miss Atwood behaved as though nothing had happened between you."

"That's about the size of it."

"How very interesting," he said, sipping his drink.

"Uh-huh, though *interesting* isn't exactly my word for it."

I emptied my shot glass and began to relate in detail my conversation with Douglas Eagleson. When my story ended, Walter downed the last of his Scotch.

"So, then, taking Mr. Eagleson at his word, it would seem that Miss Atwood is indeed hypersexual and chooses to lead a double life," Walter said thoughtfully as he poured us each another shot of Black & White. He added, "And given what appears as her wanton bestowal of favors to a variety of crude males, she's plainly also a fairly good actress when it comes to her more restrained side. Or at least we can say she portrays her prosaic persona believably."

"Or maybe she portrays a nympho believably. Or both," I

said sourly. "But let's not be too hasty, Walter. I still haven't completely ruled out her being bughouse crazy."

That got Walter to cradle his elbow with his left hand, begin kneading his chin with the fingers of his right hand, and look up and off to one side. I focused on my Scotch for a moment to let him ruminate. But soon I was mulling things over myself.

It's funny how the mind works and how ideas get jostled and slammed together so that other ideas take shape. Such a jostling and slamming was going on in my head to the point where Ethan Calmer's hiring me out of the blue while I was nosing into Rune Granholm's murder rammed into my initial suspicion that Rune had been blackmailing someone with pictures he'd taken of something they didn't want known. That bumped up against Mercedes Atwood's second life of slumming it, which then collided with those pictures Rune had taken of two couples at a roadhouse ....

"Walter, get those pictures you're keeping for me, will you?" I asked, rising from my chair.

The undamaged side of his face had a quizzical look. But instead of following up this look with a question, he went and found the pictures from where he'd stashed them between two books on his bookshelf. He handed them to me.

I put my shot glass next to Walter's on top of the workbench. I then quickly flipped through all the pictures, checking for any detail I might have missed previously. I was particularly interested in the four roadhouse shots.

These I laid out alongside our whiskey glasses so Walter could join me in perusal of the two pictures of two men and two women at a table boozing, laughing, or kissing, and two pictures of one of these couples dancing.

"What exactly are we looking for, old thing?"

"Not sure yet, Walter."

And then I saw something in two of the shots that made me laugh. Up went Walter's good eyebrow.

"I thought his smug face looked familiar when we met," I said.

"And whose familiar smug face might that be, old top?"

I tapped an index finger on the face of a man in two of the pictures. He was sitting at a table behind the couples when all were seated.

"That there is Richard Liles."

"Ah, the man in 'Security' you talked with."

"The very same. The glorified bodyguard. But in these pictures, it's hard to know if he's guarding a body or merely shadowing one."

Walter picked up the pictures and studied them more closely. "Maybe both, or maybe neither. Difficult to say."

"True. But let's revisit the blackmail angle with Liles as Rune's possible victim. If so, then what in the world is significant about these shots of him? See anything?"

Walter shook his head. "He's not looking at the camera or at anyone shown in this picture. And given the rather complacent expression on his face, it's impossible to determine whether he's the least concerned about anyone around him. He looks to be a man having a drink. Simply that."

"Okay, but intentionally blending in with a crowd is right in keeping with Liles' line of work."

Walter nodded and handed the pictures to me. I pored over every face visible till another one made me smile widely.

"Why the Cheshire Cat grin this time, old socks?"

I held up the pictures of the dancing couple so that Walter could see the attractive woman dancer I was pointing to. "You uncrinkle the laughing face on her and that could easily be Mercedes Atwood." I next handed him the pictures with Liles in it. "And though you can't see her face quite as well in these boozing and kissing shots, that's obviously Mercedes Atwood as well."

Walter took the pictures from me to give them each another quick look and then handed them back. The left side of his face appeared to form a smirk. "This certainly opens up a range of ideas."

"Uh-huh," I said as I picked up my shot glass and resumed my chair. I took a sip of my drink and added in a bland tone, "Dollars to doughnuts, Rune was blackmailing Mercedes Atwood. She'd probably pay dearly to keep the upper crust from knowing that she parties with the crumbs and scraps of the lower crust."

Walter nodded as he put the pictures down on his bench and returned to his stool and drink. "Very possibly. But tell me, Gunnar, why would Rune have written the name Richard Liles on that notepad?"

I shrugged. "Maybe Mercedes had hired Liles as a bodyguard. Maybe he and his men provide her that service when she needs it. It makes sense she'd take some precautions when she's slumming it. So, maybe Liles spotted Rune taking these pictures. Or if Rune took them without anyone knowing, maybe he somehow tumbled to Liles' bodyguard job and got hold of him later to tell him what he had on Mercedes. Either way, Liles probably took it upon himself to intervene for his client, or she insisted he do so. But instead of paying Rune off, Liles killed him."

"Conceivable, old thing. Or, perhaps Mr. Liles was himself being blackmailed," he said in a light tone. "Mr. Liles' failure to shield his customer from negative publicity would certainly mar the reputation of his business. Perhaps that was the blackmail angle of your friend Rune."

"Rune wasn't my *friend*," I reminded him. "But you make a fair point, Walter. However, I still see Mercedes Atwood as his obvious target. What she had to hide and lose would stick out like a sore thumb to the Rune Granholm I knew."

Walter didn't say anything.

"What I'd like to know is how Rune might have discovered Miss Atwood's secret life," I said.

Walter considered that a second. "Didn't Rune's landlady

mention that he'd begun his picture-taking venture about a month ago?"

I nodded. "She said he'd quit a painting job to take up with his photo scheme."

"And didn't Miss Atwood's Japanese gardener tell you that she had plumbing, plastering, and *painting* done about a month ago?"

"You're thinking Rune might have been her painter."

He nodded. "Looked at in hindsight like this, it would hardly be a happenstance if he had been. Rather, it would be the event that put in motion a chain of other events."

I shrugged. "That would fit. If so, then maybe after Rune finished painting her bathroom, Mercedes invited him into her drawing room for some moonlighting."

"No pun intended, I gather," Walter said with a smile. "But yes, the next event. And, it's certainly possible, old thing, given Miss Atwood's apparent sexual proclivities. But how would that explain these pictures Rune took?"

That had me stumped. I tried to put myself inside Rune's conniving head.

"After their impromptu tryst, perhaps Rune concluded that where there's a lot of smoke, there's got to be far more fire to discover. So, maybe he bided his time and finally shadowed Mercedes to one of her haunts with his camera in hand."

"Possibly. Or it's conceivable Rune discovered that Miss Atwood was under surveillance," Walter said thoughtfully. "Maybe he did a little digging. That could explain why he wrote down Liles' name. He knew his role."

"Whoa, Nelly. Talk about free-ranging ideas, Walter."

His very faint smile barely budged the unspoiled side of his mouth.

"For now, Walter, I'm sticking with the idea that Mercedes Atwood seduced a very willing Rune Granholm, which put him wise to her double life, and that he shadowed her after that—probably in disguise, knowing his flair for the dramatic. And

Rune did this in order to take some incriminating pictures. If he did try and blackmail her, maybe that's how and why Liles got involved. I figure Liles to be her bodyguard, shielding her from certain annoying aspects of the dark underbelly when she goes sightseeing. It makes complete sense he'd act as her go-between if she were being shaken down."

We were both quiet for a minute or so.

"Have you considered that it's probably no accident that you were hired by Ethan Calmer almost immediately after your talk with Richard Liles," Walter said grimly.

"Yeah, that's what I'm thinking. Too pat, given this business. But it doesn't completely hang together in my mind yet," I said grimly.

"Gunnar, you said you detected that Richard Liles' demeanor changed toward you at some point in your conversation."

"Yeah, his sneer practically transformed into all sweetness and light after he sized me up as being what he called an *urbane* gumshoe. Funny what mentioning Occam's razor will do for you."

Walter went on, "He gave you two of his cards and asked for one of yours. If Richard Liles is somehow involved with Rune's murder, then given your evident urbanity, old top, perhaps our Mr. Liles began to perceive your investigation into Rune's murder as a genuine threat."

"You say the kindest things, Mr. Pangborn."

Lost in thought, he ignored my comment. "Hence, his hint at a job offer was meant to divert you. And his acquiring your business card gave him a quick means to find you later on."

"I never mentioned it, Walter, but when I later called on Mercedes Atwood, there was a green Dodge Sedan parked across from the entrance of Broadmoor. It was still there when I left."

"Interesting. Very interesting. If Mr. Liles is somehow connected with your being hired by Ethan Calmer, then he would have known when you were to meet with Miss Atwood.

He could have assigned one of his minions to be there to get a good look at you, and possibly follow you. So again, your summons by Ethan Calmer seems to be hardly a coincidence, old thing."

"Uh-huh, but Calmer told me it was Dag Erickson who referred him to me," I said in a tone I didn't mean to sound so surly. "Calmer had to know I could easily check up on that."

"Not a problem, old socks. Isn't it possible—very likely, even—that Ethan Calmer already knew Dag occasionally uses your services? If so, then he may have simply phoned him to confirm the fact, and then used that conversation as a stratagem for when he spoke with you."

"Could be, Walter. But Calmer's devotion to his lady love seems to be the genuine article. So, I'm inclined to see Calmer as an oblivious cat's-paw in this whole affair. If Liles or Mercedes is pulling the strings—or they both are—then once my name was put forward, a clueless Ethan Calmer could have simply called Dag to see if he'd vouch for me. My guess is there are no menacing phone calls. Never were. Whether on the advice of Liles or not, Mercedes probably cooked up the whole thing as an excuse to hire me through Calmer, and so, he's simply acting in good faith."

Walter nodded. "Very plausible. And, all meant to sidetrack you from your investigation into Rune's murder."

"Uh-huh." Given the possibilities Walter and I had deduced from the pictures, I was now in possession of evidence the police would definitely want to know about. But something else had changed: now I had a client. I owed it to Ethan Calmer to protect his interests while I continued to sort things out. As I saw it, the possibility of losing my license in order to do that was a risk I had to take for now.

Walter broke into my thoughts by asking, "But why do you suppose Miss Atwood tried to seduce you, old top?"

"Well, maybe it's what you suggested before, Walter. She

probably did it to embroil me in her nasty secret and make it my secret as well. Her way of keeping a close rein on me."

"Hmm ... possibly. But while we've come up with a conceivable explanation for certain facts as we know them, it still lacks a fully satisfying cohesion."

"Sure. Like I said, it doesn't quite hang together yet. But it's enough for me to go on from here."

"And *where,* pray tell, will you go from here, old socks?"

I killed what was left of my Scotch and said, "Well, as my old partner Lou Boyd used to say, 'When you don't know what to do next, see if you can shake things up.'"

Walter curled the left corner of his lip a little and said nothing.

"One thing's for certain, Walter ... I sure as hell am done checking into Miss Atwood's *old* flames, because I've got a feeling it'll be far more useful for me to get acquainted with some of her *new* flames."

Chapter 15

―

IT WAS A LOW-KEY Sunday that began with me waking from a dream that featured Douglas Eagleson. He and I were a couple of American servicemen on leave in London's West End near Piccadilly Circus during the war. Eagleson led me into a building that became a seedy house of ill repute once we'd gotten inside. Mercedes Atwood's housekeeper Nadia Forsgren took money from each of us and told us some of the girls would join us directly. Then Nadia disappeared and Eagleson was walking off with a tall, brown-haired floozie who was a dead ringer for Jimmy Wesley's wife Dorothy. The Wesleys were our next-door neighbors, and Jimmy was extremely jealous. In my dream, I wondered sadly if he knew what his wife was up to when she was away from home. Suddenly, Mercedes Atwood and Cissy Paget showed up wearing nothing but black bullet bras, tap pants, and stiletto high heels. Arm in arm, they laughed hysterically as if they'd heard the funniest joke ever told. Their laughter soon stopped and they went back to being their composed, attractive selves, except that their face makeup was downright clownish for its heaviness. They looked ghoulish, but in a sensual sort of way. Each girl took one of my hands and began escorting me to a nearby stairway. I asked Cissy how long she'd been working as a Piccadilly Commando, and she looked at me like I was an idiot for even asking the question.

The dream shifted and Walter and I were on barstools having drinks in a bar. A properly dressed and very stoical Mercedes Atwood was our bartender. An air-raid siren began to wail and I woke up feeling sad and crumby inside, and really glad the dream had ended.

It was an odd coincidence that jealous Jimmy Wesley's wife had been in my dream because of a message my landlady gave me that morning.

On weekends at Mrs. Berger's, we fixed our own breakfasts. Sten and Walter were seated at the table eating and I was at the stove scrambling a couple eggs when Mrs. Berger joined us in the kitchen. I nodded at her and she eyed me speculatively.

"I almost forgot, Gunnar. Yesterday afternoon, Shortstop wanted me to ask you if you'd come over and talk to him about something."

"Shortstop" was what Mrs. Berger called our disabled neighbor, Jimmy Wesley. Jimmy was a former British commando whose war wounds had left him with a stiff left leg and a shuffling gait—the origin of her nickname for him, I guessed but never did ask. It wasn't that Mrs. Berger was unkind. Mainly she was just crass.

"Did Jimmy say what about?" I asked.

"Nope. He just got that twisted look on his face, as if the sky was falling and the world was coming to an end," she said, doing a fair imitation of Jimmy's grimace. "But I'd lay odds it has something to do with his green-eyed monster."

I groaned.

She then thought to add, "Shortstop's sphincter has got to be so tight shut that if he were to break wind his ears would wiggle."

No one disagreed.

"And I swear, the man wouldn't know a table napkin if it bit him. Why, if you boiled any of the shirts he wears, you'd have soup stock." Then she added, "Anyway, be sure and see what Shortstop wants, okay?"

"I'll go see Jimmy right after breakfast," I assured her.

So, after breakfast, I shuffled over to Jimmy Wesley's house and knocked on the front door. Six-year-old Jimmy Jr. and four-year-old Harold answered. Jimmy Jr. wore his customary knowing sneer. Harold seemed to always have a stuffy nose and usually wore a cap with side flaps that covered his ears and strapped under his chin.

"Hi boys," I said. "Would you go tell your dad that Gunnar from next door is here to see him?"

I stayed on the porch as they ran off, leaving the door wide open. Two minutes later, I heard Jimmy's shuffling steps and then saw the man himself enter the small foyer.

We exchanged greetings.

"Thanks for comin', mate," Jimmy said in a hushed British accent. His current grimace was the one Mrs. Berger had mimicked earlier, and he tossed a nervous glance over his shoulder as he put his right leg over the threshold and then dragged the left one along before closing the door behind him.

Jimmy Wesley was somewhere between thirty and thirty-five years old. He was about five feet eight, short-legged, long-waisted, and wiry overall. He had wavy, sandy-colored hair atop a narrow forehead, a stony chin, and fidgety somber eyes. He wore brown slacks and a blue sweater vest with a V-neck that showed food stains on the white shirt he had on underneath. When he talked, his slim fingers often moved and flexed.

"Mrs. Berger said you wanted to see me. What's on your mind, Jimmy?" I asked evenly.

"I'll get right to it, mate. That I will," he said, his voice no longer hushed, his fingers flexing. "You know what a lovely girl my Dorothy is, and I'm sure you understand the special worries it brings a bloke like me—you bein' a man what knows what's what."

I told him I understood. And I did.

"The thing is, Gunnar, we're havin' a problem with some sneaky fella that's been comin' round tryin' to spy on my Dorothy at evenin' time."

"A Peeping Tom?"

Jimmy nodded. "So they call 'em."

Dorothy Wesley was an American Army nurse when a recuperating Jimmy first met her. She was now about twenty-eight years old. At almost six feet tall, she was a regular Mutt to Jimmy's Jeff in the height department. Besides being tall, Dorothy was long-limbed, robust, and well-made—not an *un*appealing build, mind you, but not exactly the kind that would turn me into a Peeping Tom. She had dark-brown hair that hung in loose natural waves and a sturdy, high forehead with severe brown eyebrows that were thick and arched over wide-set, lackluster eyes. Though she had a nice nose, her mouth was a bit wide and her lips were usually unsmiling. All in all, Dorothy had a fairly average face that achieved a superficial prettiness from makeup and warranted only a quick once-over. But Jimmy believed with all the ardor of a religious fanatic in fixed denial that his Dorothy was gorgeous—which goes to show you that one man's ceiling is indeed another man's floor.

"Have you actually seen this Peeping Tom, Jimmy?" I asked.

He shook his head. "No. But we *hear* him. That we do, mate."

Fortunately for Dorothy Wesley, Jimmy trusted *her* implicitly. But he was extremely jealous of any man who came into Dorothy's orbit—at least until he got to know you, and you'd proven to his satisfaction that you weren't trying to steal his wife's affections or favors.

"Tell me all about it," I said.

"Well, the past two nights, right when Dorothy's toweling herself off, fresh out of her nightly shower, there's a tap, tap, tap on the window, like he's tryin' to get her attention. But both times it's happened, when I made my way over to deal with him, he's already slid on down the tree he's climbed and is long gone. As you know mate, I'm not as speedy as I once was," he said, reaching down to pat his leg with his left hand. "But tonight, I plan on stickin' by the window to wait for him to show."

"So, what do you want from me?"

"I was hopin' that maybe you could be my ground crew outside. Maybe nab him when he tries to make his escape?"

I didn't say anything for a long moment. "Show me which window you're talking about."

I followed Jimmy around the side of his house, where he stopped and pointed up to a second-story bedroom window with the branches of a large elm tree way too close to it. Its top branches reached up past the roofline.

"You see, mate, he climbs up that tree there and then escapes down it," Jimmy said excitedly. "If I waited on the ground for him, I could maybe nab him, but I wouldn't be able to catch him if he broke free and ran off. But if I was to surprise him up top and you was to wait for him down below, you could easily nab him and hold him."

I looked up at a stem of the branch nearest the window. Jimmy started to talk, but I signaled him to stay quiet. I waited a few minutes until I heard the tap, tap, tap noise made by the tip of the stem as it bumped against the window when moved by a slight breeze.

"There's your Peeping Tom, Jimmy," I said, pointing up at the offending stem. "You trim that branch back, and Dorothy won't be bothered anymore."

It took a little more persuading, but Jimmy finally agreed to my interpretation of the facts.

"I guess things ain't always how they look," he said quietly.

"Uh-huh. Nor what we imagine."

Let's just say, I'd seen movies with less plot.

Chapter 16

—

T HE NEXT DAY, MONDAY, marked a week since Rune had been murdered.

At breakfast, I asked Sten if he happened to know the name of the painting company Rune had worked for a month or so back. He didn't, but before he left for work he made a quick phone call to someone he thought might. A guy named Leif Eklund.

Sten hung up the phone, and on his way out the door to join Sully, he hollered over his shoulder, "Leif told me Rune worked awhile for Sandberg and Sons."

There was no way I was going to call Mercedes Atwood and ask her if Sandberg and Sons had done her painting. I thought about calling and seeing if maybe Nadia Forsgren would know, but decided not to risk even that. Instead, I went into the pantry, looked up Sandberg and Sons in the phone book, and dialed.

After one ring, a friendly but twangy voice answered, "Sandberg and Sons. Pete speakin'. How can I be of help today?"

"Hello there, Pete, my name's Tor Berglund. I work for Miss Mercedes Atwood over here in Broadmoor. You sent someone out to her home to do some painting a month or so back. We're in need of some more painting, and we were wondering if you could send the same man out. He did such a swell job that last time. I think his name was Ron or something."

"Uh, sure … lemme check." I heard a dull thump and some papers rattle, and a moment or two later Pete happily announced, "Yeah. Record shows we painted a bathroom for you, alrighty. But the worker's name wasn't Ron, it was Rune … Rune Granholm. I'm afraid he don't work for us no more. But say, listen, we'd be more than happy to send out another painter just as good."

"Oh, you say he left you, huh? Well, I know Miss Atwood especially wanted to have this Rune fellow come back, so I think I'd better check with her and call you later on with whatever she decides. She's very particular. You understand, I'm sure."

Pete said he understood, and I cradled the phone.

Time to shake things up.

THE COFFEE AND LEMONADE from earlier had finally caught up with me, so Kirsti wheeled me over to the cafeteria men's room. I'd just managed a return hop, skip, and an awkward jump back out to my wheelchair and to her helping grasp, when she said, "I know you want to get to certain details in your own good time, but I'd like to ask something about how things were back then. In Seattle, I mean."

"Shoot," I said, settling into my little chariot.

She swung my wheelchair around and began to push me back over to the outside courtyard as she continued talking.

"Were there a lot of detectives in Seattle back then?"

"Back in the *old* days, you mean?" I said with a chuckle. "Surprisingly, yes. Remember, blue eyes, when it comes right down to it, a lot of what private detectives did was fairly routine, and still is. Sometimes people wanted a person found, but often it was merely a lost item or a missing pet. Once I located a stolen Chihuahua, for instance. Or, a guy might hire you to help break up his daughter's romance with the wrong guy. Or a merchant believed one of his employees had sticky fingers and wanted you to find out who it was. Or then again, maybe a man or a woman suspected their mate of infidelity, so you were hired to follow them."

"Did you do much of that last kind of work, Gunnar?"

"Not too much. Not if I could help it," I added a bit too sourly. "And of course, then as now, some detectives worked as doorknob rattlers, providing various types of security and surveillance, and even personal protection."

When we reached our spot in the outer courtyard, and she was again seated on the wood bench facing me, I said,

"You're probably too young to know this, but for years Seattle was home to the famous Luke May, known as the 'scientific detective.'"

"Never heard of him."

"I'm not surprised. Why, some called Luke May America's Sherlock Holmes."

She merely nodded and turned on her recorder.

"But even back in 1950, when Seattle was just a cultural jerkwater, it had its fair share of detective agencies. Most of them were downtown, nestled somewhere on either Second, Third, or Fourth Avenue. Richard Liles hung his shingle in the ten-story Elihu Brown Building on Fourth. That's where I was headed …."

IT WAS JUST AROUND lunchtime when I got downtown. I went through a huge lobby with tall, cream-colored walls and large octagonal pillars of cream-colored marble, black and cream-colored terrazzo floors, and ornate cream-colored lanterns hanging from a high-beamed, cream-colored ceiling. Apparently, all cream lovers were being made to feel extremely welcome as they hunted for the elevators.

I was the sole passenger of an elevator operator wearing a

tan bellboy hat and uniform. Despite the getup, he hadn't been a boy in decades. He was a sallow-faced old plugger who'd probably been plugging away since the building opened just before America went off to fight the Kaiser.

He gripped and deftly worked the lever with long, bony fingers that would have looked less like talons if he'd been better about clipping his fingernails. It triggered in me that speculative thinking that can go on when you're alone for even a little while with a complete stranger who has one or more distinctive characteristics, be they appealing or just peculiar. So, as the elevator reeled and heaved and gradually throbbed up the shaft, I wondered what kept an old guy like this from using nail clippers on a regular basis. Do you just give up on some of the smaller details as the years go by, or do you do so gradually, a case of being reduced by sheer attrition? Or do you just wake up one morning and decide you're not going to trim your fingernails as often as you used to? And if so, what about his toenails? If he's tossed the towel in on those, then is his toe jam running amok?

Old Talon-Fingers left me off on the fifth floor after telling me in a flat, gravelly voice that Puget Sound Security was two doors down on my right.

When I telephoned earlier, I'd been fully prepared to talk to Richard Liles. But another plan of action fell in my lap. A sultry female voice told me that Mr. Liles was out of the office till the next day. It suited me just fine that Dickie-boy was gone, though I didn't tell *her* that. The sultry female voice sounded friendly enough, so I figured I'd stop by and learn what I could from one or two mice while the cat wasn't on hand to interfere.

I quietly opened the reception-area door and peeked inside. Light-gray carpet blanketed the floor from one end to the other. The room itself had those relentless, cream-colored walls and modern-looking furniture made of metal that included a large desk, a coffee table, a few smoke stands placed here and there, and chairs that were upholstered with what looked like black leather. On top of the coffee table were the mandatory magazines piled high around a couple of ceramic doodads that looked exotic and Oriental. Behind the desk but off to the right was a closed door that probably led to Richard Liles' private office.

Next to the desk were two black filing cabinets, one with its top drawer pulled wide open. The young woman standing right beside it really caught my eye; she was sleek and straight as a Corinthian column. She was turned my way, intently studying a file as if it were a rich man's last will and testament making her the sole beneficiary. Standing there like that, she reminded me of the secretary in that Edward Hopper painting *Office at Night*—only this room was just the reception area and far plushier, and the girl even more dazzling.

I closed the door behind me and cleared my throat so as not to startle her. She glanced my way.

It had looked like it was going to rain, so I had my gray raincoat draped over my left arm. On my head was a Dobbs brown fedora known as the Gay Prince, which I'd purchased the year before at Klopfenstein's downtown. I took it off and wedged it above my raincoat when our eyes met.

She put the file on the desk top and treated me to glittering eyes and straight white teeth that sparkled between parted full lips painted crimson to match her fingernails. She was slim but round-hipped, and while her bust was average size, she seemed to embody the brassiere ad that pledged: firm, striking, and well-defined.

She sashayed toward me in a black and white pullover crepe dress that had no form other than what her shapely figure gave to it.

I met her halfway and we shook hands.

"Oh yes, uh-huh, you must be Mr. Williams. And right on time, too. I'm Miss Voorhees. Joyce Voorhees. I'm Mr. Liles' personal secretary. We talked by telephone earlier." I heard a hint of business college in her polite speech.

Seattle had to have had its share of Voorhees, but when I'd called earlier, and learned that like Ethan Calmer, Richard Liles also had a secretary with the last name Voorhees, I was only a little bit surprised and a great deal suspicious.

"I met another Voorhees this morning. A girl named Lillian. I had some business in a law office in one of those tall buildings over on Second Avenue near Cherry. She's the receptionist. Are you two related?"

Joyce beamed. "Oh yes, uh-huh. Lillian's my cousin. In fact, I helped put her on to that job."

"The two of you are close?"

"So-so," she said wistfully. "Enough so that I know she's got a big crush on someone in that office."

"A lot of that going around."

"Oh yes, uh-huh."

On the phone with Joyce earlier, I'd posed as a businessman named Kenneth Williams who was concerned about his younger sister being followed by an unwanted suitor. I'd expressed my intention to engage Puget Sound Security to watch over her, and had said I was extremely anxious to get the ball rolling. Joyce Voorhees had told me that though her boss was away on business, she was fully authorized to hear me out on the particulars so as to get things underway. I'd put on my nicest and most expensive brown three-piece suit for the occasion. To top it all off, I wore a pair of horn-rimmed glasses with clear glass, which I normally kept stowed in the glove box of my coupe for those times I wanted to appear as Gunnar the Bookworm or Gunnar the Highly Respectable.

Aside from fourteen carats of diamond bracelet on one wrist and a narrow-banded watch on the other, the only jewelry I could see on Miss Joyce Voorhees were silver disks the size of dimes on her earlobes.

Unlike her cousin Lillian, Joyce Voorhees wasn't overly scented with jasmine. When we'd shaken hands, I sniffed only a faint scent of sandalwood. Like Lillian Voorhees, she was in her early twenties, had a heart-shaped face, and was beautiful. There the resemblance seemed to end.

Joyce wasn't a strawberry blonde. She had dark-brown hair with a crisp, sharp part on the left side and with luxurious soft curls that didn't quite reach her shoulders, brushed out and guided back away from her face. Her ivory skin made her thin dark eyebrows seem even more pronounced. She had a cute button nose, the narrow bridge of which was proportionately flanked by big brown eyes with lustrous beaded eyelashes—it must take a practiced and steady hand to make them look that good. Her lashes practically reached out and swatted you when she batted them, and batting them seemed to be a habit with her.

Joyce looked like she was about to make a suggestion when I heard the outer door open. She shot the newcomer a sharp glance.

"What can I do for you, Mr. Holt?" she inquired frostily. It was plain that Joyce didn't cotton to this Mr. Holt whatsoever.

"Boss man said I could come by for my pay. I was tied up on a job when the eagle flew," Mr. Holt said in a flat nasal voice. "He told me you'd have my check for me."

I turned around for a peek at him, putting a hand up to my spectacles for effect as I gave him a quick once-over.

Lo and behold, standing just inside the room was the lean, hatchet-faced driver of the green Dodge Sedan—the one I'd seen parked across the street from the entrance of Broadmoor the day I'd visited Mercedes Atwood. There were way too many coincidences going on around me to be genuine.

I looked back at Joyce, whose brooding gaze was riveted on Holt. "Oh yes, uh-huh," she said stiffly, all sweetness drained from her tone and face. I'd concluded that *Oh yes, uh-huh*, was her favorite phrase, rain or blow. She glanced my way and said in a low, cooing voice, "Please excuse me for a few minutes, Mr. Williams."

"Certainly, Miss Voorhees." I admired her faucet-like talent for turning her flow of congeniality on and off at will.

Joyce left her spot and went through the inner door to whatever awaited her beyond, so that suddenly my life lost some of its meaning. I managed to divert myself by turning my eyes back to Mr. Holt, who had just finished ogling the dear departed. Whoever that Italian sage was, he was right. Sex is indeed the poor man's opera.

Holt looked at me and used a worn-out line he'd probably said hundreds of times before about hundreds of different girls, "Gal has a rump shaped like a ripe peach."

In Joyce Voorhees' case, I couldn't argue. So I didn't. Just as I thought he was all talked out about Liles' secretary, he proved me wrong.

He winked at me, nodded at the inner door and said in a voice that sounded like it was passing through a sieve, "One time I got a good look at her in a crop top and a pair of short shorts, so I seen her legs naked from the hips down. Long, tapering legs. Very shapely." He squinted his eyes and puckered his lips to indicate his admiration, while slicing a big "s" in the air with his right hand. "But she's never given no guy here the time of day, seeing as how she had her sights set on the boss. She's *his* main squeeze now."

I nodded that I understood, so giving me another wink and a nasty grin, Holt added, "You can bet the boss man keeps her singing out her 'Oh yeses' and 'Uh-huhs' all through the long night, if you catch my drift."

Maybe my broad shoulders offset the horn-rimmed glasses, because Holt obviously figured me as a job applicant. Otherwise, I'd have given him a failing grade in good sense and public relations. Instead, I just gave him a bland smile that could mean most anything at all while I studied him more closely.

Holt held his gray fedora in his left hand and started running his right hand through his sorrel-colored hair. His leer was gone and his lips were stretched to form their usual thin, straight line. He was a weedy little man with deep-set, dull eyes and a long, high-bridged nose on a dyspeptic-looking face. It was the face of a man with few friends and one that even a mother might struggle to love. He could have been thirty-five or forty-five. Hard to tell. He had on a loose-fitting blue whipcord suit that he wore carelessly. For one brief moment, he leaned forward and his coat opened so that the round-handled grip of the gun holstered under his left arm could be seen. A big gun for such a little man.

We'd both been giving each other the up-and-down, because when I looked back to Holt's face, I met narrowed, quizzical eyes.

"You look like I know you. We met before, Mac?" he asked in a guarded tone.

"I highly doubt it," I said casually. "Williams is the name. Ken Williams. I'm just up from Portland for the day." It was possible he'd gotten as good a look at me as I did of him that day I spotted him when I drove by his sedan. I hoped not. Eyeglasses aren't the best disguise, despite what Clark Kent might have us think. I quickly changed the subject by asking, "Do you like working here?"

He shrugged. "It pays the bills. But I suppose I get a kick outta some of the people I come across. It can be real entertaining."

Appearances are indeed tricky. It's not like the guy was overwhelming me with subtlety and wit, but I started thinking Holt had more imagination than I'd given him credit for at first blush.

Joyce Voorhees rejoined us. She shot me a smile and then blasted Holt with a withering glare as she quickly crossed the room to him with restless hips and long fierce strides that made her legs seem a blur and caused the halves of her ripe-peach bottom to alternately move up and down as quickly as a couple of pistons firing. When she reached Holt, she poked an envelope at his chin. He took it, and with a swift, springy step, he was gone.

When the door had closed, Joyce turned to me and said primly, "Again, I'm sorry for the interruption. All part of doing business. You understand, I'm sure." She said it in a pleasant, cuddly voice, batting her beaded lashes and wearing an innocent smile that was almost persuasive.

I told her I understood. But her behavior with Holt, and my brief chat with him, had convinced me that while Joyce was a truly gorgeous brunette, she had eyes too calculating to go with such a pure-hearted smile. I'd been wary of her when I walked in simply because she was Richard Liles' secretary. Now that I knew she and Dick were pillow talkers, I was warier still.

She asked me to please follow her into Mr. Liles' office and added, "I'll leave the office door open to hear if someone comes in, but we'll still have more privacy that way."

Joyce moved past me. I gladly followed. But gone now were the quick fierce strides. Instead she gently swayed her hips and casually displayed the kind of taut, rounded calves that a model working for the Powers Agency would envy.

Joyce left the door slightly ajar when we entered Liles' inner sanctum. It didn't disappoint. It struck me as being a downtown annex of his mansion-wannabe over on Capitol Hill. It was about the same size as the reception area, with the same basic coloring, and with the same light-gray carpet blanketing the floor. But there the similarity ended. To my immediate left was a brown-leather couch that for length could easily sleep two. To my right was a gray filing cabinet and a small gray safe. Beside the safe was a bookcase and a portable bar, both made of dark wood. Next in line was a brown-colored compact refrigerator. Straight ahead of me and near the fridge was a large mahogany desk, with a blotter, a typewriter, a cradle phone, a notepad, a pen set, and a glass ashtray thick with butts. In front of the desk were two armless klismos-style chairs with curved saber legs, brown leather seats, and arched S-shaped backs. In one corner off to itself was a television-radio-phonograph console housed in a cabinet that was also probably of mahogany. Beyond the desk, the blinds were open and the windows stared toward buildings across Fourth Avenue.

Joyce Voorhees circled behind the desk and parked her bottom in a tall, brown-leather chair. I could tell it wasn't the first time her bottom had been parked there. When she completed that maneuver, she asked me to please be seated. She batted her eyelashes, leaned back in the chair, and pretended she wasn't a pleasure to look at and easy to listen to.

Putting my fedora and raincoat between the cradle phone and the blotter on the large desk, I sat in one of the klismos chairs.

"Please, call me Joyce, Mr. Williams."

I met that with an only-if-you-call-me-Ken.

That pleased her and evoked a delighted, "Oh yes, uh-huh."

"Well now, Mr. Will ... I mean, *Ken*. I believe I got the gist of things on the telephone, but please tell me in more detail how Puget Sound Security may be of assistance to you," she said soothingly.

"Well Joyce, as I told you, it's my kid sister Eileen," I said, meeting her level gaze. "I fear for her safety. A man she went out with a couple of times won't leave her alone. She tells me that wherever she goes, he shows up. From what Eileen says, he sometimes waits outside her apartment. Sometimes he even takes pictures of her. She's sick of this. But, like I said, I'm the one concerned for her safety."

Joyce leaned forward and snatched up the notepad from the blotter and a pen from the pen set. "Have you called the police?" she asked as she started writing on the pad, pulling her lower lip with her teeth.

"No. You see, that's the problem, Joyce. Eileen hasn't and won't call the police, and she forbids me to do so. She's told this guy off a few times, and she believes it will all blow over eventually ... But, Eileen's sometimes too plucky for her own good, if you know what I mean." I paused, adjusted my eyeglasses and did my best imitation of a mildly frantic older brother.

Joyce took her teeth from her lip. "Oh yes, uh-huh. But *you* don't think it will blow over," she said in a comforting, melodious tone.

"No, Joyce. No, I don't," I said firmly.

As she took notes, I spent the next ten minutes or so providing Joyce with a little background as to how my imaginary sister met this make-believe fellow—how long they supposedly dated and how long since that had purportedly stopped. And then I added more about the little I knew of him. That kind of thing. The details came fairly easy. I simply drew on similar situations of which I had hard-won firsthand knowledge.

As Joyce busily jotted down notes, she occasionally chimed in with her signature "Oh yes, uh-huh" in sympathetic acknowledgment.

I was about to spring on her what I'd come to spring on her when she asked, "Could you describe him to me, Ken?"

Her question was right on cue.

"Better yet, I can show him to you, Joyce. I happen to have a picture." I reached for what I had in my inside coat pocket.

I leaned in over the desk and handed her the same picture of Rune Granholm I'd shown her boss the day I'd talked with him.

She looked at the picture, not blinking, not saying anything for maybe thirty seconds as her innocent smile slowly became an uncertain one and a flush crept over her ivory skin and slowly deepened. Her thin, dark eyebrows arched in a surprise that didn't seem feigned. She raised her lovely eyes, which now flickered with suspicion and fear as they bore into me.

I pretended to sound surprised as I said, "You seem to know him. I can tell. You've seen him before, haven't you? Have there been other girls? Is that it? Is this guy some sort of sex fiend?" I tried to sound a bit rattled. "I knew it. I just knew it. I told

Eileen she was naïve to think this whole thing would just blow over."

My outburst seemed to reassure the girl. Her world started to make some sense again as the suspicion and fear in her eyes were replaced with mild bewilderment followed by the plausible realization that Rune must have been a cad and troublemaker on several fronts. Her red cheeks began to slowly fade to pink.

I'd quit talking and looked at her expectantly.

"Oh ... yes ... uh-huh, I've seen this young man before," she said a bit absently, gingerly handing me back the picture as if it was contaminated. Apparently, she didn't think having it would be of any help. "But the circumstances are foggy. I meet so many people, Mr. Williams, and I become acquainted with such a wide variety of situations. You understand, I'm sure. But if I were you, I wouldn't leap to any wild conclusions just yet." Joyce flipped a page or so back in her notepad and examined something she'd written. "You said this fellow has sometimes taken *photos* of your sister?"

I nodded, putting Rune's picture back in my inside coat pocket.

She nodded slowly in turn. "Oh yes, uh-huh. I seem to recall something of that nature. I'm not sure, so I'll have to check into it, but I believe this young man may have had something to do with making a nuisance of himself with his camera—that kind of thing. But as I say, I'll have to do some checking into it to be certain. You can appreciate that, I'm sure. Especially if we're going to do work for you that directly involves him. We'll need to first determine that there's no ... *um* ... no conflict of interest. You understand, I'm sure. For now, I have ample information from you that I can pass on to Mr. Liles when he returns tomorrow. Oh yes, uh-huh. In the meantime, Mr. Williams ...."

I think I'd successfully allayed any knee-jerk suspicions I'd aroused in Joyce by showing her Rune's picture. But, as hoped,

I'd definitely struck a nerve, because the girl stood up and started to give me the ever-so-gracious here's-your-hat-what's-your-hurry treatment.

She moved out from behind the desk to escort me to the door. I stood but didn't go anywhere.

If I left then, Joyce Voorhees wouldn't be calling Kenneth Williams any time soon, and it would be greatly preferred if he didn't call her either. But if he did call her, he'd be told that a conflict of interest prevented Puget Sound Security from handling the difficulties of his kid sister. *So, sorry ... I'm sure you understand.*

According to what Richard Liles said to me, his secretary told the cops that she couldn't find any record of Rune Granholm having phoned or visited the office. Maybe. Or maybe not.

Rune's picture hadn't been in the newspapers when his murder was reported. But it was apparent that Liles' secretary recognized Rune from his picture, so it was as plain as the cute button nose on her beautiful face that she'd seen him somewhere. What's more, she'd just volunteered that she knew him to have caused problems with his camera. That particular item wasn't in the newspapers either.

Joyce smiled primly and nodded me toward the door as if to will me to move in that direction. I didn't budge. Instead I growled, "Cut the crap, Joyce. We both know who that guy in the picture really is—or I should say, who he *was*. That's what I really came here to find out. What you know exactly. That, and to give you a message to pass on to your boss."

She looked at me with a pitiable blank expression, as if she'd just been asked a radio quiz question for a big-money prize but didn't know the answer, or anyone who did.

Chapter 17

—

IF SOMEONE *COULD TURN* as red as a beet, it was Joyce Voorhees. She was also frozen in place. All that moved were her eyelashes, blinking so swiftly that a passing fly might think it was a windstorm.

I took off the horn-rimmed glasses and tucked them in my front right coat pocket.

Joyce's lashes stopped moving as suddenly as they'd started and her brown eyes grew almost as wide as a couple of fifty-cent pieces. There was fear in those eyes again.

"Who are you?" she asked in a small voice, putting a hand up to her lovely neck.

"My name is Gunnar Nilson."

Like the photo, she knew the name. "O-oh yes, uh-huh .... Y-you're that private eye that talked to Dick ... *I mean*, Mr. Liles."

"Uh-huh. And I have those pictures and negatives your boss wanted to buy from that guy in the photo who's now dead."

The panicky look on her face told me I'd hit a bull's-eye.

"I see," she said nervously. "So, what ...." She paused to clear her throat. "What exactly is the ... *message* you want me to pass on to Mr. Liles?" She spoke with a slight quaver, her mouth gaping, her face a little less flushed now.

"Tell your boss that if he or his client still want to deal, they're dealing with me now."

She nodded once, mouthing my words to herself as she would a phone number she was committing to memory.

I was actually enjoying this. I really was. You get your amusement where you can find it. I reached into my shirt pocket for a clove and popped it in my mouth.

Joyce's color had returned and she was biting her lower lip. The girl must have gone through a tube of lipstick per week. She was teetering back and forth ever so slightly on the balls of her feet until finally her blank look became a little less blank and just a wee bit foxy. A clever idea seemed to have formed, because when she stopped teetering, her eyes gleamed as they slowly measured me. They were sly eyes now.

Her lips quirked at the corners and a playful smile started to take shape. She started batting her beaded eyelashes coyly, and in what I could only describe as a gear switch from businesslike to coquettish, she said in a lilting voice, "You know, Mr. Nilson, I'm *fully* authorized to write checks for Mr. Liles. Or, if you wish, you could go with me to the bank and I could arrange for a cashier's check or simply cash in exchange for the pictures— and the negatives too, of course. I happen to know the amount Mr. Liles is willing to pay for what you're selling. And since I have Mr. Liles' every confidence, is there any reason why you and I can't handle these negotiations while he's out of town?"

Joyce's proposition got me curious. And there it was again: that faucet-like talent of hers that had impressed me earlier. I'd already found out what I'd mainly come for, but if there was more to learn from this girl, I was quite willing to be her pupil—particularly as I sensed she meant for me to be teacher's pet.

So, I said, "I don't see why not."

That pleased her. It pleased her quite a bit. "May I call you *Gunnar*?" she purred.

Since I liked to be purred at, I said, "Sure."

That pleased her too.

I smiled a friendly, toothy smile but wasn't feeling it, not now that it was looking more and more like Dick Liles and his office sweetie were involved in Rune's murder.

However, seeing as how Joyce Voorhees had curves to make the switchbacks of a mountain highway jealous, I was willing to stick around to parley and possibly tumble to another piece or two of the puzzle in the process. *Oh yes, uh-huh.*

Joyce was plainly a girl who planned ahead, for suddenly she got busy creating the appropriate atmosphere for our tête-à-tête. She minced on over to the window and closed the blinds. Next, she whisked over to the open communicating door, and as she left the office, she said in a hushed voice, "We'll not want to be disturbed. I'll go hang the 'Out to Lunch' sign on the outer door and lock it."

The cynical side of me wondered if Joyce might be hatching some sort of badger game. Maybe Dick Liles was actually still in town and she was telephoning him to beat it on over to discover the two of us in a compromising position. Maybe, but not likely.

When Joyce came back, she fiddled with the dimmer switch near the door till Liles' office had the muted and low-key lighting of a seedy nightclub. The girl was obviously a practiced hand at tending to such mood-altering niceties in this particular office.

"Have a seat on the couch, won't you? I'll join you in a moment," she said as she practically floated over to Liles' desk. I saw then she was no longer wearing her black T-strap high heels. She opened a desk drawer and retrieved a tube of lipstick that she used to repair the damage her lip-biting had done. If she was shooting for that shimmering luster promised by Madison Avenue, she'd aced it.

I loosened my tie and sat down in the mid-section of the long leather couch as Joyce clicked on the radio to a station previously dialed in. As soft music played low, she waltzed over to the portable bar for a bottle and two glasses. When she bent over to rob the small fridge, her crepe dress nicely mapped out the rolling topography of her thighs and rump. Getting caught with her in flagrante delicto seemed a risk worth taking.

Gunnar the Daring.

As ice tinkled in the glasses, I brought up Holt. "You don't much like that guy who stopped by for his pay."

"That's putting it mildly. The man's a *pig*," she snapped in disgust. "A genuine heel. He's always saying nasty things and making passes at me when nobody's around. I've yet to report him to Mr. Liles … but it doesn't matter, because I have a hunch Mr. Holt won't be working for us much longer."

"*Oh* … why's that?"

"He moonlights. A *lot*. Which would probably be okay if it didn't cut into what he's supposed to be doing for us."

So, Holt served *two* masters. Interesting.

Joyce finished making our drinks and pranced over to me like a nubile wood nymph about to get frisky with the local satyr.

I took the glass she handed me as she carefully sat down beside me on my left. She was positioned sideways so as to better face me, her legs crossed and parallel, with one pressed tightly against the other. If I'd tried to sit that way I wouldn't have been able to walk for a week. At the moment, you just might have been able to slip a thin Mercury dime between where her stockings rubbed up against my left pant leg—if that's how you chose to spend your time. Through the reinforced toes of her sheer nylons, I could see that from the tips right through to the quicks, her toenails were painted to match her lips and fingernails. Quite the ensemble for a painted lady—and I don't mean the butterfly variety.

I tasted my drink. It was mainly whiskey with maybe a thimbleful of ginger ale tossed in to make it behave.

Joyce swallowed about a third of her highball before leaning over and placing the glass down on the floor. As she leaned back, she laughed softly. Batting her eyelashes a few times, she flashed a titillating smile that gave my frontal lobe a sound shaking then reverberated on down to my toes, curling nine of them.

Joyce's eyelids drooped as she gazed steadily at me. She stroked her left thigh with her left hand, smoothing out her already smooth dress in the process. Her head tilted to one side and then toward me as she earnestly said, "Since the war, Mr. Liles has worked very hard to build a good reputation in Seattle. And now he wants to grow the company."

Her tone of voice and how she spoke of Dick Liles told me she was proud of him and then some.

"In fact, that's why Mr. Liles is in Portland, today. He's checking into details for opening a branch there. It's one of the reasons he has to keep a tight rein on the funds he has available."

"And this concerns me, *why*?"

She reached her right hand over and touched my left arm a moment before pulling it back to cover what little cleavage showed above the heart-shaped neckline of her dress. Her eyelids had drooped now to where she was seeing me through her lashes.

"I get it. You're toying with me, aren't you?" she said softly.

"Suppose I am. I'd still like you to explain things in your own way."

"Those *pictures*," she said with a thin sigh. "Particularly *now*. Those pictures taken at that sleazy dive could do real damage to Mr. Liles' good name and business. Let alone whatever other pictures that young man—that *Rune* fellow—said he'd taken, which I suppose you have now as well?"

This last was a question more than a statement. While it was news to me that Rune had other pictures—or claimed to have had them—I still responded with a knowing nod.

Joyce's plan-ahead nature became downright palpable again, for without taking her eyes off me she nonchalantly slipped both her hands under her hem and hiked it up a bit so she could detach her nylon stockings from their garter straps as she continued talking.

"Normally, Mr. Liles would have probably just weathered the storm and ignored such a threat," she said gloomily, leaning forward a bit to deftly peel off her right stocking, which she then flung to the floor.

"I was caught completely off guard when that ... that *Rune* barged into our reception area and described his pictures to me in detail," she said as she removed her left stocking. "He said his pictures were proof that Dick couldn't protect a client from possible scandal ... let alone his willingness to try and cover up licentious behavior for money."

"Damned if you do, damned if you don't."

"Exactly. And like I said, I was caught flat-footed, and I started to beg and plead with Rune not to ruin Mr. Liles' reputation and prospects. I-I'm afraid I gushed. I tend to blurt things out when I get stressed."

"It happens."

She nodded. As she tossed the second nylon to the floor, she added, "Too late I realized I'd really blundered by giving him even more to hold over Dick than he'd probably realized."

I didn't say so, but I think Joyce was giving herself way too much credit. Shark that he was, Rune had probably already seen plenty of blood in the water to form his own notions about Mercedes Atwood and Dick Liles even before talking with Joyce. However, the girl's version did explain her obvious personal need to help set things straight for her boss.

Joyce crossed her legs again in that sideways and parallel fashion of hers, displaying generous portions of her naked thighs. Holt hadn't exaggerated. Her legs had contours a dancer in a cancan kick line would give her eye teeth for.

"I know it's not nice to say, but when Dick and I learned that young man had been murdered, we hoped we were in the clear … that maybe the pictures were stashed away and would stay hidden … or be simply ignored as unimportant if found. I know *I* was beginning to hope that was indeed the case … but then, *you* showed up today," she said faintly, "and, *well*—here we are."

"What was Rune's asking price for the pictures?"

Her thin eyebrows arched and there was a flicker of distrust in her eyes. She suddenly uncrossed her naked legs and leaned back, absently twirling a strand of her hair with the index finger of her slim right hand. Her other hand tugged at the edge of her neckline. "Y-you mean *you* don't know?"

She looked away from me to her discarded stockings for a brief moment, as if willing them back on her legs.

"I'm simply wondering if *you* do … and just how much Mr. Liles trusts you to know."

That put her suspicions to rest. She nodded and squeaked, "Oh yes, uh-huh." She put one leg atop the other again and added, "You're *testing* me, aren't you? I get it."

She'd assumed I'd simply pick up where Rune had left off, and that I'd naturally demand the very same payment in hush money that he had. Plainly, she'd invited me to stick around so she could persuade me to drop my asking price.

Gunnar the Persuadable.

She lifted her left hand to her collarbone, and then her neck, and finally she daintily fondled her lips with her fingertips. Between assaults by her teeth and her fingers, her lipstick didn't stand a chance.

"So, as you … er … as you know then, Rune demanded *six* thousand dollars for the pictures and negatives," she said in an almost hoarse whisper.

I suppressed an urge to whistle. Rune figured he'd been dealt all the right cards and had clearly tried to shoot the moon.

"Of course, Mr. Liles considered his asking price highly *unreasonable*," she said with a sharp, disdainful emphasis on the last word. In a sweet voice, she added, "I'm hoping you'll be far more reasonable in what you demand …."

She let that last word hang in space for a while as she studied my face.

I took a healthy swig of my drink before putting the glass down on the floor.

This reminded Joyce of her own drink, because she leaned over and reached for her highball. She swirled it a bit before bringing it to her mouth, and then tipped her head back so she could toss down the rest in one swift gulp. After returning the empty glass to the floor, she delicately licked her upper lip.

"Did Liles' client squawk at the cost of getting hold of the pictures? Was that it?"

Her pretty brown eyes got round. She looked genuinely puzzled. "You don't seem to understand. No client was being blackmailed, Gunnar. That young man … that *Rune* was only targeting Mr. Liles."

It was naïve of the girl to think that Rune would set his sights so low. Obviously, Dick Liles hadn't taken his sweetie into his complete confidence after all. Surely Rune's shakedown had to have included Mercedes Atwood. She stood to be hurt the most from the pictures I'd seen. Besides, Mercedes was the well-heeled party. While Joyce mentioned that Rune had other pictures, I'd believe that only when I saw proof. Rune was probably blowing smoke to help raise the ante. Once he'd stumbled on Mercedes' nasty secret, he'd feel free to exaggerate all he wished as to what he knew and what he had as proof. That was Rune through and through.

"So, tell me what your boss man considers a *reasonable* price for the pictures?"

Joyce carefully unlaced her bare legs and leaned into me as

she hooked her right hand around my neck and grabbed the front of my shirt with her left. She pulled my head toward hers.

"Kiss me," she said thickly.

I kissed her once, firmly.

"Again," she breathed.

I kissed her again—a long and lingering kiss this time. I pulled my face away and looked at her. She was dreamy-eyed and her body was relaxed. She gave me a lopsided smile and her eyelids started fluttering like the tapping castanets of a hopped-up flamenco dancer.

"Mr. Liles is willing to pay *two* thousand dollars," she said softly.

"Not a penny more?"

She shook her lovely head several times till her soft curls wobbled. Her pupils were dilated and the nostrils of her cute button nose were flared. She wrapped both arms around my neck and repeatedly thrust her lips into mine as she ran the fingers of one hand through my hair and tugged on the back of my neck with the other. I soon learned this was but a measly preamble of what was to follow, because next she pitched her shapely frame hard up against me and began slathering my lips and face with amorous kisses as if they were soft butter being spread on warm toast.

I found Joyce extremely persuasive. However, eventually she began chiming in with an "Oh yes, uh-huh" or two, which frankly killed the mood for me. So much so, that I finally pulled my face free of hers and asked, "Why didn't your boss try to get Rune to drop his price for the pictures? Why'd he have to go and kill him?"

She jerked away from me with a shocked look on her face. "Dick … didn't *kill* him," she said breathlessly. "He … just couldn't have. From what I read in the newspaper, Dick was with me at the time of the murder … so he couldn't have done it."

"Liles was with *you*? *Where*?"

"That's just it … we were in his car in a parking lot over near Green Lake. Dick was supposed to meet that fellow Rune near the bathhouse to make him a counteroffer and then pay him if he accepted it. In fact, Dick called him from a phone booth to confirm the meeting maybe an hour before we were to meet up. So, like I said, Dick couldn't have killed him. You're wrong about that, Gunnar. And Dick *was* going to try and get the price down. He really was."

A man with Liles' contacts and resources would have no problem getting hold of Rune's telephone number and address, careless as Rune could be. And the bathhouse meet-up squared with what Rune had told me at the Flying Clipper.

"What time did Liles make that call?"

"A little past eight thirty or so. Ten minutes or so past, at the most. Dick wanted to be at Green Lake well ahead of time. Dick's that way. The meeting was for nine thirty. Rune told Dick he would be there just before he ended the phone conversation all of a sudden. Dick said it was as if Rune had been interrupted by something or maybe someone."

That put the call roughly ten or fifteen minutes before I showed up at Rune's doorstep. So, maybe the killer had arrived and interrupted Liles' call, and then I showed up and scared off the killer.

"I swear, I'm telling you the unvarnished truth, Gunnar. Dick *didn't* kill your friend. He just couldn't have."

"I believe you." Well, I should say I believed she believed it.

Her surprise at the idea that Liles had murdered Rune seemed genuine enough. And since the story had rushed out of her mouth so quickly, it smacked of the truth. She did say she was a blurter.

But, if Liles had found out where Rune lived, he could easily have arranged for an underling or hired gun to shoot Rune, while giving himself an alibi. I saw no point in pressing the point with Joyce, especially since she was again pushing her lips and body at mine with renewed vigor.

I'd had no qualms about sampling Joyce's charms under a pretext when I'd believed she was somehow connected to Rune's murder. And given the kind of sacrifice she was obviously willing to make for her boss, I confess that I was sorely tempted to put her long legs and restless hips through the paces, should she offer. Pretty lowdown of me, I know, but there you have it.

Gunnar the Would-be Vigilante.

However, I had a change of heart. The more I talked with Joyce, the more I saw her as just a hapless pawn on Liles' chessboard, and a fairly likeable pawn at that.

So, when she gently pulled away and in a thin, tired voice said, "A section of this couch opens up into a full-size bed," I'd already begun to change course—as unbelievably hard as that was for me to do. And when she gave me her lopsided smile, gathered up her hem with both hands, and started jockeying her rump from side to side so as to pull her pullover dress up and over, I stopped her.

BEFORE I LEFT, I assured Joyce that I indeed had the pictures Liles wanted, but that I was no blackmailer. All I sought was information. I also told her I wanted to talk with her boss, and that he was welcome to have the pictures and negatives in exchange for answers.

Lately, refusing the favors offered me by gorgeous women was becoming an annoying habit.

Gunnar Cold-Shower Nilson.

ONCE IN THE ELEVATOR with old Talon-Fingers, I popped a clove in my mouth, sighed quietly, and said out loud, "Nuts."

"*Gesundheit*," said the old plugger.

"Ah, go cut your toenails and tend to your toe jam," I muttered at him. But I don't think he caught it.

Chapter 18

—

I WASN'T DONE SHAKING things up for the day.

Before I left the lobby of the Elihu Brown Building, I ducked into a phone booth. Nadia Forsgren picked up after the second ring. I told Nadia, in a firm but agitated voice, that it was important that I see Miss Atwood pronto. I had something crucial to discuss with her mistress, and it just couldn't wait. That's all it took for Nadia to give me a green light.

Horns honked and engines growled on Fourth Avenue when I came out of the lobby and put my raincoat on. It was beginning to drizzle as I started walking the few blocks to where my coupe was parked. I suddenly felt eyes watching me. It was a bit irrational, since there were plenty of eyes all around, what with the sidewalk loaded with pedestrians scurrying hither, thither, and yon. I blamed my little escapade with Joyce for triggering that bit of sixth sense for looming danger that had carried over from the war. Emotions are funny things. I dismissed the feeling.

But not entirely.

When I got behind the wheel of my Chevy Coupe and looked in the rearview mirror, I saw a trace of lipstick on my upper lip.

When I'd entered the elevator, what must old Talon-Fingers have thought but not said? *Tsk, tsk, some people's children.*

I put renewed life into my coupe. As I nosed it into traffic, I spotted a green Dodge Sedan behind me, but with a couple of other cars nestled between us. The drizzle didn't help my rearview vision any, so I couldn't tell if the sedan was actually trailing me, or even if Holt was behind the wheel.

After driving down Fourth Avenue a ways, I looked behind me. The green Dodge was still there, but staying at a respectable distance. I still couldn't make out the driver.

I stayed on Fourth Avenue for a few blocks and then took a right. The green Dodge stayed right with me. At one point, I gave it an opportunity to snuggle up a little closer, but it didn't.

I figured there was little reason to worry. If it was Holt, it probably meant he'd recognized me. And if he was shadowing me, he'd have no problem locating my office or learning where I lived, even if I shook him. Still, I did what I could to lose him as I worked my way over to Aurora Avenue North, and after a bit I didn't see the Dodge anymore.

If Holt had been the driver, I'd either shaken him or maybe he wasn't all that interested in the direction I was headed.

Strictly speaking, I wasn't doing the job Ethan Calmer had hired me to do. Not in the manner he'd hoped, anyway. But I still saw myself as working for him, or at least looking out for his interests. Time would tell if he appreciated it, let alone paid me for my trouble.

The rain was beating out a wild symphony on the roof of my car by the time I reached Broadmoor.

The oblong section of Miss Atwood's long driveway still contained the blue Cadillac Sedan, the newer model red Buick, and the weather-beaten Dodge Coupe off to one side all by itself. The coupe still looked lonely.

I rang the bell. Nadia Forsgren opened the door and greeted me in her usual commanding voice, though she actually looked a little pleased to see me when I touched my hat and gave her a polished smile.

I removed my hat and raincoat as she led me through the huge vestibule across the oak-paneled reception room. Then it was up the broad sweeping staircase till we reached the long quiet hallway with its blood-red runner that Mercedes Atwood had guided me down that first day. Nadia led me along the hall to the door of the dark-paneled study.

I heard the clickety-clack-clack of a typewriter. The typing stopped when Nadia rapped on the door a few times and then left me like a soft breeze blowing quietly under a Nomad's tent flap just before a coming sandstorm. At least that's how it struck me at the time.

"Please come in, Mr. Nilson," said a voice that sounded like Mercedes Atwood's muted by a closed door. I opened the door, stepped inside, and shut it behind me.

She stood up to greet me. Behind her was one of the two matching chairs placed next to the heavy dark desk with the typewriter. A piece of typing paper was rolled halfway into the machine. Next to the typewriter sat a vase packed with Oriental lilies. As the room was small, the huge white flowers gave off a scent powerful enough to hang a picture on.

"Casa Blanca," I said, nodding at the flowers.

"Yes. I see you know your lilies. I cut them in the greenhouse this morning."

Mercedes Atwood was wearing a plain gray wrap dress that made her look like a prison matron. Granted, the material and tailoring would suggest she was *head* matron, but a matron nonetheless. On her feet were white socks and a serviceable pair of black, wide-heeled, round-toed oxfords that didn't take away from the image she was creating one little bit.

"Mr. Nilson, I expect that your reason for being here is extremely important for it to justify your barging in on me like this," she said in her distant, untouchable manner. "Please be seated."

She sat and then I sat. "Looks like I've interrupted some letter writing," I said breezily.

She glanced woodenly at the typewriter then back to me. "If you must know, I'm writing an art collector who wishes to buy some rare Oriental porcelain from my father's collection."

Just to be impish, I said, "Are you again referring to that pair of Foo Dog incense burners that Mr. Calmer seems to love almost as much as he does you?"

"Indeed," she said coldly, a tiny hint of surprise in her eyes. But my flip remark didn't stop her from adding, "As much as he adores the set, Mr. Calmer believes I should sell them to a collector willing to exhibit them full-time. But, as I've told him, selling them is out of the question. Which, if it's any concern of yours, is what I'm trying to explain in this letter. Mr. Nilson, I assume you're not here to discuss flowers or the management of my father's collection."

"Uh-huh," I said absently. It felt a little crazy, both of us pretending that we'd never exchanged more than a cordial handshake. But the imp in me hoped to get a rise out of her by what I said next. "Funny thing. I'd assumed we'd be having this meeting on the main floor in the drawing room."

Her only reaction was to knit her brows in thought and then say in what passed as her far-off voice, "The *drawing room*? Why, I *never* use it. That room was like a sanctuary for my father when he was at home, between trips. It's where he entertained close friends and special visitors. Nadia dusts in there, of course, but if you must know, I've not stepped inside that room since my father died."

I let her words ricochet around the room awhile. She'd spoken with a straight face … but then again, when didn't she? Not much dumbfounded me anymore when it came to people and their behavior. But her reaction to my comment— or her *lack* of reaction—left me thunderstruck, and feeling like this conversation wasn't going to be as much fun as I had anticipated.

"I must say, you make such odd remarks at times, Mr. Nilson," she said quietly, staring at me with that poker-face of hers meant for keeping all kinds of secrets. She leisurely placed one matronly leg atop the other before adding, "But really, I must insist you get to the point of your visit. Nadia told me you had something crucial to tell me. I gather it has to do with the telephone calls I've been receiving. At least I hope that it does."

"You continue to receive the calls?"

She nodded. "One every day. I'm having Nadia answer the phone, but he always manages to beguile her to where I end up on the line. It's very unsettling."

"Message still the same?" I asked, fishing a clove from my pocket and slipping it in my mouth.

"Always," she said, sounding annoyed—or as annoyed as she could sound. She began fidgeting her raised foot so that her serviceable oxford became a bit blurry. "But Mr. Nilson, you could easily have asked me these questions by telephone."

I gave her a cool hard look that became an impish grin.

She uncrossed her legs, cleared her throat, and said, "Please, Mr. Nilson. What is it you came to tell me? What is it that's so crucial?"

"Several days ago, and just before your fiancé hired me, I met with a guy named Rune Granholm in a bar over in Fremont."

At the mention of his name, I watched her closely to see what reaction if any it would create. Nothing.

I went on, "Rune and I were never close but I was good friends with his older brother. As a favor, Rune wanted me to go with him later that night to a meeting he'd set up near the bathhouse at Green Lake. He told me he was holding someone's gold Cartier watch as security for money owed him, and he was to meet this fellow in order to trade the watch for the cash he had coming. Rune said he wanted me along in case things didn't go as planned."

"This is all well and good, I'm sure, Mr. Nilson," she said

flatly. "But what can such shenanigans possibly have to do with me and the phone calls I've been receiving?"

"Patience, Miss Atwood. It's important that you hear me out."

She gave a crisp nod of her head, laced her fingers together and carefully parked her hands on her lap as I continued, "Frankly, Rune's story struck me as more than a little fishy. He'd always been a bit on the shady side, so I didn't really believe he was being completely up front with me. But I agreed to go along with him anyway. Silly of me, I know, but there it is."

"Why on earth would you do that? Particularly if you didn't believe he was being truthful?"

"Mainly, because I was curious as to what kind of fix he'd got himself into. That's me. I'm as curious as they come."

She considered that a moment. Giving me a vacant stare, she said, "And what kind of *fix*, as you say, had he gotten himself into?"

"I can only guess, Miss Atwood. You see, when I went over to his place a little later that evening to accompany him, he was deader than a dead dog. Someone had shot him, and probably with his own gun."

Her gasp was like the sound a mosquito might make if it sneezed. Still, a big gasp for her. "How very dreadful."

"Yes. Dreadful."

"Who in the world could have done such a thing? And *why*?"

"Who and why indeed. Turns out Rune was trying to blackmail a couple of people."

She shuddered infinitesimally. It struck me as a genuine shudder despite its subtlety. That bothered me. I was hoping for a little embarrassment or discomfort at the least, maybe a panicky look at the most. What I got was a toned-down version of the reaction most people have at hearing something distasteful. That's it. And even that passed quickly.

I needed another clove. I took one from my shirt pocket and slipped it in my mouth before saying anything more to the cold fish sitting in front of me, as sedate and poised as a magician's assistant being sawn in half before a theater full of worried or bloodthirsty spectators.

The whole conversation went downhill from there. Downhill as far as getting any kind of telltale reaction out of her. I didn't confront her head on, and I didn't accuse her of anything specifically. I don't know why. Maybe because her apparent ignorance of what I did tell her seemed so real. Eerily real. My talk of Rune and his blackmail scheme didn't appear to register with her at all, other than it being an utterly new and dreadful story.

It was painful.

Painful to me, anyway.

Of course, Miss Atwood quite naturally wondered what my point was in telling her something so unpleasant. I managed to dodge the question by asking her if she was sure she'd never heard anything about what I'd just told her.

"No. Never. Why would I? And how is it relevant?" she asked in the composed voice of an undertaker helping a customer choose between two costly coffins.

"Not sure yet." I gave her what I hoped was an inscrutable look and asked, "Do you know Richard Liles of Puget Sound Security?"

Her face had a strange, grave dignity as she said, "Why, yes. I've met Mr. Liles once or twice in Mr. Calmer's office. He seems to be a very capable man. From what I understand, Ethan's ... *I mean*, Mr. Calmer's firm has used the services of Mr. Liles' company on more than one occasion. But again, I must ask, how is this relevant?"

"It may not be, Miss Atwood. I just needed to run these things by you. You can probably imagine that a lot of things pass under my nose that raise red flags when I'm on a job such as yours. I never know when something may have a critical connection or not. So, it pays to ask questions, even if they don't seem to make sense at the time."

After telling her I'd keep her posted, I quickly excused myself. I quietly closed the study door as if leaving a patient in a loony bin.

Nadia Forsgren saw me out. Before she shut the door behind me, I asked her, "Does that old Dodge Coupe in the driveway belong to you, or is it Isabella's?"

For a split-second, I saw alarm in her eyes.

"Oh no," she said in a voice that was not at all commanding. "That's one of Miss Atwood's cars."

"She has *three* cars?"

Nadia nodded, which only heaped insult on my injury, for surely that lonely old coupe had to be the car Mercedes used when she was slumming.

Maybe it was me. Maybe I'd bumped smack-dab into normalcy and just didn't realize it. Too jarring. Too overwhelming. I could hear the whispered comments now, some sympathetic, some pitiless, "If only the poor sap had been a little less or maybe a little more human, he might not have snapped."

Well, at least Mercedes Atwood hadn't tried to seduce me this time around. Thank goodness for small favors.

Chapter 19

———

THAT EVENING ON THAT same Monday, I was half-lounging on my landlady's slightly dilapidated living-room sofa while opposite me, Walter Pangborn had nestled in her Boston rocker. The rain was still pounding away outside, and periodically when a breeze glommed onto some raindrops we'd hear them *bam-bam-bamming* as they slammed into the front window. I'd missed dinner, but I think my sad-sack appearance from the day's travail had moved Mrs. Berger to take pity on me and heat up what she'd served. At the moment, my stomach was happily grappling with the beef stew I'd sent its way.

Sten Larson was off at one of his dimly lit haunts playing cards or shooting pool. Mrs. Berger was also planning to leave us and walk a couple of blocks to a sick friend's house to serve her the rest of the beef stew. Walter and I had each offered to drive her there, but she'd said no and donned a yellow sou'wester, a yellow slicker, and a pair of black rubber boots for her trek.

After Mrs. Berger left, Walter suggested we aid our digestion with gin and bitters, which he concocted for us in a couple of his special tumblers. Normally, he made this particular drink only on Saturday nights during spring and summer, but after I told him about my talk with Mercedes Atwood and gave him a slightly abridged version of my visit with Joyce Voorhees, he decided to break out the Gordon's Distilled London Dry.

When I say I told Walter a slightly abridged version of my visit with Joyce, I mean that I left out the part about me toying with taking full advantage of what Joyce seemed willing to offer me. Instead, I depicted myself as merely playing along just to get her talking. I don't think Walter believed it for a second, but it made me feel better to tell it that way.

Gunnar the Expurgator.

"What a curious and sad relationship Miss Voorhees has with Mr. Liles," Walter said, "that she'd be so willing to grant her sexual favors to another man in his behalf. Not unheard of, I realize, but still, very sad and very strange."

"It's a screwy relationship, if you ask me," I said.

Walter nodded. "But probably not all that surprising, old socks, when you consider the varying experiences of people and the emotional needs they acquire, especially during their childhood," he said solemnly, pausing to give me a probing stare. He added, "I'm sure it took a Herculean effort to pull yourself away from the lovely Miss Voorhees' enticing clutches."

It seemed like a good time to say nothing. Walter's stare started to make me a teensy bit uncomfortable before he finally broke it off and took a sip from his tumbler. He went on, "In most affaires de coeur, old thing, the focus of one's love is but a projection of one's needs. So, in his own peculiar way, Mr. Liles probably fulfills some basic or central need in Miss Voorhees. And vice versa, of course. For her to behave in the fashion you've described, my guess is that her sense of worth and self-respect have such yawning holes that she's moved to try and fill them by whatever plaudits and signs of approval she can garner from Mr. Liles—and possibly even from you, in this particular instance. It's sad, really. Very sad."

"Uh-huh, very interesting, Dr. Freud. But whatever the girl's motivations, at least I was able to learn a few things from her."

"Undeniably, old thing. Rune Granholm was indeed a blackmailer. That's now established. And as we'd already surmised, while seemingly benign on their face, those four pictures he took at the roadhouse would be very damaging to Mr. Liles' business plans and would definitely create a scandal for a woman of Miss Atwood's social standing. But as you suggest, there must surely be more to it than that, and the pictures in your possession are probably just a fairly minor tip of a pretty outrageous iceberg of Mr. Granholm's devising."

"Uh-huh. I think it's still safe to assume that Mercedes Atwood successfully seduced Rune the painter, which made him suspicious and led to his following her around with a camera. Rune was a real schemer. That kind of cloak-and-dagger tomfoolery would have been right up his alley. Rune either knew who Dick Liles was or he doped it out when he observed Liles' hovering presence around Mercedes when she was out on the town. Whatever the case, something got Rune to stop by Liles' office and tell Joyce about the pictures he'd taken. Joyce's reaction confirmed for him that he definitely had something to sell."

"So, Gunnar, who murdered Rune Granholm?"

"Probably some hireling of Liles or Mercedes or both, Walter. I'm still working it out." I took a sip from my tumbler. My voice sounded weary to me when I added, "I believed Joyce Voorhees when she said Dick Liles was with her at the time of the murder. That Green Lake rendezvous rings true, especially as Rune wanted me to go with him to the bathhouse for his meet-up. Since his pictures weren't developed when he needed them, he had to stall Liles somehow. Which is why he wanted me to tag along—in case things went sideways. Even so, Liles could still have arranged for Rune to be murdered beforehand, while giving himself a solid alibi with Joyce."

Walter raised his good eyebrow and then finished his drink.

Putting his tumbler on the floor, he asked, "But you also suspect Miss Atwood had some role in all this?"

I nodded. "I haven't completely ruled her out as Rune's murderer. Accustomed to slumming it as she is, it's not hard for me to imagine her getting adventurous. It would be right in keeping with her character … the *unrestrained* side of it, at least. So, I can easily see her knocking on Rune's door and confronting him, and then putting a bullet in him, whether she planned to do so or not."

Walter sat quietly, the unspoiled side of his face wearing a slight trace of sorrow. He intoned gloomily, "Mr. Granholm's hush money demand was certainly excessive. That could very well have persuaded Miss Atwood to take matters into her own hands. As you know, blackmailers have a way of making never-ending demands for more money. So what now of Mr. Calmer, Gunnar? In view of his secretary being the cousin of Mr. Liles' secretary, do you suspect complicity on *his* part?"

"Anything's possible, Walter. But I seriously doubt it," I said. "From what I've seen, Calmer appears to genuinely love Mercedes Atwood. I'm still betting he doesn't have a clue about her secret social life. That's just how it reads to me. And if Calmer doesn't know there's a secret to protect, then what possible motive for murder could he have?"

Looking meditative, Walter stood up and went over to the pantry where he'd left his pipe and tobacco pouch on the counter. When he came back and sat in the rocker again, he asked tonelessly, "So, what do you make of the two secretaries being cousins? Don't you find that kind of coincidence a worrisome detail?"

"Not really," I said. "Joyce said she helped Lillian get her job with Calmer, but that they aren't all that close. Mercedes Atwood told me that Liles has done work for Calmer in the past, which might explain how she learned about his bodyguard services. It would also account for how Joyce knew of a position opening up with Calmer that her cousin Lillian could fill. So, at least for now, I'd say their being cousins seems incidental."

As he considered that, Walter stared at the mouthpiece of his pipe. He then filled and lit it.

I went on, "Liles worked for Mercedes Atwood. Figure then that they were *both* being blackmailed by Rune. When I talked to Liles about Rune and showed him his picture, it must have spooked him. He knew I was nosing around on my own dime. So, he probably persuaded Mercedes to convince Calmer to hire me on some phony pretext in order to keep me from snooping around any further. It all fits. And, you have to admit, it did work for a time."

Smoke drifted from the bowl of Walter's pipe as he asked, "What's your thoughts about Mr. Holt being parked outside Broadmoor in his green Dodge Sedan, and his possibly having followed you today? Do you think Mr. Holt has been keeping an eye on you for Mr. Liles?"

I grinned. "He's either keeping his eye on me for Liles, or for Mercedes Atwood herself. Joyce told me Holt was moonlighting. It could be that Mercedes hired him to keep tabs on me, to make certain I wasn't looking under rocks that are best left undisturbed. Since she knew when I was coming to see her that first day I called on her, she could easily have arranged ahead of time for Holt to be parked and posted outside Broadmoor so he could put the eye on me."

A sardonic smile showed on the undamaged side of Walter's face as he blew smoke to one side and said, "An interesting construct, but it's still quite a lot of guesswork, old thing, however sound."

"Yeah. I've got to turn all this theorizing into something more solid."

"How do you propose to do so?"

"Good question. I've shaken things up at Liles' office. By now, Joyce has probably telephoned her boss and given him my message. He'll be back in Seattle tomorrow, so some sparks are bound to start flying."

At that moment, a gust of wind slammed raindrops up against the front window with a loud *bammedy-bam-bam* that startled both of us.

After we'd traded quick looks at the window and each other, Walter got back to our topic. "How do you account for Miss Atwood's odd behavior today?"

I sighed. "Beats me, Walter. Thinking about it now, her lack of reaction to what I said doesn't really bother me too much, since stoicism is practically her stock-in-trade. That deadpan manner is like breathing air to her. What disturbs me is that when she told me she hadn't been in the drawing room in years, she almost convinced me she was telling the truth. She actually seemed to believe what she was saying."

"Maybe she did, old thing. Maybe she did."

"Well, you've definitely got me on tenterhooks with that remark, Mr. Pangborn."

"Ah yes, tenterhooks," he began, staring up at the ceiling. "An expression that means in a state of tension or anxiety … taken from the hooks used by fullers to hold cloth taut on a frame. Fabric so stretched was in a state of tension … and hence—"

"Walter."

"Uh … yes, old thing. Sorry," he said, giving me a sidewise look. "What I've been thinking, Gunnar, is that Miss Atwood may have more than one personality."

"*What*? First, you tell me she's a nympho. Are you now telling me she's also a schizophrenic?"

"She may indeed be a 'nympho,' to use the term. But I'm not suggesting that she has schizophrenia, which as I understand it has to do with confused thinking, hallucinations, and a distorted perception of what is real. No, to my mind, Miss Atwood's behavior may indicate something else that I've been reading about."

"In those books you borrowed from Dieter Feinberg?"

He nodded.

"I have a feeling that you're about to take me skating out

where the ice is really thin … but I'll put the skates on. So, what's your theory, Walter?"

Walter went on solemnly, "Simply put, old thing, it's possible that Miss Atwood has a mental disorder evidenced by her *having*—not just *displaying*—at least two, and possibly more, distinct personalities that alternately control her behavior."

"So, what you're telling me is that she *is* bughouse crazy after all."

"I wouldn't go so far as to say that, old socks."

"Well, it would be a helluva lot simpler if you did. I mean this whole situation is making *me* a little nuts," I said sourly. "So, just how'd you come up with this idea, Walter?"

"Actually, the possibility first occurred to me when you said that the seductive Miss Atwood referred to the two women that work for her as 'those two old ladies.'"

"You're kidding."

"No, not at all. Her seductive behavior was one thing. But after the stoical Miss Atwood initially described the two women who had been her surrogate mothers as *family*, you said that later on, as a seductress, she referred to them as 'those two old ladies.' That struck me as very odd. It seemed so dramatically disrespectful and callous and totally out of character, let alone so unnecessary for one simply seeking sexual gratification on the fly."

"Don't you think that's a bit of a stretch, Walter?"

"I'll concede that it might be. However, when you later told me what Mr. Eagleson had to say, I started to believe my theory had real merit."

"Explain, oh wise one."

Walter ignored my sarcasm. He'd let his pipe go out, so he lit a match and held it to the bowl as he said, "Mr. Eagleson told you that when he saw Miss Atwood in a roadhouse made up like a loose woman, she didn't seem to know him when he addressed her."

"Walter, don't you think she simply pretended not to know

him for her own reasons? That's how I took it. That's how Eagleson took it."

He stared at me over his pipe bowl. "Perhaps, Gunnar. But her behavior could also be explained as evidence of a distinct personality, one utterly different from the stoical, well-behaved Miss Atwood."

I just looked at him.

He got his pipe drawing and started to blow smoke. He went on, "Humans can be quite fragile and complex. Weak nerves and an excitable temperament can be affected in unusual ways by stresses in childhood. Recall, even Mr. Eagleson told you that he often wondered if the death of Miss Atwood's mother and her father's frequent absences might have done something to her emotionally. It's possible that both experiences could have genuinely harmed her psyche."

"Honestly Walter, this is a bit too rich for me."

"I completely understand your reluctance to embrace this theory, old top. It's a controversial explanation that has declined in favor owing to hoaxes and the popularity of schizophrenia as a diagnosis. Still, some defend it, and believe that emotionally traumatic experiences can cause unusual and long-term disorders. And, there may be something else about Miss Atwood's life of which we're ignorant, but that also has a significant bearing."

"Okay, but—"

"It *could* explain why Miss Atwood told you that she hadn't been in the drawing room for years. You did say she was very convincing in telling you that."

"Still …."

Walter blew smoke to one side and said, "Again, it's just a theory, old socks. It's just a theory. And I remind you, I'm nothing more than a dime-store analyst."

"Uh-huh."

Walter stared at his pipe a moment then looked up and said, "Did Nora tell you about last night's excitement over at the Wesley's?"

I shook my head.

"Mind you, I'm ignorant as to when exactly it all happened. Our radios must have drowned out whatever noise occurred— either that, or we were all asleep. Nora and I learned about it only after you left this morning. It seems that Jimmy confronted a Peeping Tom attempting to peep through their bedroom window. The fellow was so startled on being discovered that he fell from the tree he had climbed and broke his leg. Jimmy stood guard over him till the police came and collected him."

I almost said, "Well, don't that beat all." Instead, what came out of my mouth was a quiet, "Huh."

Gunnar the Thunderstruck.

I related the conversation I'd had with Jimmy to Walter, and what my conclusion had been.

Walter quietly chuckled and said, "Well, sometimes it's bound to happen, old top, that the loud clattering sound of hooves means that zebras are approaching, *not* horses."

Chapter 20

———

TUESDAY MORNING, I WOKE from a war dream. I used to have them quite often. I dreamt I was in a squad made up mostly of replacements. A guy named Leahy and I were the only battle-hardened old-timers—a real repple depple SNAFU of the first magnitude. We were in a grassy field with only a few trees and rocks for cover, and we were pinned down by unrelenting machine gunfire coming at us from two different directions. As we hugged and kissed the earth, we naturally assumed it was the Krauts laying down the fire, but then over to my right Leahy shouted out that it was the French underground firing on us by mistake. "They must think we're Krauts!" Leahy screamed. I looked over his way but he wasn't there anymore. The entire area where he and two others had been lying flat to the ground was now just a smoldering patch of soot. I woke in a cold sweat, glad to be out of the dream. It was particularly troubling because Leahy had actually survived the war.

I grumbled and fumbled my way to the bathroom that Walter and I shared on the second floor. I still hadn't gotten used to the swan motif that Mrs. Berger had recently inflicted on the room, with swan-shaped soap, a swan soap dish, and swans printed all over the plastic shower curtains. Even the towels had swans on them.

Doing my best to ignore the swans, I shaved and showered and got into the same brown suit and hat I'd worn the day before.

When I came down to breakfast, Sten had already scrambled off to an early job with Sully, and Walter sat alone at the table reading a book as he ate. He told me that Mrs. Berger was in the small bathroom off the kitchen.

"Nora is performing her oil-pulling ritual," he said absently, knowing he didn't need to explain any further.

I had orange juice, bacon and eggs, toast and jam, and three cups of coffee. When I asked what he was reading, Walter told me it was one of the books he'd borrowed from the scholarly Dieter Feinberg.

Mrs. Berger had returned to the kitchen during most of my meal, and warned me a time or two about my not chewing my food enough as she skimmed sections of the newspaper.

My Longines said 8:50 when I got outside. The rain had stopped, but there was a slow-moving row of broken clouds that the sun was peeking over like a hopeful quarterback looking for an opening above the heads of the opposing players on the line of scrimmage.

I drove the less than five minutes it took me to get to my office over on Market Street.

Luckily, Miss Olga Peterson was busy with a customer in her flower and knickknack shop as I entered the Hanstad Building. Busy or not, Olga spotted me as I went by and we exchanged waves. That woman had sharper eyes than Natty Bumppo when it came to seeing what she wanted to see, when she wanted to see it.

As I reached the second floor, I heard typing. Aggressive typing. Violent typing. I opened the door to Dag Erickson's suite. Cissy Paget was at her desk hammering away on her

Smith and Corona as if she was playing the *Hungarian Rhapsody No. 2* on a grand piano. She even appeared dressed for a recital in her elegant getup: a smart brown business suit with a tan blouse open at the neck to show a necklace with a single pearl.

Cissy looked up from her typewriter and stopped typing when she saw me. She removed her glasses and gave me a thin, frail smile.

"Behind on typing, are we?" I asked.

She nodded vigorously, which encouraged an adventurous strand of her hair to swing down and touch her forehead. She tried to remove it with a flick of her head but it stayed put.

"Any messages for me?"

"Not a one."

I nodded and said, "I was hoping to talk to his nibs. Will he be in this morning by chance, or is he in court for the duration?"

"Neither. Dag's got a nasty cold so he's at home all day today." That turned her frail smile into a robust one that showed me several teeth. Cissy respected her boss. Liked him even. But Dag Erickson was a high-strung employer who was generous when it came to sharing his stress. Too much time with him in close quarters gave Cissy a headache.

I'd never been one to get in the way of a performing artist. After trading a few pleasantries, I left her so she could get back to her piano solo.

I let myself into my small waiting area and then closed the outer door but left it unlocked. My mail was on the floor where it had fallen from the mail slot, so I picked it up and unlocked the inner door, which I left wide open.

Along with my hat, I put my mail on my desk. I opened the one window Dag's building remodel had left me to welcome in some morning air before I sat down at my desk.

Pulling the phone in close, I dialed Dag's home number. He answered after the fourth ring. He sounded a little stuffed up.

After a bit of chit-chat about nasty colds, I asked, "What do you know about a fellow shyster named Ethan Calmer?"

Ignoring my shyster crack, he said, "He's the junior partner at Mumford and Calmer. We have more than a nodding acquaintance, but not much more. I've run into him a time or two at Longacres Racetrack. We've also bumped into each other here and there at a restaurant. That sort of thing."

"What kind of lawyer is he?"

"I've never seen him in action, but the word is he's a little better than mediocre. His late father was Mumford's original partner for many years. Ethan replaced his father. Mumford is definitely the legal genius and the workhorse of the firm. Since Ethan seems to be good with people, I suspect he holds up more of the public relations end of things. Why the interest?"

"Calmer's got me doing some work for him. He told me he knew that you occasionally use my services. I just wondered how well you knew him."

"Again, not well, I'm afraid. And of course, now you've got me curious. But you know me; I'm not one to pry."

"*Oh?* And during what week of which month of the year is that the case?"

He let that one slide. It must have been the cold. Dag Erickson was in his mid-forties but as lean as when he was twenty. He didn't exercise, he just had one of those metabolisms no amount of money can buy. A dapper dresser with rimless spectacles perched on the bridge of his aquiline nose except when he slept, he looked every bit like the prissy and punctilious attorney that he was.

"Do you know Calmer's fiancée, Mercedes Atwood?"

"Not really, no. I've seen her at some museum events I've attended. And she was with Ethan at the Georgian Room some weeks back when I was there for dinner, where he introduced us. A very lovely woman to look at, albeit extremely reserved. I suppose you know she's the daughter of Chester Atwood of local fame?"

"Uh-huh."

"Well Gunnar, now you've got me positively intrigued."

"For now you're going to have to stay intrigued, Dag. But maybe someday soon, I'll have an interesting story to tell you."

"Over a frosty libation?"

"I'll insist on it."

I thanked him and we hung up.

I went through my mail and had just taken the book *Shane* from my desk drawer to read a page or two when I heard the outer door open.

A weedy little hatchet-faced man with deep-set eyes quietly entered the small reception area and just as quietly shut the outer door behind him. This time he wore a dark brown fedora, a tan suit, and two-tone wingtips. The whole ensemble looked one size too big for him, but I think it was just the way he'd look in whatever outfit he put on. Holt had that kind of frame.

His lips formed that thin smile of his. Whether real or a pose, he was wearing one of the most menacing faces this side of a penitentiary. He was hugging a dark raincoat with his left arm and hand. If Holt were still a growing boy, then maybe one day he'd actually grow into the long-barreled semi-automatic pistol he was holding in his right hand—dubbed a Broomhandle Mauser from the shape of its grip. The Chinese simply called it the "box cannon."

In his flat, nasal voice, Holt said, "It maybe took me a sec to place you, but I knew who you was when I seen you at the office yesterday, even with them cheaters on."

"Is this a business or a social call?" I asked, not needing an answer. My eyes were taking turns studying the sneer on Holt's face and staring down the barrel of his Mauser.

"Strictly business, smart guy," he said, adding with a menacing tone: "Put your hat on. Me and you is gonna take a ride."

Art imitates life. No doubt about it. But the tough guy remark was merely Holt mimicking a B-movie for effect. So, his tone didn't scare me. But his gun looked lethal enough, so I grabbed my hat off the desk, planted it on my head, and slowly stood up.

"Who you working for on this one, Holt? Dick Liles, or is there a higher bidder?"

"Funny, ain't we?"

"Funny peculiar, or funny ha-ha?"

"You'll learn plenty soon, smart guy. But first, show me you ain't armed," he said in his dull, pinch-nosed manner while waving his Mauser at my coat.

I opened my coat and showed him all I had on inside was my shirt and tie. I then patted my coat and pants pockets flat for him.

"I'll be wrapping this here Kraut howitzer of mine in my raincoat. Don't forget I've got it as we stroll on out of here."

Holt shut the outer door behind us but before we went anywhere, he insisted I lock up.

"Don't want anyone wonderin' why you'd gone off and been so careless, now do we?"

As I put my keys back in my pocket, I said, "A man who figures the angles."

He glared at me and growled, "Move."

I moved. As we ambled past Dag's suite, I heard Cissy's typewriter fiercely clacking away. When we reached the bottom of the stairs, the sounds of Cissy's key-pounding were replaced with the thud and clap of Miss Olga Peterson's orthopedic shoes crossing the lobby floor from her flower and knickknack shop. Business that morning must have been slow.

"Mr. Vance …. Oh, Mr. Vance … wait up a moment, won't you?" said Miss Peterson.

I stopped to face her. Holt stopped too, but I felt the nose of his Mauser prodding the small of my back through layers of cloth. It was hard to ignore, but I managed.

The scent of Miss Peterson's over-spiced perfume reached us

before she did. It was always a bit much to take, but glancing back and seeing Holt's discomfort made it bearable.

"My stars, Mr. Vance, but it's been ages since we've spoken to one another," she said cheerily when she reached us, giving my arm a squeeze that was sure to leave a bruise. I was "Philo Vance" to her from the day we first met. I quickly realized correcting her would be futile, so I never did.

Miss Olga Peterson had a pudgy face that wasn't unpleasant, but would have never won a beauty contest. She was somewhere between fifty and sixty, and though her hair should have been gray it was the color of faded mustard. Her thick body was encased in a shapeless dark-blue dress generously covered with large white polka dots.

"Is this a client or a colleague, Mr. Vance?" she asked, beaming and nodding at a mirthless Holt.

"He's sort of a colleague," I said lamely as I eyed Holt. He'd suddenly decided to do his best version of a friendly smile for her. A very feeble smile and an extremely poor version.

"My stars, but your line of work must be exciting at times," she purred enthusiastically.

"Well, it's certainly not dull, that's for sure. How would you describe it, Holt?"

"Dangerous." He practically hissed the word.

Miss Peterson was delighted. Her eyes got as big as golf balls and her lips formed a large circle before they switched over to a grin that would make the Cheshire Cat envious. Not meaning to, Holt had told her just the kind of thing she desperately wanted to hear.

Holt's Mauser poked me again and he said, "We're gonna be late, pal. We better go. *Now*."

I smiled and nodded at Miss Peterson and Holt followed me as I started to walk toward the front entrance.

As we exited the building, she called after us, "Be careful, you two. And Mr. Vance, please be sure to give Mr. Pangborn my fresh greetings."

Cars were parked on both sides of Market Street, but I didn't see a green Dodge Sedan anywhere. A few pedestrians were in sight, but none seemed in the take-notice mood.

"Head to the right," Holt snapped.

I did so. We walked two blocks till we came to an alley.

"In the alley."

He continued to follow my lead into the alley, where Holt's Dodge Sedan was illegally parked next to some overflowing garbage cans. A couple of shabby-looking tabby cats were sniffing around where some of the trash had spilled to the ground. As we came closer, they scattered. A back door of a nearby café was ajar so that pancake and bacon smells wafted our way and made me a little nauseous.

When we'd reached the back of Holt's car, he said, "Your choice. Trunk or backseat."

He wasn't kidding.

"Backseat," I said as I opened the rear door on the driver's side.

"Scooch on over and lay down so your head is behind the front passenger seat, so I can better keep an eye on you."

The rear seat handles were made of metal, and the one next to where my head would be had one bracelet of a pair of handcuffs already clamped to it.

"Slap that cuff around your right wrist," Holt barked. "That'll keep you from tryin' any funny business on the way. It'll also keep you from seein' the route we take. The boss don't want you knowin' where we're goin'."

I got in position as directed and put the cuff on. It beat the trunk. At least he hadn't sapped me. Apparently, his impersonation of B-movie characters had its limits.

Holt climbed behind the wheel and within a minute the motor started purring and throbbing like a large contented cat right after a mouse meal. I felt like the mouse.

I tried to engage Holt in conversation a couple times as we

moved along, but no success. He drove as if he were all alone, which just added tedium to the tension. And believe me, from where I rode, describing the trip would be mind-numbing.

Since we started in Ballard, we rode in town a good while, confirmed by fleeting glimpses of passing buildings, the average speed we were going, the recurring stops and starts, and the surrounding noises of people and cars. However, eventually my brief peeks were of blurred greenery as our speed became pretty consistent, and our stops far less frequent. And since the Dodge's motor was the only real noise, I concluded we'd entered the countryside beyond Seattle—especially since the switchbacks, dips, and rises I felt made it seem like I was riding a roller coaster.

"BEING ABDUCTED LIKE THAT would be scary enough," Kirsti said, turning off her recorder. "But, not knowing where I was being taken ... I mean ... that would be even worse."

"Uh-huh. I'll admit, it was more than a little unnerving, having no idea what that gun-wielding little weasel had in mind for me," I said wryly. "Later I was able to determine that Holt had driven us to a summer house on the west side of Beaver Lake out on the Sammamish Plateau. Familiar with that area, are you?"

"Just a little bit," she said, showing me an eighth of an inch gap between her right index finger and thumb.

"Well, just like Seattle itself, the Sammamish Plateau started off being logged. Over time, the logging of the west and east sides of Beaver Lake led to random development in the 1920s. Eventually summer homes and resorts with rental cabins sprung up before and after the war. All in all, the resorts did a brisk trade. I'd been to a weekend dance or two at one of the resorts before the war, and one or two afterwards as well."

"I'll bet you did," she said, flashing a smile at me.

"You probably don't know this, blue eyes, but that movie actor Clint Eastwood taught lifeguard training classes at

Beaver Lake one summer, just a few years after what I'm telling you about took place."

"Clint who?"

"Skip it."

Kirsti clicked her mic back on.

I COULD TELL ASPHALT had been replaced by gravel when I heard unrelenting snap, crackle, and popping noises that easily surpassed those of any milk-drenched breakfast cereal on the grocery shelves.

After about five minutes, Holt's Dodge jerked to a stop and spilled me roughly onto the floor as he cut the motor. As I remounted my perch, Holt got out and opened the rear door that my shoes had been snuggling up against. He tossed his keys at me.

"Leave your wrist cuffed, but unlock yourself from that handle, and climb on out. And don't even think about tryin' to pull somethin'," he said in his high-pitched nasal twang. He moved back from the car, waving his long-barreled gun at the ground.

I got out and stretched, using it as an excuse to take a quick look around. The Dodge was parked on a gravel driveway behind a newer model Oldsmobile Sedan. We were in a partly shady, partly sunny clearing. Evergreen trees were on three sides of us, and a lakeshore and a small pier were on the fourth side about forty or fifty feet from where we stood. Across the lake, I spotted two or three cabins nestled in the trees. A rowboat sat peacefully on the lake with two men in it who weren't fooling anybody with the thermos they were passing back and forth while pretending to fish. It was doubtful they could see us because of the mixed lighting we were in. Well beyond the fishermen, a canoer fiercely paddled his craft as if he was a frontiersman escaping a canoe of hostiles in hot pursuit.

I ended my stretching and turned away from the lake. I saw

that the driveway belonged to a fair-sized two-story wood structure with a brick foundation and composition roof. If I was keeping score, I'd say it was much closer to a home than a cabin. A wealthy man's idea of a cabin. It had four wooden steps that led up to what was probably a wrap-around porch. On the front porch to the left of the front door were four comfortable-looking brown wicker chairs. Two chairs flanked each side of a small table top of wooden planks that jutted out just below a front window nearest the door, supported by a frame made from pipes that was securely fastened to the outer wall of the cabin.

Holt pointed to the house and followed me up the steps to the porch. He indicated one of the chairs next to the table top but farthest from the front door and so facing it. "Plant your keister in that one," he said.

I planted my keister.

He pointed at the handcuffs dangling from my right wrist and told me to clamp the other bracelet around the nearest pipe of the table top's support frame. This routine was getting old, but since the little man was still wig-wagging his Mauser in the air, I did as he said.

"I'm just the delivery man," he said in his dry, adenoidal manner. "That job bein' done, I'll be takin' off for a while. But you ain't seen the last of me. Not by a long shot. We're a bit early, and I see the lights are off inside. Be patient. The boss'll come out for you soon enough." As he left the porch, he added, "S'long, sucker."

I waited for the gravel to start groaning and complaining under the spinning tires of Holt's Dodge before I leaned over and took a look inside the window through the gap made by partly opened curtains. No lights were on, but here and there a little outside light leaked in and bounced off the high points of a few pieces of furniture.

It was one of those quiet mornings out in the sticks when you feel far removed from the hustle-bustle world and can escape what weighs on you for a while. But I didn't, so I couldn't.

Finally a bird chirped angrily in a nearby tree. "That makes two of us, brother," I said under my breath.

I watched the fishermen out on the lake for about ten minutes. I toyed with the idea of calling out to them, but didn't. Somebody in the cabin would likely hear me before they did— *if* they did. Besides, they probably couldn't see me, so what was the point?

Their booze was evidently gone because one of the fishermen started rowing them away. As they moved off, a soft dull thump sounded in the cabin. I leaned over and looked inside again. It was the same as before. But as I was pulling my head back a light switched on inside that drew my eyes.

Beyond a living room that was still partly in shadow, I could clearly see an open area divided between a moderate-sized kitchen with too many brightly colored tiles and a smaller breakfast room with knotty-pine wainscoting. What I saw next was a definite upside that took the edge right off the obvious downside of my situation.

A young woman with her back to me was busily making coffee at the kitchen counter. She had reddish-yellow hair that almost touched her shoulders. She was nimble too, and either music was playing or she was humming a tune to herself, because as she filled the coffee pot with water over at the sink, her legs, hips, and torso shook and shimmied to some sort of rhythm like a clothes-peeler hired to vibrate for the drunken members of some local lodge. She was a real pleasure to watch. She had a nice, curvy figure, and at the moment she was being generous with it since the panties she wore were definitely knitted to stretch and spring back with every intense movement of her rear end. Clearly, to this girl, this cabin was a place to have fun.

The girl's legs were unusually long and well-toned enough to belong to one of George Petty's calendar girls. She suddenly began stamping her bare feet and scooping and tossing coffee into the pot to a beat that a Sub-Saharan tribal dancer would relate to. He'd relate to her garb too, because all she had on were those panties, which really made her performance compelling while not overly taxing my imagination.

The girl had striking shoulder blades and an elegant indentation down the middle of her back. But what really caught my eye was when her head turned for a moment so that I got a good look at her profile. The coffee was on its way to boiling, and reaching for a skillet off to her right was Ethan Calmer's beautiful secretary, Lillian Voorhees.

I was both surprised and amused as I continued to goggle.

I figure cumulative experience with humanity's underbelly had blunted my sense of decorum and propriety. And I suppose what made me feel justified in prolonging my peeping was that it wasn't my idea to be there in the first place. The way I saw it, if Lillian had some part in my abduction, then her unwitting burlesque act was *her* problem, not mine.

Still, my grandmother Agnette had done what she could to instill some standards of decency in me, so I was about to look away from my windfall peepshow when the sound of a loud horn behind me from the far side of the lake caused Lillian to spin around and face my direction. She held the skillet in front of her, which hid her bare breasts, so my eyes shot right up to meet her thick-lashed ones just as they bore into mine. Her eyes got as big as Yakima apples and her lips formed an uppercase "O."

Lillian dropped the skillet, clasped her hands to her chest, and made a dash for the stairs.

The floor show had ended.

Gunnar the Voyeur was duly announced.

Chapter 21

—

I EXPERIENCED EINSTEIN'S EXPLANATION for relativity, because five minutes managed to drag themselves by, feeling more like five hours. Finally, the front door of the cabin opened and Ethan Calmer stepped out onto the porch. As he closed the door behind him, he surveyed my face while I carefully mapped his.

His far-too-many teeth glinted in the kind of eerie, ingratiating smile you usually only see on a hotel clerk in the off-season.

His brown hair was pillow-tousled, so not quite as wavy as when we first met, and I noted dissipation lines around his eyes and mouth that I hadn't noticed before. Maybe it was the natural light. Or maybe Calmer was just looking a bit different to me, now that I was getting to know him better than I wanted to.

"Ah, Mr. Nilson … Lillian said she spotted you out here on the porch," he said in that fast-talking way of his.

She spotted *me*? That was rich. But it suggested the girl hadn't bothered to tell her boss about giving me a free show.

He went on, "You're early, but that's not a problem. You're being here is what matters."

I didn't say anything. He continued standing.

Calmer wore a light-blue polo shirt. Despite being open at the neck, it seemed a little too tight around his broad shoulders, accentuating his pudginess. He wore gray slacks and an even grayer pair of loafers. Clearly he wasn't staying at this cabin on business. Not the law firm's business, anyway.

"You and Lillian," I said, pausing to let my words drift a bit. "So, it's *that way* between you."

He slowly nodded.

"And Miss Atwood?"

"Ah yes, Mercedes," he said, taking an open pack of Lucky Strikes and a lighter from his pants pocket. "I'm afraid that all along, she's been merely a suitable means to a highly satisfactory end—a fact that, if you haven't deduced it already, your nosy nature would have discovered soon enough, I'm quite sure. And frankly, that's why you've been escorted here." He was definitely showing me the gets-along-with-people side of his personality.

"*Escorted*, huh? And it's my nosy nature that's to blame?" I grabbed a clove from my shirt pocket with my free left hand and slipped it into my mouth. "Do tell."

With a nod, he took a cigarette from the pack and sat in the wicker chair across the table from me. He placed the open pack and lighter on the tabletop with his left hand as he rolled the unlit cigarette around with the fingers of his right.

The front door opened again and a casually clad Lillian Voorhees minced smartly out onto the porch, carrying a metal tray. Calmer stood up. I might have too, if I could. But I did tip my hat. It seemed the least I could do. I don't think she noticed.

Lillian came over to us and placed the tray on the table. It held three mugs of steaming coffee, a small creamer, a little bowl filled with sugar cubes, and a ceramic ashtray.

"Thank you, my dear," Calmer said in an oily voice.

She smiled at him. I could tell immediately he was more than a little soft on her, and that they weren't at this cabin to merely do the rough-and-ready romp. But then again, up to a few minutes ago I'd believed he was gaga for Mercedes Atwood, so what did I really know about this guy's feelings?

"Will you have some coffee, Mr. Nilson?" Lillian said, her smile gone now. Her eyebrows were arched and her eyes were narrowed to slits with a go-to-hell message aimed right at me.

Lillian had put on a shirt with pink and white stripes. She was still being generous with her long legs, as she wore a pair of red fly-front corduroy shorts. On her feet were white Grecian sandals. I'd hoped that she didn't douse herself with perfume out here in the country, but I was disappointed. A big whiff of jasmine came wafting my way, carried on the outdoor air. It was as hard to take, as usual, but also, as usual, she was easy to look at.

With my free hand, I reached for the cup nearest me, hoping she hadn't spit in it. I watched as she pulled an empty chair over next to Calmer's but a little away from the tabletop. He sat down again and so did she, after first snagging a mug off the tray.

As Lillian eased into her wicker chair, she held her mug in both hands up close to her nose. She gave me the nasty eye over the rim as she leisurely crossed her pliable legs.

Calmer was busy lighting his cigarette, so I winked at the girl and gave her a one-sided smile. Let's just say, if it wasn't a mean scowl on her face, then I don't know a mean scowler when I see one. Despite that, hers was a face made for staring at—and stare at it I did, until it softened into aloof and stony.

Glancing at the cabin, I said just to say it, "Nice digs."

"It serves," Calmer said. He drew in a lungful of smoke and let it out in raggedy wisps. "My father had this place built in the early thirties."

I looked at him and said, "I have a hard time believing that my snooping alone would embolden you and Miss Voorhees to become party to kidnapping."

The portion of Lillian's face showing above her cup looked crimson and uneasy. Her eyebrows furrowed, forming little vertical lines between them.

"*Kidnapping* is such a nasty word, Mr. Nilson. Please ... think of it more as, temporary *detainment*," he said, dropping ash into the ashtray.

"That's the lawyer in you I hear talking."

Calmer shrugged his broad shoulders, putting a strain on his polo shirt. "Well, it *could* turn into a *voluntary* detainment, if you're willing to hear me out, and if you're a reasonable man."

"For sake of argument, consider me reasonable. I'm listening."

He smiled. "First, Mr. Nilson, I'd like to hear something from *you*. Surely, being a seasoned detective, with all that's been going on, you must have drawn some conclusions by now?"

I grunted. "Apparently too few of the right kind."

"You're being modest. Tell me what you've worked out thus far. I'd truly like to know." Calmer was beaming like a man holding a winning ticket to a sweepstakes. My eyes went to Lillian. She still held her mug close to her nose, but there seemed to be a playfulness in her eyes now.

I took a big sip of my coffee and said, "There are no menacing phone calls. There never were. Not genuine ones, anyway. It's probably been you calling Miss Atwood using a disguised voice."

"You're half right," he said. "The calls have indeed been fake, but Mr. Liles has been making them for me. Go on."

I mulled that one over before saying, "It was no coincidence that you summoned me to your office *after* I'd stopped at Dick Liles' house to question him about Rune Granholm. I must have set off an alarm of some sort."

Amusement flickered in Calmer's eyes as he unhurriedly blew a plume of smoke, while Lillian decided to cross her legs the other way for a change.

"I was hired so you could divert me. Liles reported to you

that I was looking into Rune's murder on my own time. So, you wanted me kept busy at something else so I'd stop looking. It's my guess you were afraid I'd find out that you'd murdered Rune—or had him murdered."

"No, no, Mr. Nilson. I had nothing to do with that young man's murder. You do me an injustice."

"This from the man that had me brought to him at *gunpoint*," I said in an annoyed tone, which he ignored. "But okay. Assuming I believe you … then maybe Liles or one of his underlings murdered Rune. Perhaps even your darling Mr. Holt killed him."

He shook his head. "Dick Liles assures me that he had absolutely nothing to do with the murder, and I choose to believe him. Admittedly, that fellow Rune was a thorn in both our sides, but we were handling him well enough—and peaceably so. We would have easily resolved matters without resorting to murder, I can assure you. No, Mr. Nilson, I'm afraid you've gone down a false trail on that one."

"All right, we'll table that for the time being. Though I'm not persuaded that you or Liles aren't guilty of murder. Otherwise, why bother to hire me to chase after a phantom? If there was no murder to prove against you, why was my snooping such a big concern?"

"Because I didn't want you to discover the specific proof against Mercedes that Rune Granholm had, or claimed to have in his possession. That's why."

"You mean the proof that your fiancée's brand of man-craziness takes her to seedy dives and sleazy roadhouses for periodic sex sprees? Is that what you mean?"

He smiled at that. "Precisely. And yes, Mr. Liles phoned me yesterday to notify me that you are now in possession of those pictures that Rune had taken … as well as whatever other incriminating proof he claimed to have of Mercedes' … er … *proclivities*."

He raised his eyebrows when saying that last part, and it

came out as more of a question than a statement of fact. He was doing more fishing that those two boozers I'd seen out on the lake earlier.

But I didn't bite. I wanted to let him think I had more than I did. I casually finished my coffee.

Calmer tried and failed to blow a smoke ring and then said, "Mr. Liles also told me the welcome news you'd given his secretary—that you aren't intending to blackmail anyone, but that you simply seek answers to some questions." He gave me a level stare before knocking some ash into the ashtray.

I nodded. "Here's a question for you. When you hired me, weren't you worried I'd find out Miss Atwood was a nympho?"

"Frankly, I didn't care if you did. I actually assumed that you eventually would. It was Rune's proof that I didn't want you to find—unless, of course, you were working for me when you found it."

Calmer could see I was confused.

"You see, if while you were working for me, you happened to stumble upon Mercedes' secret life, then I'd be able to make use of your discovery for what I eventually have planned. Of course, at first I would have pretended to disbelieve your findings, but then later on—when it suited me—I'd feign acceptance. However, I was concerned that should you find Rune's particular proof while snooping into his murder on your own, it would jeopardize my plan."

He could tell I was still in the dark, so he went on, "As you may have surmised, Dick Liles' secretary is under the impression that he alone was being blackmailed. That was my idea. I thought it best that the fewer who know of Mercedes' wild dalliances, the better. And I do genuinely hope you were being truthful about *not* being a blackmailer."

He went on in a smug tone, "Mind you, it's not just her undue need for seedy liaisons, Mr. Nilson. I've become convinced that Mercedes genuinely has some kind of mental problem. I know this will sound like something right out of *Ripley's Believe It*

Or Not!, but it's as if she's two different people, living entirely separate lives. What's more, I don't think she even realizes it— that each of her personas is unknown to the other. Apparently, she's been deranged in this way for several years, at least near as I've been able to determine."

"And yet, you went ahead and got engaged to her."

"And for good reason." He smiled at me as if I was an earnest but stupid child. "As I told you, Mercedes is a means to an end. Nothing more."

"Well, I have to admit, I'd wondered why you were attracted to her—aside from her good looks, that is." It came out of my mouth a bit too fast and a little too sarcastic.

Lillian tittered, staring over at Calmer through thick, long-lashed, bedroom eyes. She then uncrossed her legs and leaned over to put her empty coffee mug on the table with one hand while taking a cigarette from the open pack with the other. I continued to watch as she lit the cigarette with Calmer's lighter and then leaned back in her chair to fill her lungs with smoke as she crossed her legs again.

I had by no means figured everything out yet, but things were shifting and changing to where some events started to make sense to me now. It was probably Lillian's earlier spicy dance number that suggested the comparison, because I got to thinking of one of those Busby Berkeley movie musicals where the scantily clad showgirls form kaleidoscopic patterns shot with a camera from overhead that suddenly transform with the dance moves of the girls. It was starting to feel a lot like that, but the pattern taking shape was not at all pleasing to look at.

A swirl of smoke from Calmer's cigarette got in his eyes. He batted his eyelids and waved the smoke away with his free hand. He killed his stub by smashing it in the ashtray and asked, "Is that the extent of what you've deduced, Mr. Nilson? Have I sounded your depths fully, then?"

I shook my head. "Don't be so hasty. A line or two of thought about motive has opened up while spending this time with you and the lovely Miss Voorhees." I nodded at each of them in turn. He wore a mocking grin. She tilted her head sideways like a globe on its axis, a sour smile twisting her red lips as she gently and unhurriedly blew a plume of smoke.

Lillian continued to look like she'd been forced to suck a particularly sour lemon. She uncrossed her legs so she could lean over and twitch her cigarette over the ashtray.

I could tell I'd piqued Calmer's curiosity because he raised his eyebrows and beamed as he had previously. Carefully lighting another Lucky Strike, he said, "By all means, please proceed."

"Well, I'd have to say everything probably hinges on two questions. Why would you knowingly marry a loony socialite who has a secret sex life to hide? And, why try to protect that secret prior to marrying her?"

Calmer's smile was pleasant, avuncular even. He fanned smoke away from his face with his hand and the smell of tobacco wafted my way.

Waving at the smoke, I said, "I've ruled out lust. You seem to have those needs taken care of already." I leered affably at Lillian.

She took a delicate puff on her cigarette while giving me a glacial smile.

I said, "You're clearly not in love with Mercedes Atwood. You say she's just a means to some end. And while you might not really *like* her all that much, I can't see that you *hate* her."

"I don't hate her. No."

I continued, keeping my tone casual, "So, what grand and glorious end is your man-crazy fiancée the necessary means to? I'm guessing *money*. You must need cash. And I'm figuring a lot of it." I pointed to his car and then the cabin. "But, by all appearances, you seem to be in the chips already. Plus, you're in a well-paid profession. Still, things are not always as they seem. And I've recently learned that you like to play the ponies."

Calmer seemed amused.

"I'll wager that pony-playing isn't the only gambling you go in for, and you wouldn't be the first person ruined by how he spends his off-hours. Five will get you ten that you've got gambling debts that far exceed what you take in as a shyster. And the odds are good that marriage to Mercedes Atwood will give you access to her collection of doodads, especially the pricey ones."

"Interesting. *Very* interesting, Mr. Nilson. And expectedly astute. Yes, unfortunately my great love for games of chance has resulted in my owing a great deal of money to the wrong kind of people. However, while my markers are held by unsavory types, still, they're being reasonable and patient. They realize that I can make good … or that I will be able to do so soon."

"Plus, once you're married to Mercedes Atwood, they've got you down on their chump list as an ongoing sure thing."

Calmer ignored that and went on in a calm voice, "Only you're unaware of a slight catch, Mr. Nilson. As are my disreputable creditors, thankfully." He spoke through a cloud of smoke. "Chester Atwood's will leaves control and disposal of his entire collection strictly to Mercedes' discretion. It stipulates that Mercedes is solely to determine whether any part of the collection be sold or not, even precluding whomever she might marry. And trust me, she won't sell *anything*. I've had that discussion with her so many times that I'm convinced there's no budging her."

It was epiphany time for me.

"Ah, but there's more than one way to fleece a wife," I said. "And as a good and caring husband, you'll quickly establish power of attorney so that you'll be duly authorized to act in Mercedes' behalf should she be somehow incapacitated or deemed incompetent. If she could be declared legally insane and committed to a nuthouse, you, as her devoted husband, would be given the official say-so over all those pricey doodads. Sell some of those and your debt problems disappear. How am I doing?"

The cigarette between his lips bobbed and weaved as he said, "Rather well, actually."

Lillian got up and reached for the tray. "Anyone for more coffee?" She spoke in a smooth, cool voice while fiddling with her cigarette and then dropping it in the ashtray.

Calmer and I both nodded and put our empty mugs on the tray, which the girl soon carried into the cabin.

"After you've plundered Mercedes' treasures, do you plan on divorcing her and marrying up with that one?" I asked Calmer, nodding at the cabin.

"Oh, probably," he said jovially. "But it's way too early to cross that particular bridge."

"Since you're talking so freely around Miss Voorhees, she's obviously okay with what you have planned for Mercedes."

He nodded and said airily, "Lillian believes that Mercedes is indeed crazy and belongs in a mental institution. And besides, Lillian's ambitions and her love of nice things have conspired to produce a rather elastic conscience."

"And it didn't even take law school to get her there."

He ignored that, so I went on, "Just how'd you happen to tumble to Mercedes' secret life?"

He quickly related a story similar to the one Douglas Eagleson had told me. Except Calmer had gone into a seedy dive all alone one night, somewhere north of Seattle. He was having trouble finding an address and was asking a barkeep for directions when he spotted Mercedes dressed and made up like a floozy and seated at a table with a scruffy group. He'd been a little more discreet than Eagleson. He approached her and the man she seemed to be with, and when he'd gotten their attention, he immediately apologized for staring and explained that he'd mistaken them for another couple he knew. To ensure that there was no ill will, he immediately insisted on buying everyone at their table a round of drinks. And then he left.

"I could tell straight away that Mercedes didn't know who I was. I hadn't surprised her in the least, and her blank look was genuine."

"Or she pretended not to know you. It's hard for me to believe she didn't."

"All the same, what I'm telling you is true, however bizarre it might sound. It's as if Mercedes is two different people, each one not knowing about the other. I'm serious. It's more than a bit eerie."

He was one to talk of eerie. But I let that go. "You've got to figure that you're not the only one of Mercedes' circle who's discovered that she gets her kicks in low dives."

"Oh, no doubt. Believe me, I've thought of that. Perhaps one or two have stumbled onto her dalliances over the years. But my guess is that they've kept it to themselves, and consider it to be none of their business. Or, if any of her crowd *have* shared it with others, it's seen as nothing more than unsubstantiated tittle-tattle or malicious gossip."

As I was mulling that one over, Lillian returned and put the tray back on the table. If it wasn't for me being handcuffed to the table frame, an observer would think we were three friends having a casual chat.

Calmer and I helped ourselves to our refilled cups as Lillian sat down and crossed her long legs again and started wiggling her raised Grecian sandal. She saw me watching her foot and stopped. Her lower lip curled. And since I happen to like lower lips that curl, it was easy to look at. That abruptly ended the curled lip.

No more free shows for me. No siree.

Calmer was busy lighting a fresh cigarette, and as I sipped my coffee, I said, "I can see that Rune wouldn't have simply hurt your scheme, he'd have demolished it. If he'd made it generally known by proofs that your fiancée was a nympho, people would rightly wonder why you'd want to marry her. Hard to explain that. Hard to then go through with it. The same goes if he'd have publicized that she was batty. Who in their right mind would marry a loon? And if you did marry her, they'd assume *you* were off *your* nut. At the very least, your motives would then be put under a microscope, and you couldn't have that. Not at all. So, Rune was as welcome to you as a tornado is to a wheat farmer at harvest time."

"Frankly, I couldn't have sized up the situation any better myself," he said in an airy and patronizing manner. "I hired Dick Liles to keep a close watch over Mercedes. She's been extremely lucky that no calamity has befallen her these past few years, given her habits. But I wanted to ensure that nothing untoward happened before we were married. So, when she's occasionally gone venturing in that old jalopy of hers, Dick has stuck to her like glue."

He seemed to expect me to make a comment, but I didn't, so he went on, "Somehow that scoundrel Rune learned of Mercedes' escapades. He also figured out who was surveilling Mercedes, so as you know, he approached Dick's secretary at his office. Long story short, Dick was just beginning to negotiate with the young man when he was murdered. But we'd have gladly paid him to keep his mouth shut. As it is, I'm paying for Dick Liles' services through the firm, and a little more of the firm's money to temporarily pay off a blackmailer wouldn't have been noticed if handled correctly. Dick and I certainly had no illusions about Rune not coming back to our trough for more hush money later on. But that didn't matter to us in the slightest. Once Mercedes and I were married and after Dick got his business plans off the ground, Rune would no longer have been much of a threat to either one of us. In my case, once I was Mercedes' husband, whatever he might wish to disclose could actually help me make a case to get her committed. So, again, we had no need to murder the young fellow. We only needed to humor him and play for time. As I said, we were handling him."

I'll say this for Calmer: he made a good case. But why wouldn't he? He was a lawyer. And, Rune did have a track record of being clever only by half. But I still had a hard time swallowing Mercedes Atwood as two separate people unaware of each other. Too airy-fairy for my blood. I saw her as simply living a double life and keeping it under wraps like so many other hypocrites have done ad infinitum. But either way, a blackmailer armed with proof of her dalliances could have pushed her off whatever shaky edge she'd been standing awfully close to, turning her into a killer.

I looked at Calmer and asked, "Do you think Mercedes Atwood killed Rune? Or had him killed?"

He looked at me with puzzled eyes. "Not for a minute. Leastways, not the aloof and very proper Mercedes. I suppose it's remotely possible—*remote*, mind you—that her alter ego might have done so ... but frankly, I highly doubt that. No, that particular persona is a tramp, not a killer. Besides, Mr. Nilson, to my knowledge, Rune hadn't tried to blackmail Mercedes. I assume he'd deduced that something was amiss with her, and decided not to bother. Impossible to know now."

It sounded plausible. I didn't tell him I suspected Mercedes had probably seduced Rune when he was wearing his painter's hat. Maybe her Jekyll and Hyde routine convinced him she was a loony loose cannon.

I shot a glance at Lillian, who again had her mug up to her nose and was eyeing me steadily. I looked back at Calmer. His eyes narrowed and he looked at me with the malignant expression of a man whose conscience knows when to step aside for self-interest.

He went on in a flat, calm voice, "And now, Mr. Nilson, you seem to have become the latest fly in my ointment. Or *are you*?" He spoke in a purring voice and with the toadying smile of a mortician helping with the selection of burial plots. "I can assure you, you needn't be. I'm quite certain that you realize it. As they say, you could choose to play ball. It would be quite simple, actually. If you were to agree to keep quiet about all of this, then once I'm finally able to sell off some of the Atwood collection, I'd make your silence profitable. That's a promise. What do you say to that? Do we have a deal?"

Calmer's proposition had taken its sweet time to finally come out of his mouth. And now that it had, I was again treated to his toadying smile of far-too-many teeth, which was more creepy than charming, and more menacing than creepy.

Chapter 22

———

I WASN'T ABOUT TO play ball, of course. Calmer was disappointed, naturally, but not too surprised. He was a man clearly accustomed to losing both cases and bets. But the dam had busted, the camel's back was broken, and we'd arrived at our wit's end.

I remained handcuffed on the front porch of the cabin as I listened to the popping and crackling sounds made by Calmer's Oldsmobile zooming off over the gravel driveway. He and the leggy Lillian had changed into business attire and were headed back to Seattle.

I replayed in my mind the last part of our conversation where Calmer had spelled out his plans for me.

"As soon as Lillian and I reach a payphone, I'll call Mr. Holt and tell him to return for you. In anticipation of this likely … *impasse* … Mr. Holt has already been instructed to drive you to a location a few miles outside of Issaquah."

He looked at me as if he expected a question. I didn't ask one, so he went on, "An old acquaintance of mine owns a large old residence there that he's renovated and converted into a successful health facility far removed from everyone and everything. You see, Mr. Nilson, he specializes in helping those unfortunates with drug and alcohol issues."

"So, I'm to be shuttled off to a cure house for dope and liquor addicts," I said. There was no masking the sarcasm in my tone, which got a titter out of Lillian.

Calmer shrugged his broad shoulders to where I thought his polo shirt would cry out in agony from the stretching it got. "If you prefer to call it that, fine. I like to think of it as a homey little sanatorium. You're to be a guest there for a few months—or however long it takes for me to get my affairs well in order, and beyond. Look on it as a well-deserved vacation, Mr. Nilson."

"Uh-huh."

"Believe you me, it will all be nice and legal. I'll draw up the necessary paperwork when I get back to Seattle. And of course, there will be nothing traceable back to me. In fact, if later checked, the paper trail will eventually lead back to no one at all."

"Another of your phantoms."

"Precisely."

"This quack friend of yours must owe you a pretty big favor," I said sourly.

"That, Mr. Nilson, is an understatement."

"He knows Mr. Holt, of course?"

He shook his head. "He and Mr. Holt have never met. My friend knows only that a man acting as my agent will be dropping you off."

Since he'd not asked the question I was expecting, I did. "Why haven't you asked me about those pictures Rune took, and whatever else he had on Miss Atwood? Don't you want what I've got stashed away?"

"Since it's not turned you into a blackmailer, and you're not willing to play ball with me, then I feel safe in assuming you haven't shared willy-nilly whatever it is you've got on Mercedes. Of course, I'll have your office searched thoroughly, and if necessary, your room at your boarding house. If that proves fruitless, then it's likely that your *stash*, as you call it, is safely tucked away and will remain so."

I studied him awhile, then I said, "And how will you explain my sudden disappearance, let alone my long absence? I'm not a hermit, you know. I have people who will wonder." At least I hoped they'd wonder. Walter would wonder.

"You sell me short, Mr. Nilson. I've done my homework on you. After Mr. Holt delivers you to your new home, he's to drive over to Idaho. He'll have with him your billfold and whatever identification necessary to establish that he is you when he stops at a telegraph office. From there he'll send two telegrams, as if sent by you. One to your landlady, Nora Berger, and the other to Dag Erickson." His breezy delivery showed he was more than a little pleased with his plan. "These telegrams will explain that your work for me has unexpectedly taken you to Montana, and that you'll be away for a couple of weeks, maybe longer. After those couple of weeks have passed, I'll again dispatch Mr. Holt to Montana to send an update from you in two additional telegrams."

Mrs. Berger, Sten, Cissy, and even Dag would likely accept the telegrams as being genuine. But Walter wouldn't be fooled. Knowing me, and what we'd talked about, Walter would smell trouble. Calmer hadn't done his homework on me as completely as he thought.

It became more and more apparent that Calmer liked his actors knowing only the parts of the script for the scenes they were in. Still, I asked him, "Dick Liles knows about this plan of yours?"

"By no means. The fewer who know, the better. That's the motto to which I strictly subscribe. No, Mr. Liles thinks every man has his price, and so he believes I'll be entirely successful in paying you off. He'll simply assume your disappearance has something do with the deal we've struck—or so I'll tell him."

"Nice. But, aren't you worried about me squawking once I'm finally let go?"

He shook his head slowly, a look of pity on his face. "My 'quack' friend, as you call him, will have turned you into a drug addict by then. Any wild accusations that you'd care to make against me once you're on the loose, I'll adamantly deny. If necessary, I'll issue some statement about how you'd been targeted while in my employ, and that this was truly sad and most unfortunate. It grieves me that you now cast blame on me. That sort of rubbish. And of course, you'll have absolutely no proof of my involvement. Should there be any serious questions raised, then my quack friend will make the paperwork readily available while claiming that he and his staff acted legally and in good faith. And again, nothing will be traced back to me."

He finished his speech in a hard, thin voice and then his mouth and teeth formed a quiet sleek grin as you might see on a nasty-minded circus clown.

Calmer continued in a sinister purr, "Now, I ask you, Mr. Nilson, who will the authorities believe? Who will people in general believe? *Me*, a respected attorney? Or *you*, a two-bit gumshoe who is down on his uppers because he's turned dope fiend?"

Any grousing by me at that time would fall mainly on deaf ears and very few caring ones. And even if it didn't, Calmer probably had enough bigwig contacts to shut down any investigation into my lunatic sob story before it got off the ground. Such is the way of the world.

"Sounds like you have it all figured out," I said lamely. Actually, it was more than a bit unnerving just how well he'd thought things through.

I looked at Lillian. A cigarette dangled from her pouting lips. Her eyes crinkled at the corners. She seemed to be brooding over what Calmer had been telling me. I sensed she wasn't entirely comfortable with it. I liked to think it was dawning on her that he probably also had ways of disposing of girlfriends who overstay their welcome. After all, she already knew what he had planned for his fiancée.

Lillian got up, flicked her half-smoked cigarette in the ashtray, and went inside the cabin. Evidently the way she kept her conscience so elastic was to stay removed from whatever started to sting and poke at it.

Since Calmer had pretty much spelled out all that he'd cared to, he got to his feet. Coolly and precisely he said, "I need to get back to Seattle for a meeting. I do hope you realize there's nothing personal in all this, Mr. Nilson."

How was intentionally inflicting injury to another anything but *personal*? But no good would come from arguing the point, so I just gave him a blank look as I slipped a clove in my mouth.

ABOUT A HALF-HOUR AFTER Calmer and his girlfriend left, the arrival of Holt's Dodge was signaled by the moaning and groaning gravel driveway.

Knowing that Holt's mission wasn't to kill me but simply deliver me to some quack gave me a slight edge I hadn't had on our trip out to the cabin. Or at least I hoped it did. I also knew what interested Holt far more than being my keeper. It pays to know your enemy.

The Dodge came to a sudden stop, and Holt made a leisurely exit. He came toward the porch quietly, his Mauser still in its holster.

"I guess you and me get to take another little ride together," he said in that dry, nasal way of his.

"What's life for, but travel, adventure, and good company?"

"Glad to hear you can still crack wise, knowin' where I'm takin' you," he said in a mean little voice that fit the mean little man.

Holt came up the steps and moved around to the side of the table where Calmer had been seated closest to the cabin door.

Taking keys from his left coat pocket, he tossed them on the table.

"You know the drill by now," he said, staring stonily at me. His right hand was suddenly sprouting his Mauser.

I took my time fiddling awkwardly with the keys and studied them a moment or two before attempting to free myself from the table frame. My fumbling didn't go unnoticed.

"Quit your stallin' and make it snappy. I wanna be on the road before we're both old men," he grumped.

"You missed a real show after you left," I said tonelessly, as I shoved the key in its keyhole. "You were gone maybe ten minutes when a light came on inside the cabin, so I could see Calmer's gorgeous girlfriend making coffee in the kitchen."

"So she made coffee," he said sharply, his Mauser pointed up and to his right. "What of it?" But I could see interest in his eyes.

"She didn't know I was watching her, is what. And she must have just rolled out of bed, because she wasn't wearing much," I said, letting that image sink into his lascivious little brain.

Having freed myself, I gingerly stood up. I took one step and pretended to falter, bracing myself against the front edge of the tabletop.

"Leg's asleep," I said, grimacing. I lifted my hands from the tabletop and carefully sidled around the front of the table by slowly moving my other leg as if it was frozen solid, and then stopped when I was facing him.

"Both legs. Just give me a sec till it wears off, will you?"

Holt nodded and said, "What was that about the girlfriend makin' coffee and not wearin' much?"

I smiled a smile of fraternal affection that even I might believe if I were to see it. "Well, the only thing she had on was a pair of tap pants that were so tight and clingy she may as well have been naked … if you catch my drift."

Holt caught my drift so well his eyes goggled and his jaw dropped.

"And as the girl fiddled away with the coffee pot, there must have been music playing on the radio, because she was shimmying and shaking like a regular bump and grind queen."

"*Yeah*? You seen her doin' that, huh?"

"Yep. Did you know she and Liles' secretary Joyce are cousins?"

He said he knew that.

"Well, if you think Joyce has long, beautiful legs, you should see the legs on her cousin Lillian."

"Yeah?"

"Uh-huh."

He moistened his lips with his tongue.

I'd reached what Mrs. Berger liked to call the tight-sphincter moment. It was for me, anyway. Holt, however, was standing relaxed and the Mauser was pointed down at the porch decking. His eyes had glazed over and were looking a little off to one side, like he'd already dropped me off at the quack's and had made that long drive over to Idaho to send that telegram.

I went on, "And let me tell you, that wiggle-waggling, round bottom of hers looked just like a quivering plate of Jell-O." I took a quick step forward and kicked Holt in the crotch with everything I had.

His right hand let go of the Mauser as both his hands went to his groin and he doubled up and howled in pain. Normally that would have evoked a small wince of sympathy from me, if I'd had time to think about it, or cared. His reaction gave me the minute or two I needed. Going from a pleasurable diversion of the mind to a mind-numbingly painful one had to be rough enough for Holt. I made it even rougher.

I stepped into him and pushed his shoulders up and backwards so I could plow into his belly with my left and sock him on the jaw with my right. He fell backwards toward the section of outer wall between the window and the door of the cabin. I'm not sure I heard a grunt when he slammed into it, but his knees buckled, and he quickly plunged to the deck right after.

He was out cold.

I used the key to get the handcuffs off my right wrist, and then kneeled down to roll him over and pull his hands behind him so that I could cuff both his wrists.

"You'll live," I told the back of his head. I also made a gag for him with his necktie. No sense letting him attract attention.

I'd intended to leave him inside the living room on a sofa I'd seen earlier through the window. It was a lot better treatment than he'd planned for me. But I changed my mind, because a peculiar idea struck me that better appealed to my sense of justice.

I went through Holt's wallet, and among some bills, I found a piece of paper with an Issaquah address and directions written on it.

Calmer said his quack friend had never met Holt. And it seemed to me, if you had a willing enough quack who didn't know the delivery guy, then he'd be fully prepared to believe what he was told. What would surely cinch the deal is if the delivery guy told the quack that his patient would probably rant and rave and insist he's not who the quack thinks he is, so that heavily sedating him for the first couple of days would be a good plan.

Funny thing, it was during my talk with Ethan Calmer that I'd pretty much doped out who'd killed Rune Granholm. I didn't have much in the way of solid proof, mind you, but I had enough to go on to make a visit and have a meaningful conversation. However, as I saw it, that visit and that talk could wait a little while longer.

So, I had plenty of time to go visit a quack.

Gunnar the Delivery Guy.

A DISAPPOINTED BUT ACCEPTING Kirsti agreed to take me back to my room. As I'd predicted, several hours of talking had taken its toll on me. I needed to rest.

Gunnar the Octogenarian.

I took a slug of water from one of the bottles Kirsti had brought as she pushed me along in my wheelchair. Some water got jostled on my lap as I bumped across the gravel and flagstone walk leading out of the courtyard.

"All I'll say, Gunnar, is that just like last time, you seem to tire out right when I'm left hanging," she said.

She didn't see my smile, since my back was to her.

We agreed to meet the following day after her shift was through, when I'd finish my story.

Chapter 23

—

Finecare Retirement Home, Everett, Washington, late afternoon, Monday, July 7, 2003

BY 3:10 THE NEXT afternoon, we were back in our spot in the outer courtyard: me in my wheelchair and Kirsti still in her green scrubs, seated on the wood bench facing me, her cassette recorder resting on her knees. On my lap was a water bottle and a meatloaf sandwich her mom had made for me and wrapped in a plastic baggy.

Kirsti looked beat from her day of care-giving. Still, despite the no-nonsense expression on her face, I noted her lipstick had been refreshed and she was managing one of her lopsided smiles for me.

"Yesterday," she began, "we quit with you telling me of your conversation with that sleazebag Calmer, and then your escape from Holt, that scary tool of his. But then you had to stop talking after saying how you'd dropped Holt off at some phony sanitarium, somewhere outside of Issaquah."

"I appreciate the recap," I said cheerfully. "It always helps to prime the old pump." I took a big sip from the water bottle and added, "So you know, I think I'll be able to tell the ending a lot better after having slept on it."

"I've got to say," she began again, "that with all that you'd learned from Calmer, and with what you'd been through … I mean, I'd think you'd be in a hurry to do something about it all." Kirsti spoke with surprising energy.

"Frankly, blue eyes, I didn't feel too rushed when it came to Calmer, since he believed I was safely out of the picture, and he had yet to marry Mercedes Atwood. So, rather than feeling rushed, I'd say I was mainly determined."

She nodded and clicked on the mic.

Tuesday, July 18, 1950

I DROVE FROM THE outskirts of Issaquah directly to my office in Ballard so I could trade Holt's Dodge for my Chevy Coupe. I parked his green sedan in front of a fire plug. Then I found my car and drove home to Mrs. Berger's.

I went straight to Walter's room.

"Greetings, old top," he said cheerily. He was seated at his workbench in front of his Remington typewriter and a large pile of notes. "I was finishing up a little editing on Nora's play."

As a genuine labor of love, Walter was helping Mrs. Berger write a play titled *The Making of a Fan Dancer*. It dealt with the ongoing perils of a lovely and surprisingly innocent young woman named Penny. It was mostly a farfetched work of fiction, but no doubt peppered with actual events from Mrs. Berger's hoochie-coochie days. The last time I'd paid strict attention, Penny had managed to escape unsoiled from a white slaver ring and was about to waltz into a Chinatown opium den.

"Come in and have a seat, Gunnar," he said, pointing to his notes. "I've steered Nora away from the opium den idea, but she wants me to come up with an exciting alternative. I assure you, a little conversation would be a most welcome break."

"Sorry, Walter, but I can't stay. I'm just here for a quick clean-up and fresh clothes, and then I've got to run. My story will have to wait. I just need those four roadhouse pictures you've been keeping for me. Also, the negatives."

"Certainly," he said, turning to retrieve them.

"I'm not in *that* big of a hurry, Walter," I said to stop him. "I'll come get them when I'm ready to leave."

I was glad to climb out of my brown suit. It had a stale, charred, woodsy odor to it, like two chain-smoking naturalists on a wilderness picnic.

I took my Silvertone Portable Radio with me into the bathroom to let it play while I shaved and took a quick shower. I'd tuned in as the news blared something about a major general of the Army being separated from his unit when North Korean troops overran some city, and then a blurb I could barely hear about a group of scientists headed by Professor Ashley Montagu publishing a statement about all men of all races belonging to the same species.

I toweled off and changed into a white shirt, a red and beige-striped Sulka tie I'd received as a gift, my navy-blue suit, and my gray fedora. On my way out, I got the pictures and negatives from Walter, promising him I'd supply details later.

IT TOOK ME AROUND thirty minutes to get to Mercedes Atwood's place. My Longines said it was 6:25 when I pulled in the sweeping oblong section of the long driveway. The blue Cadillac, red Buick, and lonely Dodge Coupe were still where I'd seen them last. I ambled over the flagstone walkway and rang the bell.

In a few minutes, Nadia Forsgren opened the door. This time her plain housedress was khaki-colored, and her wide-set eyes looked puzzled as they probed mine.

"Mr. Nilson ... is Miss Atwood expecting you?" she asked doubtfully, her Scandinavian accent strong as ever, her voice as commanding as when we first met.

I touched my hat and smiled ruefully. "No, Nadia. I'm not here to talk with your mistress," I said. "I was hoping to talk with you, if I may. I promise not to keep you any longer than I have to, but it would be good if we could have some privacy."

Still puzzled, she nodded and asked me to follow her. I removed my hat as she led me through the huge vestibule across the reception room, on past the staircase, drawing room, and living room, and then down the hallway toward the kitchen. She motioned me to the adjacent dining room where we'd talked that first day.

"This room. We can talk in this room," she said in a voice that was a little less authoritative now. She explained that Miss Atwood was napping and Isabella was away visiting friends. "Please sit."

I sat.

"Would you like some coffee?"

I said no thanks, so she sat down and began to silently stare at me.

My hat rested on my lap. As before, we were seated at the corner of the bare, rectangular table—me at the head, and Nadia seated to my left. A nice, relaxed, comfy position. The table acted as a kind of buffer between us, our angle to one another giving her the choice of looking over at me or straight ahead if she felt uneasy. So, the seating arrangement suited me just fine, since I was sure she'd soon be feeling uneasy.

"You recall that Miss Atwood asked you and Isabella to fully cooperate with me in my investigation?"

She nodded and asked, "You found the man making those terrible phone calls?"

"Yes, and no," I said quietly. "Turns out it was simply a cruel hoax."

"I … I don't understand."

"Yeah. I kind of wish I didn't," I said wistfully. "In my line of work, things aren't always as they seem. I'm hired to look after my client's interests, and I try to. But since I'm also hired to nose around, I sometimes come across unpleasant facts. Ugly secrets, even. Sometimes they're even secrets about my client."

She stared at me blankly. I went on, "Given the odds, and what they know of their own family, I think your average person suspects that most families have at least one or two relatives with peculiar, or even nutty behavior. The odd duck uncle here, a screwball cousin there. That kind of thing. Do you know what I mean, Nadia?"

Her eyes told me she knew what I meant.

With a faint smile, I said, "In one family I worked for, the grandfather put eggs in his slippers to pre-warm them overnight so they'd boil quicker in the morning. Or, so he thought."

That earned me a wan smile.

"Actually, doing what I do for a living, I've come to believe that if most families were put under a microscope, they'd all look somewhat screwy to the rest of us."

She slowly nodded her agreement.

I reached my hand in my inside coat pocket and pulled out the pictures and negatives. "Since a picture speaks a thousand words, these should give my tongue a rest."

I handed her the four roadhouse shots.

She looked them over. She didn't exactly flush to the temples, but her cheeks turned rosy.

"Of course, you must know about your mistress's secret. Her *other* life, that is. You've probably always known, haven't you? I don't see how you couldn't."

She nodded and her thin eyebrows arched higher than normal. The flush in her face deepened.

"And *Isabella*? How much does she know, or … *understand*?" I asked delicately.

Nadia smiled sadly and shook her head. "Isabella is a hard worker. A *good* worker. But not a thinker. *Ja* … she don't know from nothing."

My smile was wry. Some people you can talk with, and

others you can only talk at. As I'd suspected when I met her, Isabella was the latter. Her particular brand of impenetrability came with a bliss I sometimes envied, but in no way sought.

I pressed on, "How long have you known?"

"*Ja* … it could have begun before her father died … but I learned of it only *after* he left us." There was a tiny glint of moisture in Nadia's wide-set eyes. "I've never approved, *but* …." She shrugged her shoulders. She mumbled something about hoping that marriage would change Mercedes.

If I had a dollar for every time I'd heard that one, I might not be rich, but I could go out to dinner quite a lot. Still, while not agreeing with her hopeful sentiment, I nodded that I understood it. And I believe I did.

Nadia had been like a mother, and now the woman she'd mothered was no longer a teenager. No surprise then that she'd view and tolerate Mercedes as a mother might a wayward and straying daughter over twenty-one. Being her employee was an added constraint.

I gave her some time to collect herself, so we just stared at each other in heavy silence for a short while. Finally I said softly, "I need to tell you some unpleasant things I've uncovered, Nadia. And then I'll need you to do something I just can't do. If you're willing, that is."

She tilted her head forward in a listening attitude.

I left out my own brief encounter in the drawing room with Mercedes' alter ego. But even though I gave Nadia the nutshell version, I saw no point in holding back much of anything else. I told her what I'd learned from Douglas Eagleson. I told her where the four pictures had come from and about Rune's blackmail attempt and his subsequent murder. I also told her the real reason Ethan Calmer had hired me, and all that he'd laid out for me at the cabin earlier in the day.

As I talked, Nadia appeared spellbound, as if she was a mother listening to a doctor's prognosis of her sick child. And in a sense, she was. I saw surprise, shock, disgust, and anger in her eyes. But mostly, anger. Anger at Ethan Calmer.

In order to explain Calmer's scheme, I had to bring up the mental-problem angle. I'm guessing it was because Nadia and I had both been born into, and grounded in a more meat-and-potatoes world, but that like me, she had a hard time believing Mercedes Atwood didn't know her socialite side from her floozy side. She believed Mercedes was sane, just loose, and that she understood full well what she was doing.

I concluded by saying, "I want you to keep the pictures and the negatives. I'm thinking and hoping you might be able to make use of them."

She was puzzled again. "*Ja* ... what is it you want me to do that you cannot?"

"Show the pictures to Miss Atwood. Tell her what I've told you. *Everything.*" Shrugging and smiling candidly, I added, "Whether she's completely sane or not, it would probably be best if you had your frank talk with her when she's her formal, ladylike self. Tell her where you got the pictures, and then explain what Ethan Calmer has in mind for her. That's probably all you can do. After that, just hope you've reached her, so she'll take steps to protect herself."

It was anyone's guess how Mercedes Atwood would react to her housekeeper's disclosures. To paraphrase something Mark Twain once said, people are more easily fooled than persuaded that they've been fooled.

Nadia said she would talk with Mercedes as soon as she rose from her nap.

After she had shown me to the door, I said one last thing to Nadia. "I'm pretty sure I won't be coming back here again. No reason to. So, goodbye, and good luck."

If that lean and bony woman didn't reach up and bear-hug me before I could turn to leave, then I don't know my bear hugs, and I never will.

Chapter 24

—

THE DAY HAD BEEN almost as long as some I'd spent in a foxhole, when time dragged on and on and on, and what chiefly concerned you was surviving whatever the next few minutes might suddenly throw at you. I say *almost as long* … but not quite. Not hardly. No kind of day ever would be.

I do know that I wasn't in a particular hurry after I'd left Nadia Forsgren, because I drove at a sloth's pace from Broadmoor over to my next destination. "In for a penny, in for a pound." It wasn't one of my grandmother's Swedish sayings, but it fit well enough. I'd come to the conclusion that telling the police about Rune's pictures would do more harm than good. So, I decided, *mum's the word.* That wasn't the only thing I planned to keep from them. And if it blew up in my face, well, so be it.

I'd hoped for a chance to assemble some thoughts, but as I drove, for some reason the show tune "Crazy Rhythm" was stuck in my tired head. Douglas Eagleson had alluded to its lyrics when describing the highbrow Mercedes Atwood becoming a no-brow by consorting with lowbrows.

Maybe "Crazy Rhythm" played over and over in my brain because this screwy case had made me a little crazy.

But hopefully, crazy like a fox. As I steered my Chevy for Wallingford, I felt I could add my own line or two to the song about what might happen if an angered lowbrow confronts a shifty no-brow. After all, Walter had merely stated the exception to the rule when it comes to the noisy clatter of hooves. Most of the time, the noise means *horses* are coming, not zebras.

There was still plenty of light out when I pulled down Burke Avenue and parked. I left my coupe and walked unhurriedly across the sidewalk and then up the concrete steps that cut through the retaining wall. When I reached the front walkway, I saw Clara Brooks sitting in her glider on the front porch, puffing away on one of her Lucky Strikes.

As I walked up the front steps, Clara smiled and said in her deep, gravelly voice, "Why, I do believe it's that young fella who was the so-so friend of Rune Granholm. That private eye fella. Am I right?"

"Right you are. I'm glad you remember me," I said cheerfully, touching my hat as I reached the front porch. "Care if I join you for another short visit?"

"Suit yourself," she said, pointing to the two metal motel chairs across from her. "My daughter and son-in-law are off seein' a movie, so it seems a bit of company won't hurt me none."

"What's the movie they're seeing?"

"Ma and Pa Kettle do … *somethin'*. O'course my son-in-law gets a special kick outta them, as the Kettles is supposed to be living somewhere over on the Olympic Peninsula, where he was raised."

Her gray hair was still done up in tight braids, though this time the housedress was brown. Like its predecessor, it did nothing to enhance her thickset figure. She was wearing the same white oxfords as before, still sockless, and both of her feet were again planted squarely on the threadbare hassock in front of the glider.

I removed my hat and put it on my lap as I sat down in the

spring-form chair I'd used the last time. And again, I felt like I was on the deck of a ship in a squall before I finally got settled in.

Mrs. Brooks stared at me steadily for a long moment with her shrewd round eyes. "You look a bit frazzled in the face, like you could use a drink. Somethin' strong, maybe?"

"What's that you're having?" I asked, nodding at the half-empty glass beside the ashtray on the small metal table next to her.

"Whiskey with a hint of 7-Up to civilize it."

"Then that's what I'll have, if you're offering."

She dropped her cigarette in the ashtray and picked up her tall glass as she swung her feet off the hassock and heaved her stocky body in the air to stand up. Despite her ample girth, she was an agile old gal, I'll give her that. As I'd noticed on my first visit, hers was the smooth and seamless movement you'd expect of an aging former acrobat. She'd have no problem at all clambering out a window and climbing down a fire escape if properly motivated.

I watched as she quickly downed the remainder of her drink.

"I'll make us both one," she said, looking down at me. "Won't be but a minute."

While Mrs. Brooks was in the house busily making our highballs, I looked out at the yard. The large elm tree still looked lonely but wasn't providing any shade worth noticing at the moment. The day had been more warm than hot, but it was getting a little cooler, as we probably had only another hour of sunlight left.

I loosened my tie as Mrs. Brooks came back with our drinks. Handing me mine, she sat back down in the glider with hers and put her feet atop the hassock again.

I sipped my drink as she took a hearty swallow of hers, licked her lips, and asked, "So, did you ever figure out who it was killed that four-flusher, Rune?"

"Uh-huh. Though not so that I can prove it. But yeah, I think

I've figured it out … or, at least I've got a pretty good idea." I gazed directly at her face.

"Huh. You don't say?"

"When it comes to murder and even manslaughter, it usually boils down to a formula that's downright clichéd."

"And that would be what?"

"Means, motive, and opportunity."

"Huh. Is that so?"

"Uh-huh. It's so."

Her small bulbous nose twitched and she said, "So, how was it you come up with this pretty good idea of yours?"

I shrugged. "Mind you, it's nothing but a guess. And, I have to admit it was pretty much served up to me on a silver platter—once I'd ruled out other likely suspects, that is. But as guesses go, I'd say it's a pretty good one."

"Huh. So then, who do you think it was killed Rune?"

"You," I said gently. "I think *you* killed him."

Mrs. Brooks didn't say anything. Her face was blank. But not an uncomprehending blank. A fleeting glitter in her eyes told me it was a composed blank. A poker-face blank. A face that could even teach Mercedes Atwood a thing or two.

Finally, she said in her frank manner, "That sure is one harebrained idea, young fella. Some might even call it an *accusation* …." She let that last word drift in the air as she took a sip of her drink and turned her eyes down to the street behind me.

"Some might, sure. And maybe it is harebrained, as guesses go. Nothing I can really prove, that's for sure. It's more in the arena of odds, possibilities, likelihoods—that kind of thing."

She was making eye contact with me again. I took another gulp from my highball to let what I'd said sink in. She hadn't lied about the whiskey to 7-Up ratio.

Mrs. Brooks stayed silent, the fingers of her left hand drumming against the glass she gripped with her right hand.

Finishing her drink, she put the glass down on the table. She reached for a Lucky Strike and the matches.

As she lit up, I said, "You told me your son Stanley takes after your husband Charles in being trusting. I'll bet he's also as honorable, and that you love that about him. You saw Rune as the rogue and user he was, and you warned Stan, but he thought you were being too hard on Rune. Again, a bit too trusting, your Stan. You probably let Rune rent the apartment above the bakery, not so much to please Stan as to keep close tabs on Rune and his influence on your son. After all, Stan is innocent and a bit naive, and he didn't know the kind of mischief a guy like Rune might hatch. But you did. Rune was trouble. He needed watching. Luckily, Stan got that job on a fishing boat for the summer. Maybe luck had nothing to do with it. Maybe you even arranged for that job. Whatever the case, it made for a good opportunity to confront Rune and evict him for failing to pay his rent."

I paused to let that register while I took another sip of mostly whiskey. I continued, "I think you went to see Rune that night he was killed. Not to murder him, but to tell him to clear out or be put out."

Mrs. Brooks raised her bushy brows and took a drag on her Lucky Strike. She kept staring at me as I went on talking.

"Rune's door was probably wide open when you came up the back steps. That's how I found it. But Rune didn't hear you because he was too busy talking blackmail talk on the telephone. You overheard him demanding money for pictures he'd taken with your Stan's camera. You heard Rune talk of meeting up with someone to collect the hush money. You were outraged. How dare Rune carry on such a swindle in the very apartment that Charles had built? How dare he involve your innocent Stan in a shakedown racket in even a roundabout fashion? I'm guessing it pushed you over the top. You probably shouted something at Rune so that he broke off the phone call and came over to where you were standing next to the armchair and sofa. You gave him a big piece of your mind. Rune probably just laughed at you and maybe even said some mocking words. It's the type of thing he'd do. He could be real stupid that way."

I paused, but as she said nothing, I went on, "Rune owned a small automatic with mother-of-pearl grips. He'd been loading it to take along with him. It was either lying on the small end table, or more than likely he was fiddling with it in one hand while he was talking on the phone. Whatever the case, I'm guessing you got in a tussle with Rune that ended when the gun went off and he hit the floor."

Mrs. Brooks blew a vague plume of smoke and watched it with half-shut eyes that crinkled at the corners.

"It's funny what a person will do when adrenaline starts to flow and shock sets in. You shut every window shade, for all the good it did. Rune owed you rent money, so you went through his pockets and wallet, making sure not to leave fingerprints. You'd think to do that because you're a reader of crime stories. But when you heard me noisily stomping up the back steps, you quickly snatched what little cash you could from his wallet, leaving a couple bucks behind in your haste. You then beat it for the window leading to the fire escape. A newcomer to the place wouldn't have readily thought about that fire escape. For what it's worth, that's what finally put me on to you after I'd ruled out others. When you walked away from Rune's place with your arms folded to hide that little automatic, no one in the neighborhood noticed—even if they saw you. And why would they? You've probably walked from the bakery to your house enough times over the years to where you'd be practically invisible."

Mrs. Brooks' scared and haggard face reminded me of some of the displaced and orphaned waifs I'd seen during the war. It also evoked pity, just as theirs had, but for different reasons.

She breathed in deep and long through her nose, and then

let it out through her open mouth. "O'course, like you told me, young fella, all this talk of yours is just a guess."

I finished my drink and said, "Uh-huh. Nothing but a guess. One I can't prove, nor will I even bother to try."

Her eyes looked a bit watery as they slowly moved over my face.

"Whether it *was* you who killed Rune or somebody else," I said heavily, "I imagine by now that little automatic with mother-of-pearl grips is keeping the fish company somewhere in Puget Sound. Or it would be, if Rune's killer has any sense at all."

As I got up to leave, she was as quiet as a thousand church mice or a thousand graves. Take your pick.

"YOU MEAN YOU JUST let her get away with it?" Kirsti burst out incredulously. "How could you do that? What in the world were you thinking?"

"Hold your horses, young lady," I said firmly. "I'm not finished with my story yet."

Chapter 25

—

WHEN I GOT BEHIND the wheel of my coupe after leaving Mrs. Brooks, I felt like I needed a long, hot bath in Arnica-dosed bathwater. But before I took that bath, I had a promise to keep. So, I went to Walter's room and laid everything out over a couple of shots of Black & White.

Walter was definitely sold on the idea that Mercedes Atwood had multiple personalities. He argued, "It's the only way it makes sense as to why she hadn't become suspicious of Ethan Calmer's scheming."

"I don't know about that, Walter. People in love will sometimes ignore or overlook a lot. You know that." I gave him a meaningful smile that he chose to disregard.

"That's if she really was in love, old socks ... but I've got to wonder. Maybe the staid and serious Miss Atwood thought it was time for marriage. Believing Mr. Calmer to be a suitable choice, she simply played her part accordingly." He took a quick sip from his shot glass. "Whatever the case, perhaps after Nadia has that forthright conversation with her, this whole affair will prove to be a powerful watershed incident in Miss Atwood's life."

"Well, at the very least, I hope it leads her to get good and clear of that shark Calmer. But Walter, I'm thinking you mean something more by 'watershed incident.'"

"I do indeed, old file. It's conceivable that on being confronted with some jarring facts, Miss Atwood will be moved to seek professional help."

"Ah ... the nut angle again."

He ignored that, so I went on. Walter listened quietly as I told him what I'd said to Clara Brooks. When I finished, he merely nodded his head a few times before glancing at our empty shot glasses and refilling them.

Walter didn't challenge my decision in the matter, or even comment on it. I figured he'd understand. He'd killed men in his Great War just as I had in mine. And like me, he'd experienced a time or two when his moral compass had been so thoroughly disrupted that the needle blurred or simply disappeared.

"WELL, I DON'T UNDERSTAND it at all," Kirsti said. She was plainly irritated and also confused. "Even if it did happen during a struggle, she killed a man. How could you just let that go, Gunnar?"

I couldn't reply immediately, as I was chewing on some of that meatloaf sandwich her mom had packed for me. She waited patiently while I swallowed, and then I said, "At the time I didn't see it that way, blue eyes. Before the war, I'm sure I'd have told the cops my suspicions about Clara Brooks. And maybe I'd do so today, though I'm not so sure about that. I had no solid proof of her guilt. Plus, at that time I was still fresh from the effects of kill-or-be-killed. It might not be nice to say it, but the way I looked at it, Rune wasn't worth what the cops and newspapers would have done to someone like Clara Brooks. And knowing him like I did, I was pretty sure Rune's brother Nils would have felt the same way."

I could see Kirsti still didn't understand. I wouldn't have either, at her age. My old partner Lou Boyd made a remark to me sometime around 1939 or '40 that I didn't fully appreciate until after I'd gone to war. He was thumbing through a copy of *Life* magazine, when he showed me a picture of young German soldiers marching down a street.

"Just remember, Gunnar lad, they have mothers too," Lou had said. He was a veteran of World War I. And, looking back, since nations had begun warring again at the time, and the U.S. was headed in the same direction, I can see Lou was trying to share a perspective that was lost on me at the time.

I took a long swig from my water bottle and said, "Listen, blue eyes, whatever the newspapers might trumpet as the reasons why men go off to war, believe me when I tell you that when it comes right down to it, you end up killing the enemy to protect yourself and the guys fighting and bleeding right alongside you. And while to this day I still believe I killed men who fought for an *evil* cause, and that some of them were likely *bad* men, I also continue to believe that most of them were probably just average Joes like me, caught up in something they had no control over."

A tiny glimmer in Kirsti's big blue eyes told me my point was beginning to register, though she still looked puzzled.

"Clara Brooks may have *killed* Rune Granholm, but she wasn't a murderer. Not in my book. Just so you know, thereafter I stopped in on her at her bakery from time to time to say hello and buy a cinnamon roll or a loaf of bread for Mrs. Berger. As far as I know, Clara never killed anyone ever again. And that's where I chose to leave it."

Kirsti thought about this for a long while. I didn't expect agreement from her, but perhaps a wee bit of understanding.

"Look, if it will make you feel better about the whole thing, a year or two after I learned that Clara Brooks had died, I ran into Detective Fitch at Seattle's 1962 World's Fair. Over a cup of coffee, we chatted about Rune's unsolved murder for a while, when he up and tells me that he and Togstad suspected Clara might have done it."

"He said that to you?"

I nodded. "Fitch told me that after having talked with Mrs. Brooks and coming up empty elsewhere, he and Togstad figured that maybe she'd shot Rune over a fight about the back rent he owed her."

"W-why didn't they do something about it?"

"Fitch said that after raking through Rune's checkered life and unsavory affairs, they figured it wasn't worth making all that trouble for the old girl without having solid evidence to go on, and particularly if they were wrong."

That quieted Kirsti for a long moment.

Finally, she broke the silence by asking, "Did you tell some of this to Cissy Paget? I mean, wasn't she going to type up a report for you?"

"Uh-huh. In exchange for which I gave Cissy a rough version of what I called the Calmer-Atwood Circus. That Friday we went out on the town."

CISSY PAGET LIVED WITH her widowed mother in a modest house in a blue-collar section of the hilly Magnolia neighborhood. While the upscale houses perched on Magnolia Bluff overlooked Elliott Bay and Puget Sound, Mrs. Paget's house faced Queen Anne Hill. But, as Cissy liked to quip, if you climbed a tall enough ladder, you just might get a lovely view of Fishermen's Terminal on Salmon Bay.

Cissy and I were in what she called "the green room"—the reason being that although the walls of the living room were painted white, as was the brick fireplace, everything else was some shade of green. There was a light-green jute braided rug, a pair of dark-green Mohair armchairs with matching sofa flanked by lime-green end tables with sea-green glass lamps and shades, and floor-to-ceiling jungle-green drapes up against the front window. It was a calming room. A room meant to tranquilize the rambunctious.

I was sitting at carefree ease on the sofa with my suit coat off and my tie at half-mast. Cissy was in the kitchen clinking glasses and ice cubes. I'd treated her to a prime rib dinner at the Georgian Room at the Olympic Hotel and then we'd gone to the Trianon Ballroom to dance till our feet got sore. Since her mother was in California visiting relatives, Cissy invited me in for a nightcap.

Steps sounded on the linoleum floor of the kitchen. "Well, that was definitely a colorful collection of loonies you had to deal with," Cissy said playfully as she shimmied into the living room with a couple of highball glasses.

"*This* coming from a girl who thinks the whole world is one large insane asylum," I said, taking my drink from her.

"You know what I mean, smart guy," she said, lifting a corner of her lip to give me a sour grin. She kicked her shoes off and joined me on the sofa as she continued, "The sex-crazed, Jekyll and Hyde socialite, her two-timing shyster fiancé, his conniving secretary and girlfriend, the ambitious and unscrupulous security guy, his loyal but horribly misguided secretary. And of course, there's the would-be Hollywood gangster type to do the dirty work. Quite a group."

Cissy switched her drink to her left hand as her eyes crinkled so that a tiny smile tugged at the corners of her mouth. "Most definitely a lively bunch of wrong-headed hombres," she added, bustling about for a few seconds as she tucked her right ankle under her left haunch to get more comfortable.

I watched her in silence as I sipped my drink.

"And yet, sadly the murder of Rune Granholm remains unsolved," she said, a small grimace on her pretty face as she looked at me over the top of her glass.

"Uh-huh. I had nothing to give the cops, and from what I hear the case remains open."

"Disappointed?"

"I suppose. But only a little. Rune was on the shady side and a risk-taker who ran with a pretty rough crowd. He regularly pushed his luck and his luck finally ran out."

"Lie with dogs, rise with fleas. I get it," she said solemnly. "Still you seem unusually settled and philosophical about the whole thing."

I shrugged. "I was a good friend of Rune's brother Nils. Not so much with Rune. I really didn't like him much. What can I say?"

She thought about that a moment and nodded once. She then riveted her lovely brown eyes on my face and said, "I've got to believe that Nadia Forsgren followed through and had that frank talk with her employer. But did you learn whether or not Miss Atwood believed her? Have you heard anything?"

"Yeah, but not directly," I said casually. "I learned from my reporter pal Sam Kelly that Mercedes gave Ethan Calmer the air. Their engagement is off."

"Well, well ... now that's something, anyway."

"Sure," I said, nodding. "What's more, sweet knees, I received a check in the mail from Mercedes Atwood that more than covers what Calmer didn't pay me."

"Ho, ho ... now that's saying plenty," she said cheerfully.

"Uh-huh."

After inhaling a little of my drink, I said, "And unless Ethan Calmer comes up with some cash pretty soon, I imagine his unsavory creditors will have something meaningful to say to him."

"Is that why you didn't tell the police about his horrible scheme?"

"It would've been hard for me to make a case against him that would've stuck ... and certainly not worth the trouble to try, especially since I can just let nature take its course."

"Well, aren't you the slyboots," she said thoughtfully, moving her nimble fingers behind my neck to give it a gentle massage.

"I did tell my police pal Frank Milland about that bogus health facility outside of Issaquah. He said he knew a couple of guys who'd be more than happy to go calling. So, Holt's detention will be a short one."

"What about Dick Liles? Any word on him?"

"No, and frankly he doesn't interest me all that much. While plainly his business ends justified his methods, he was just a glorified cog in this whole thing. Liles saw Mercedes Atwood as a loon, and it didn't matter to him if she eventually wound up in an institution. But as far as I could tell, he wasn't in on the nastier aspects of Calmer's plans. He's just a shady, run-of-the-mill businessman with just enough scruples to make himself appear sufficiently honest to further his aims."

"And what of his girlfriend, the alluring Joyce Voorhees?" she whispered huskily, giving me a cool, significant stare.

"Don't know. And at the moment, I don't care."

"Good answer," she said, leaning in so close that for a second I thought she might be trying to guess my weight and shoe size. Instead she pulled my head closer and we kissed. She pressed her lips hard against mine for a few seconds and then gently broke free and said softly, "Fancy a chaser for that nightcap, tough guy?"

"Oh yes, uh-huh …."

That won me a playful slug in the arm.

"I'D HAVE SLUGGED YOU too," Kirsti said, clicking off her recorder. "Real hard."

"I believe you."

Since Kirsti's mother had assumed that I overstated my bygone appeal to women, what I chose not to say was that afterwards Cissy grabbed my tie and got up off the sofa, dragging me along with her. She led me from the serenity of the green room into a neighboring one that lent itself to rowdiness.

Gunnar the Understater.

BORN INTO A BLUE-COLLAR family in Seattle, Washington, and raised in the suburbs of the greater Seattle area, T.W. Emory has been an avid reader since his early teens. In addition to fiction, he likes biographies, autobiographies, and the writings of certain essayists. He also enjoys reading secular and religious history, and is a dabbler in philosophy and sociology. Moreover, he likes reading reprinted collections of old comic strips such as *Thimble Theatre* (aka *Popeye*), *Moon Mullins*, *Captain Easy*, and *Li'l Abner*.

After taking on various odd jobs that included brief stints assisting a grounds-keeper, working in a laundry, washing dishes, waiting tables, and doing inside and outside painting, he got into drywall finishing and eventually became a small-time drywall contractor.

In addition to writing, T.W. Emory enjoys cartooning as a hobby. He is second-generation Swede on his mother's side and third-generation Norwegian on his father's, which helps explain the Scandinavian flavoring in his two novels, *Trouble in Rooster Paradise* and *Crazy Rhythm*.

He currently lives north of Seattle with his wife, two sons, one cat that is companionable and another that is aloof and rather ditsy.

For more information, go to www.twemoryauthor.com.

Seattle, 1950. When men were men, thanks to WWII, and fine dining meant a steak at Canlis.

TROUBLE IN ROOSTER PARADISE

T. W. Emory

Oldster PI Gunnar Nilson tells the story of a case he handled in Seattle, 1950. A client hires him to find the killer of a young beauty who worked at Fasciné Expressions, a "rooster paradise" where pretty girls charm male customers into spending big. The heady fragrance of perfumed female can make it tough for a guy to think clearly, especially when the killer is breathing down his neck.

An Excerpt from

Trouble in Rooster Paradise

Chapter 1

———

An assisted living home in Everett, Washington
Monday, June 2, 2003

"WELL, YOU'RE A WELCOME improvement," I told the
pretty young woman standing at the threshold of my
open door.

"*Excuse me*?" she asked.

"You're not wearing scrubs yet, but you're looking in on *me*,
and you've got that concerned caregiver face worn by all the
staff. So, I gather it's *you* who's replacing Amazon Sally."

"*Amazon Sally*? Oh, you mean Sally Jennings."

"Uh-huh. A big Amazon of a girl. Her height reminded me
of a tall waitress I knew back when telephones were black and
a call cost a nickel." I turned my wheelchair to face my visitor.

"I didn't get a chance to meet Sally, but yes, I'll be taking over
for her, starting tomorrow." My cheery caregiver entered the
room and came over on a sleek pair of legs with cute dimpled
knees that brought back memories of a girl I once knew—one
who liked to dance to music with a heartbeat.

The new girl was standing in front of my wheelchair now,

so I had to glance up to see her shrewd eyes and moving lips.

"I'll be working here for the summer. I'm not on duty yet, but I wanted to pop by and meet everyone." I detected a hint of community college in her voice. "My name is Kirsti Liddell, Mr. Nilson."

"Nice to meet you, Kirsti. And please, call me Gunnar." We shook hands.

Kirsti Liddell wore a light blue blouse, red twill shorts, and tennis shoes. She was on the tall side of short, had big blue eyes, blonde hair cut in a pageboy, and a pert little bust that didn't jounce as she moved about. I placed her age at about twenty.

"I understand you'll be with us until your broken leg mends," she said in a dulcet tone.

"Right," I muttered. "You might say I found out the hard way that it's high time to pay someone else to clean my gutters."

Kirsti gave me a broad smile. Her airy, nimble movements provided a stark contrast to the sumo wrestler clunkiness of her predecessor. And whereas Amazon Sally had reeked of salve and her breath of far too many cigarettes, Kirsti's scent was vanilla and jasmine. In my day, Big Sal was what we called a B-girl. Kirsti would have rated a hubba-hubba.

Kirsti and I got better acquainted in the next couple of days. She was a nail-biter who favored multicolored ankle socks. By the third day I'd sized her up as one of those terminal romantics, the type who have more than five senses, hear tunes we don't, and view ordinary events as headline news. By the close of her first week, she was remembering to call me Gunnar and I was calling her Blue Eyes. By the second week of June, she was electrified to find out what I used to do for a living.

"Why you've been holding out on me! Mrs. Johnson says that years ago you were a private investigator in Seattle."

"That biddy's the one who's the snoop."

"It must have been exciting."

"That was donkey's years back."

"What?"

"A long time ago. Long before Seattle became the current land of Oz."

"You mean the Emerald City?"

"Yeah, whatever."

"I'll bet you've faced danger."

It was her doe-in-the-crosshairs eyes that got me yammering. "Well, I suppose I've seen my share of mean streets. Sure. And I've been in more than one place where staring wasn't just impolite, but hazardous to your health."

"I'd love to hear all about it. You'll have to tell me."

After that Kirsti regularly quizzed me about my private eye days each time she came to the room. Her grillings reminded me of an ex-landlady of mine who fancied herself a playwright hunting up background material.

With big eyes made even bigger, Kirsti asked, "Did you ever find a missing person? Or deal with a murder case? Did you ever have to … you know, kill anyone?"

"Well, I wasn't exactly Peter Gunn, but—"

"Who?"

"Skip it."

A few times she came by after her day ended and we talked for half an hour or so. I was glad to oblige. She was far easier on the eyes than most of the natives at Finecare. Plus, frankly, I was flattered by the attention. Granted, it was the attention a granddaughter might show her granddad, but still, it had been ages since an attractive young female had shown me any kind of interest. And I appreciated it. So much so, that at Kirsti's behest I began jotting down some of my recollections in a tablet—just a few words or phrases really, enough to remind me of a person, place, or thing. She got me prying into the undusted rooms of my mind. I was sweeping out memories from way back to just after the Second World War. Some were a hoot to recall, while others, well ….

By the third week of our acquaintance, she asked if she could visit on a Sunday to pick my brain.

"Don't you have a social life, blue eyes?"

"Don't you want a social life, Gunnar?"

I couldn't argue with her there.

"During our brief visits you've told me bits and pieces about your detective days, but I've been thinking that if we got together on a Sunday, maybe you'd be okay with telling me about one of your cases from start to finish. I mean, if you think you're up to it. *Talking* with me for several hours, that is …."

I made a dismissive wave with my hand. "Trading in ill winds as I did, *talking* was a big part of my business, blue eyes. And despite what some of the keepers here might think, I'm still no slouch at it." I gave her a level stare and smiled. "I can assure you, *my* ability to talk isn't the issue. It'll be *your* ability to listen."

"That's awesome. And besides, Gunnar, if it makes you feel any better, I'm being a little bit selfish. Who knows? With your permission, of course, I might be able to transform your memories into an extra credit paper when I return to school. You know, human interest, that sort of thing."

I told her she had my permission. "I'll even sign an official release form if you need me to," I said with a chuckle. And since she assured me the drive into Everett was a quick one for her, I was persuaded the extra visit would be no real imposition.

COME SUNDAY THE 22ND, I refused to go the string-tie route, but I did wear a new flannel shirt. She said she'd come by around mid-morning. My note tablet sat on my lap. I kept up a steady *rat-a-tat-tat* with my fingers on the old Sucrets tin in my pants pocket that held my stash of cloves. I'd already sucked on five since about 8:00 a.m.

The corridor still smelled of assembly line pancakes when Kirsti finally showed up. She stood in the doorway, tote bag in hand and arms akimbo. I received a merry little look and a sorry-I'm-late. I countered with a nonchalant expression and an I-wasn't-going-anywhere-anyway. She wore a blue drawstring skirt that hugged her flanks and a white tank top that made her breasts look unusually abrupt.

"You're wearing sandals," I said as she went around behind me. "You paint your toes."

"It's nice out," she said. "And I sure do."

The distant sound of rattling dishes was dying down as she wheeled me through the corridor. My bumpy ride over the gravel and flagstone walk finally ended when we reached the outside courtyard.

She made chirping glad sounds as she parked my chariot and then planted herself on the wood bench facing me. Showing me her tote bag, she said, "Since you told me you like them, I made you a couple of pastrami sandwiches on rye for when you get hungry later."

Deeply touched doesn't begin to describe how that made me feel.

"I hope you don't mind, but I'd like to tape our conversation," she said, slamming a fresh cassette into the recorder she'd taken from the bag. "Just try to ignore the microphone and please be as candid as possible."

I smiled and fetched another clove.

"I'm not squeamish," she said, "and you should know by now I'm no prude."

"It's not as if I worked in a slaughterhouse, blue eyes."

She smiled, but her bright eyes narrowed. "Come on, Gunnar. You know what I mean. You started to tell me something the other day but then you shut right up. I saw the sparkle in your eyes. You said something about a dead body that led you into rooster paradise. I want you to tell me about that."

I looked from her to the mic she held in her hand.

"Like, what did you mean about the rooster thing?" she asked.

"You're positive you're not a prude?"

"For sure."

"A couple of ground rules," I said solemnly. "First off, I'm gonna need to take an occasional pee break."

"I'll wheel you over to the men's room whenever you say so."

"And second, I'm pretty sure I'll be all talked out at some point. So, figure on me having to finish this story in another installment. Maybe two."

"I think I can work with that," she said good-naturedly.

"Keep in mind that when I was young, a woman who smoked and wore pedal pushers was liberated, and if you spoke of 'feminism' you meant soft, ladylike, and sometimes sexy."

"Uh-huh."

"And blue eyes, you have to understand I'll be taking us back a ways to when being correct politically had to do with how you cast your ballot and not how you spoke."

"I'm with you."

I sighed.

"Kind of funny that it's June, because what I'm about to tell you happened during one week in June, back in 1950. Telephones then weren't like they are now, with all their beeps, hums, and tunes. Not hardly. No, most of them had a bell sound that was harsh and shrill. A call late at night, for instance—well, it was like a fireman's summons."

"Uh-huh," she said, clicking on the mic. "I'm all set."

I wasn't sure I was. But what the heck.

From T.W. Emory and Coffeetown Press

———

THANK YOU FOR READING *Crazy Rhythm*. We are so grateful for you, our readers. If you enjoyed this book, here are some steps you can take that could help contribute to its success and the success of this series.

- Post a review on Amazon, BN.com, and/or GoodReads.
- Check out T.W.'s website (www.twemoryauthor.com) and blog (www.twemoryauthor.com/blog), send a comment, or ask to be put on his mailing list.
- Spread the word on social media, especially Facebook Twitter, and Pinterest.
- Like T.W.'s Facebook page (TWEmory), and Coffeetown's page (coffeetownpress).
- Follow T.W. (@tw_emory) and Coffeetown Press (@coffeetownpress) on Twitter.
- Ask for this book at your local library or request it on their online portal.

Good books and authors from small presses are often overlooked. Your comments and reviews can make an enormous difference.

77595874R00154

Made in the USA
Lexington, KY
29 December 2017